T0110300

CHARLES JACKSON

THE LOST WEEKEND

Charles Jackson was born in 1903 and raised in the township of Arcadia, New York, in the Finger Lakes region, where much of his fiction is set. After a youth marred by tuberculosis and alcoholism, Jackson achieved international fame with his first novel, *The Lost Weekend* (1944), which was adapted into a classic movie by Billy Wilder and Charles Brackett. Over the next nine years, Jackson published two more novels and two story collections, while continuing to struggle with alcohol and drug addiction. In 1967, after a fourteen-year silence, he returned to the best-seller lists with a novel about a nymphomaniac, *A Second-Hand Life*, but the following year he died of an overdose at the Hotel Chelsea in Manhattan.

Blake Bailey is the author of *Farther & Wilder: The Lost Weekends and Literary Dreams of Charles Jackson*. His other books include *A Tragic Honesty: The Life and Work of Richard Yates*, finalist for the National Book Critics Circle Award, and *Cheever: A Life*, winner of the National Book Critics Circle Award, the Francis Parkman Prize, and finalist for the Pulitzer and James Tait Black Memorial Prize. He edited a two-volume edition of Cheever's work for The Library of America, and in 2010 received an Award in Literature from the American Academy of Arts and Letters. He lives in Virginia with his wife and daughter.

THE LOST WEEKEND

CHARLES JACKSON

THE LOST WEEKEND

With an Introduction by Blake Bailey

Vintage Books
A Division of Random House, Inc. | New York

FIRST VINTAGE BOOKS EDITION, FEBRUARY 2013

Copyright © 1944 by Charles R. Jackson. Copyright renewed 1971
by Rhoda Jackson
Introduction copyright © 2013 by Blake Bailey

All rights reserved. Published in the United States by Vintage Books,
a division of Random House, Inc., New York, and in Canada by
Random House of Canada Limited, Toronto. Originally published
in hardcover in slightly different form by Farrar & Rinehart, Inc.,
New York, in 1944.

Vintage and colophon are registered trademarks of
Random House, Inc.

The Cataloging-in-Publication data is available at the
Library of Congress.

Vintage ISBN: 978-0-307-94871-7

Designed by Joy O'Meara Wispe

www.vintagebooks.com

146028962

To My Wife

And can you, by no drift of circumstance,
Get from him why he puts on this confusion,
Grating so harshly all his days of quiet
With turbulent and dangerous lunacy?

—*Hamlet,* III, 1.

CONTENTS

INTRODUCTION

Blake Bailey

The Lost Weekend—a novel about five disastrous days in the life of Don Birnam—was written in the early 1940s, a time when alcoholism was widely regarded as a moral failing rather than a disease. The publisher, Stanley Rinehart, realized the book would need all the clinical validation it could get, and sent advance copies to medical schools around the country. Dr. Morris Fishbein, editor of *The Journal of the American Medical Association,* claimed that the novel captured "the very soul of the dipsomaniac" ("I found myself at the end . . . full of sympathy and a desire to help"), while another specialist, Dr. Herbert L. Nossen, called it "expert and wonderful—the work of a courageous man."

Fiction writers also tended to be enthusiastic. Sinclair Lewis, who knew whereof he spoke, found *The Lost Weekend* brilliant on every level—"the only unflinching story of an alcoholic that I have ever read"—and subsequently made a point of mentioning Charles Jackson as one of the few American writers who showed promise of greatness. Another alcoholic writer, however, seemed almost traumatized by the novel: William Seabrook, nowadays forgotten, was then well known as the author of *Asylum* (1935), the record of his incarceration at a mental hospital in Westchester County. "Here's my honest reaction to *The Lost Weekend* by Charles Jackson which I read word by word to the end with increasing pain and anguish," he wrote Jackson's publisher.

I hate the goddam book almost as much as I hate my own inflamed conscience. "There go I but for the grace of God" and all that stuff, in that horrible, hopeless, cumulative nightmare this guy's devil-guided pen (or portable) has envoked [sic].

I've suffered as a drunk but not like that and hope to Christ I never will. It's the only book that ever scared me. It should be soberly read by every white-collar souse in America. If it doesn't scare the liver, lights and daylights out of him as it did me, it means the poor bastard has softening of the brain and is already sunk. . . .

As it happened, Seabrook was then in the midst of a final alcoholic relapse; twenty months later he'd kill himself with an overdose of sleeping pills, though friends claimed it wasn't a matter of deliberate suicide so much as "another drastic attempt to accomplish what he had tried, vainly, all his life to do—to get away from himself." Jackson would have understood only too well.

Nor was Jackson surprised by his novel's stunning success, since, as he put it, "Almost everybody has somebody in their family who's a drunk but who's worth worrying about." Within five years, *The Lost Weekend* sold almost half a million copies in various editions and was translated into fourteen languages, syndicated by King Features as a comic strip, and added to the prestigious Modern Library. Its critical reception was no less impressive: "Charles Jackson has made the most compelling gift to the literature of addiction since De Quincey," Philip Wylie wrote in *The New York Times*. The trailer for the classic movie summarized the matter nicely: "Famous critics called it . . . 'Powerful . . .' 'Terrifying . . .' 'Unforgettable . . .' 'Superb . . .' 'Brilliant . . .' AND NOW PARAMOUNT DARES TO OPEN . . . THE STRANGE AND SAVAGE PAGES OF . . . *The Lost Weekend*."

The movie, released less than two years after the novel, almost swept the Oscars—winning Best Picture, Director, and Screenplay, as well as Best Actor for Ray Milland, a Welshman hitherto known as a competent light comedian for supporting roles. A near teetotaler, Milland had been coached in the ways of drunkenness by the novel's author—a balding, impeccably groomed middle-aged man whose weird combination of wistfulness and zest put the actor in mind of "a bright, erratic problem child." At the time, Jackson was working at MGM on a screenwriting assignment and was bemused to find himself the most popular man in Hollywood. Everyone, it seemed, had read his book and experienced an almost Seabrook-like shock of recognition, regarding Jackson (as one journalist put it) "in the manner of a returned war hero . . . of a man who had been through hellfire and emerged bloodshot but unbowed." By then Jackson had been sober for almost a decade and was appalled by how readily people identified him with his narcissistic, crypto-homosexual, writer-manqué protagonist. "One third of the history is based on what I have experienced myself," he told Louella Parsons and others, "about one third on the experiences of a very good friend whose drinking career I followed very closely, and the other third is pure invention."

In fact, *The Lost Weekend* is autobiographical in almost every particular, though ultimately it's a little misleading to confuse Don Birnam with his creator. Whereas it's Don's curse to see his own alcoholic self-deceptions objectively, before he can quite enjoy them, Jackson the novelist had managed to remove himself once further—that is, by objectifying both the deluded *and* self-knowing Don. The first is the artist-hero of Don's never-to-be-written masterpiece, "In a Glass"—the brooding, dissolute apotheosis of the boy who, twenty years before, had stared into his bathroom mirror in hope that poetry-writing had wrought some telltale change, some outward sign of his cherished superiority ("Clods"), now preserved only by alcohol: "Suppose the clear vision in the bathroom mirror could fade (as in some trick movie) and be replaced by this image over the bar. Suppose that lad— Suppose time could be all mixed up so that the child of twenty years ago could look into the bathroom mirror and see himself reflected at thirty-three, as he saw himself now. What would he think, that boy?" As Don excitedly considers the possibilities— gloating over the clever multivalence of his title, "In a Glass" (the whiskey glass, the mirrors past and present)—for a moment he becomes not only the hero but the author, too, of this "classic of form and content," a kindred of Poe and Keats and Chatterton at whom his boy-self would have "nodded in happy recognition."

But of course the book doesn't exist, could *never* exist, and Don catches himself yet again—smiling tipsily, fatuously, into a barroom mirror. This, again, is the Don who is both tragic clown and audience ("staring back at the performer in silent contempt and ridicule"), while hovering above is the triumphant novelist— Jackson—and hence the implicit irony of Don's self-loathing diatribe:

> "In a Glass"—who would ever want to read a novel about a punk and a drunk! Everybody knew a couple or a dozen; they were not to be taken seriously; nuisances and trouble-makers, nothing more; like queers and fairies, people were belly-sick of them; whatever ailed them, that was their funeral; who cared?—life presented a thousand things more important to be written about than misfits and failures. . . . Like all his attempts at fiction it would be as personal as a letter—painful to those who knew him, of no interest to those who didn't; . . . so narcissistic that its final effect would be that of the mirrored room which gives back the same image times without count, or the old Post Toastie box of his boyhood with the fascinating picture of a woman and child holding a Post Toastie box with a picture of a woman and child holding a Post Toastie box with a picture of a woman and child holding . . .

And yet Jackson—producer of that evocative Post Toastie box—has written just such a novel as "In a Glass," and here we are reading it.

But of course the author understood that there was more to addiction than narcissistic escapism; indeed, many addicts (especially among the comfortable middle class) *begin* life, at least, as peculiarly lovable, promising human beings—all too aware, later, of the heartbreak they cause. "|W|hy were so many brilliant men alcoholic?" Don muses. "And from there, the next |question| was: Why did you drink?" Naturally Don can give any number of answers—and does—while understanding, too, that answers don't matter "in the face of the one fact: you drank and it was killing you. Why? Because alcohol was something you couldn't handle, it had you licked." This is the epiphanic "bottom" to which the addict must descend before seeking help— and yet Don keeps drinking. One thinks of the tippler in *The Little Prince,* who drinks because he is ashamed and is ashamed because he drinks—an insidious cycle of remorse that can either save or destroy the alcoholic: that is, either shame him into stopping once and for all, or goad him into further escape and final destruction. Not for nothing is *Macbeth* invoked again and again in the novel, the original title of which was "Present Fears" from Act I, Scene 3: "Present fears / Are less than horrible imaginings. . . ." Thus Don (named for the "Great Birnam Wood") constantly weighs his remorse over past misdeeds with his fear of what lies ahead—the "horrible imaginings" of a future that is, after all, only logical in light of the past:

> *Obviously there was the will in him to destroy himself; part of him was bent on self-destruction—he'd be the last to deny it. But obviously, too, part was not, part held back and expressed its disapproval in remorse and shame. . . . But the foolish psychiatrist knew so much less about it than the poet, the poet who said to another doctor,* Canst thou not minister to a mind diseased. . . . Raze out the written troubles of the brain?, *the poet who answered,* Therein the patient must minister to himself. . . .

Only Don can save himself, and yet (as poor William Seabrook and other fellow sufferers are apt to foresee) he almost certainly won't. In the early chapters there's a kind of black, picaresque comedy to Don's misadventures, grading subtly into tragedy until the climactic horror of his delirium tremens—which serves, superbly, both to recall the comedy and foretell Don's ultimate self-destruction, as his wheeling, drunken bat-self murders (and seems gruesomely to copulate with) the passive mouse: "The more it squeezed, the wider and higher rose the wings, like tiny filthy umbrellas, grey-wet with slime. Under the single spread of wings the two furry forms lay exposed to his stare, cuddled together as under a cosy canopy, indistinguishable one from the other, except that now the mouse began to bleed. Tiny drops of bright blood spurted down the wall; and from the bed he heard the faint miles-distant shrieks of dying." This, then, is the consummation of Don's narcissism—subject and object merging in death—though at the novel's end we leave him alive if not very well ("Why did they make such a fuss?"), preparing for another binge.

Don Birnam remains the definitive portrait of an alcoholic in American literature—a tragicomic combination of Hamlet and Mr. Toad, according to *Time,* which in 1963 reprinted the book as part of its paperback "Reading Program" of contemporary classics. The editors of *Time* were pleased to mention that Jackson himself was doing just fine: a devoted family man (the married father of two daughters) and chairman of the Alcoholics Anonymous chapter in New Brunswick, New Jersey—a man who now freely admitted that he was indeed Don Birnam, and hence his many hospitalizations for drug- and alcohol-related collapses in the twenty years since his famous first novel had been published. To be sure, he could afford to be candid by then; very few people had any idea who Jackson was, and even those happy few tended to muddle the matter. "I have become so used to having people say 'We loved your movie' instead of 'We read your book,'" said Jackson, "that now I merely say 'Thanks.'"

The Lost Weekend, after all, is something of an anomaly: a great novel that also resulted in a great (or near-great) movie—somewhat to the author's woe, as there are far more moviegoers than readers of literary fiction; the upshot, oddly enough, is that the movie has all but supplanted the novel as a cultural artifact (and never mind the five other books Jackson published in his lifetime). For his part Jackson never stopped fighting against his later obscurity, and finally was even willing to sacrifice his hard-won sobriety in order to resume writing, which he'd found all but impossible without the stimulus of drugs or alcohol. A recurrence of tuberculosis resulted in the removal of his right lung in 1963, and while recuperating at Will Rogers Hospital in Saranac Lake, Jackson was given medication that not only reduced his pain but restored his creative impulse. By 1967 he was back on the *Times* best-seller list with a novel about a nymphomaniac, *A Second-Hand Life,* and was eager to resume work on his long-awaited "Birnam saga," the first volume of which was to be titled *Farther and Wilder*. According to his editor at Macmillan, Robert Markel, Jackson had finished at least three hundred pages of this magnum opus when, in 1968, he took a fatal overdose of Seconal at the Hotel Chelsea, where he'd been living with a Czechoslovakian factory worker named Stanley Zednik.

He died, of course, as "the author of *The Lost Weekend,*" the way he'd been invariably identified throughout his career, no matter what he wrote. Within two years, however, even his most famous novel went out of print, its main subject no longer a matter of such lurid, salable sensationalism—due in part to its own influence as "the *Uncle Tom's Cabin* of alcoholism," as Walter Winchell called it. "[S]ince the publication of Charles Jackson's somber novel about an alcoholic," *Life* magazine had reported in 1946, "an unprecedented amount of attention has been paid to the drinking of alcohol and the problems arising therefrom." Jackson's insights were widely cited by such organizations as AA, the National Council on Alcoholism, and the Rutgers Center of

Alcohol Studies (where Jackson's devoted wife, Rhoda, worked for almost fifteen years), until at last the American Medical Association was roused to recognize alcoholism, officially, as a treatable disease.

Jackson, who'd spent so many years "on the circuit" giving talks for AA, would have been pleased by the ongoing shift in public perception, if perhaps a little exasperated where his own work was concerned: "I'm a writer first of all, and a non-drinker second," he insisted again and again, to little avail. This was a man who'd written arguably the first serious American novel whose foremost subject is homosexuality, *The Fall of Valor* (1946), as well as a short story collection, *The Sunnier Side* (1950), that was acclaimed as the midcentury equivalent of *Winesburg, Ohio*. That said, his greatest book is undoubtedly *The Lost Weekend,* and it deserves to be rediscovered foremost as a work of art. Among writers, to be sure, its most boisterous advocates tend to be famous drinkers, too—but then, who better to attest to its enduring power? "Marvelous and horrifying . . . the best fictional account of alcoholism I have ever read," said Kingsley Amis, a supreme authority in such matters. Let the reader be assured, then, that this is a work of canonical importance, for every conceivable reason.

PART ONE

The Start

"The barometer of his emotional nature was set for a spell of riot."

These words, on the printed page, had the unsettling effect no doubt intended, but with a difference. At once he put the book aside: closed it, with his fingers still between the pages; dropped his arm over the edge of the chair and let it hang, the book somewhere near the floor. This in case he wanted to look at it again. But he did not need to. Already he knew the sentence by heart: he might have written it himself. Indeed, it was with a sense of familiarity, of recognition, that his mind had first read through and accepted that sentence only a moment before; and now, as he relaxed his fingers' grip and dropped the book to the floor, he said aloud to himself: "That's me, all right." The book hit the rug with a soft thump and the Scottie looked up from its basket. "You heard me, Mac," he called out. "That's what I said!" He glared at the sleepy dog and added, loudly, burlesquing his fear and his delight: "It's *me* they're talking about. Me!"

He had been alone for nearly an hour. When Wick left, they had had one of their familiar and painful scenes, a scene in which he played dumb, as usual, leaving to his brother the burden of talking around the subject and avoiding any specific mention of what was on both their minds.

Wick had stood in the open door and looked back and said, "I wish you'd change your mind and come with us, this afternoon."

From the deep chair he smiled at his younger brother. "I know you do," he said, "but I can't. I'll be much better off here." He was aware that he was acting and looking like a romantic invalid and he tried to curb this.

The brother came back in and closed the door. "Listen. We've had the tickets such a long while. And Helen'll be disappointed and I'll be disappointed. You know she's only going because of you."

"I'll hear it on the radio."

"Today's Thursday, not Saturday."

"Oh yes. I forgot."

"And you look all right," his brother went on. "Nobody would think there was a thing wrong with you—it's all in your imagination. You look perfectly all right."

"Wick, I could never sit through it. I'd spoil it for you and Helen and I'd be miserable myself." Unintentionally he made the pathetic, the disarming admission: "Wick, I've only just recovered—it's only been three days. I couldn't *con*centrate."

The brother looked at him searchingly, almost sadly, he thought. "I wouldn't keep asking you, Don, if I didn't think it would do you good. It would do you so much good."

He smiled again, hanging onto his patience for dear life. "I'd run into someone I know and I can't see anybody."

"You wouldn't see anybody."

"Oh yes I would. And besides there's Helen. I can't have even her see me."

"Helen's seen you like this dozens of times."

"There—you see? I do show it."

"You're exaggerating all this, Don, and just indulging yourself. Listen, Don. If I'm willing to take off the rest of the week, to take you away for a long weekend in the country—just the two of us and Mac—I should think you could do this one thing for me. *Please* come with us."

He looked at the Scottie curled up in its basket, absently watching the two brothers. After a long pause, while he gathered his breath and his brother regarded him in that worried puzzled way, he said: "I don't mean to be stubborn but I'm not exaggerating and I'm not really indulging myself. Please try to understand. One more day and I'll be all right, but today—I can't go out now and I certainly can't go sit through *Tristan*. Tonight, when we get together in the car and drive away, fine. But not now.—Wick, I'd go to pieces if I went out now."

"How?" the brother asked. "And anyway, I'd be with you."

He shook his head. "Wick, won't you please go and forget about me? I can't see why you want me to go when you know I don't want to."

"You know why I want you to go," the brother said. "I mean," he added quickly, "I just don't want you to be alone when you're feeling like this."

"I'll be all right," he said, pretending not to notice the slip. He sighed, already fatigued with the familiar argument, but he believed he could keep it up forever if only it ended, finally, with his brother leaving him alone. "Will you *stop* worrying about me?"

"All right"—and he saw, with relief, that Wick had reached the point where he was afraid of pressing him too far and even now pretended to be pacified. "I'll tell Helen you didn't feel well enough. Will you be ready when I come back?"

"Yes," he said. "I'm ready now. I feel much better since I shaved and dressed." The shaving and dressing was probably what had precipitated this whole tiresome thing, it had given Wick ideas, but he couldn't take it back now.

Wick didn't seem to have noticed. "Mrs. Foley will be in about three o'clock to clean up a little. I've left a dollar on the radio in case you want her to get you anything."

"I won't want anything."

"What are you going to do—you're not going out, are you?"

"Oh no, I'm not going out." He smiled, and added, "You don't believe me, do you?"

The brother looked away. "I just thought maybe you'd be taking Mac out."

"No. Mrs. Foley can, if he wants to go out."

"All right," the brother said again. "I'll have the car sent over and we can get going by six-thirty at the latest. It may be cold down there; after all, it's October; but a weekend in the country will do you a lot of good. Both of us."

Don smiled again. "Thursday to Monday—that's pretty long for a 'weekend.'"

"That's all right, the longer the better. And listen,"—Wick was working it up for his benefit, trying to act enthusiastic, trying to show he had forgotten the tiresome pleading and was convinced that he would stay where he was, safe and sound—"let's not come back till Tuesday, or even Wednesday. Well, Tuesday—I can arrange it all right with the office."

"Sounds wonderful, Wick. Hear that, Mac?" He laughed. "One of those *long* weekends in the country, that you read about!"

"I'll be late," Wick said, turning. "Goodbye."

"Give my love to Helen."

"You're sure there isn't anything you want?"

"Thanks, Wick, I don't want anything. Have a good time."

"You'll surely be here?"

"Here?"

"When I come back."

"Of course I'll be here!" He was reproachful, hurt, and his brother turned at once toward the door.

"Goodbye."

"Goodbye. Give my love to Helen!"

The door was closed; and he smiled to himself as he realized what an effort it had cost Wick not to look back once more. He smiled because he was relieved to be alone again and because he knew so much more about this whole thing than his brother did. Poor Wick, he thought, and at once he began to feel better. "Well, Mac," he said aloud, "it seems that we're going to the country." He got up and went over to look at the dollar bill lying on the radio. Then he came back and sat down again in the big chair.

There was a small Longines traveling clock on the ledge of the bookshelf at his elbow and it said 1:32. He picked it up and wound it, remembering the generous Dutchman who had given it to him that winter in Gstaad and how the Dutchman's feelings had been hurt because he hadn't got around to thanking him for two days. He set it back on the shelf and looked about the room.

Now that he was alone, with five hours staring him in the face, he began to sense the first pricks of panic; then knew at once it was something he only imagined. "What to do, Mac, what to do?" The dog opened its eyes, lifted its head from the cushion, and relapsed into sleep again. "I get it," he said. "Bored!" He spoke up sharply, not even thinking of the dog now. "What the hell have *you* got to be bored with!" His eye fell on the gramophone. He walked over to it and lifted the cover. The last record of a Beethoven sonata was on, the *Waldstein*. He turned the switch and set it going; but before the record was halfway through, its jubilant energy and hammering clanging rhythm oppressed him, and he reached to shut it off. As he lifted the arm of the pickup, the trembling of his hand caused the needle to scrape across the record with a strident squawk that brought the Scottie to its feet. "Relax, dog," he said, and came back to his chair.

The time had to be filled, he couldn't just sit here. On the bookshelf at his elbow was a collection of monographs on modern painters. He leaned forward to examine the titles, then chose the Utrillo. He pulled the book down and spread it open on his lap. There were a few colored reproductions but these were scarcely more colorful than the black-and-whites. He thumbed through the drab pages, stopping now and again to linger over some scene of a deserted melancholy street, or a little grey lane hemmed in by sad plaster walls, and a feeling of almost intolerable loneliness came over him. Even the village squares or the open places in front of churches had this loneliness, this desertion, as if everyone had gone off for the day to attend some brilliant fair, leaving the town desolate and empty behind. In imagination, in memory, he stood in just such a little street now, as he had when he was a child—at sundown, after supper, on a summer evening, standing alone in the quiet street and listening to a steam calliope playing far away on the edge of the town, at the fairgrounds, before the evening performance of the circus. He closed the book and put it back on the shelf, remembering that moment so clearly and well that tears of pity came to his eyes—for the child, for himself, for the painter, he did not know whom.

"I must be in lousy condition to get so worked up over—over nothing," he said. "Or do I want to?" He addressed the waking dog. "Do I, Mac? *You* tell me." He stared at the dog. "Well?" The dog stared back. "Am I indulging myself, as your pr-r-r-roud master said"—trilling the "r" like an actor—"am I putting it on, is it all my imagination? Or if not mine, whose?" There's a thought for today, he said to himself. He stood up. "Mac, you're exaggerating, nobody would think there was a thing wrong with you! You look perfectly all right! And when I say you look all right, then, God damn it, you *feel* all right, do you hear?" He was having fun now, but even as he reached the pitch of his enjoyment he tired of it, and so did the dog. Who's loony now, he said to himself apathetically, as he sat down again.

His fingers touched the edge of a small book tucked in beside the cushion of the chair. He pulled it out and looked at the title. It was a copy of James Joyce's *Dubliners* his brother had been reading. He opened it and began to read at random, articulating the words very carefully in a whisper, paying elaborate attention to the form of each word but none to what he was reading. It was like the time, on similar occasions, when, keyed-up, desperate, he went out in search of a French movie, and sat in some airless movie-house all afternoon concentrating on the rapid French being spoken from the screen, because he believed a few hours of such concentration, even though he didn't listen to the sense, had a steadying effect. So he read now for some minutes, thinking that he might even read the book right through and then through again before his brother came back. Wouldn't that surprise him? he said to himself with a smile, while his lips formed other words: *The barometer of his emotional nature was set for a spell of riot.* The smile faded, he stared and read again.

The burden, the oppression was gone. He felt positively light-headed, joyous. The words had released him from the acute sense of suspense he now realized he had been under since his brother left. This is what he had been waiting for, what he had probably known all along in the back of his mind was bound to happen. It was as though a light-switch had been snapped on or a door sprung open, showing him the way. He dropped the book; and after he had exhorted the dog, saying, "It's *me* they're talking about. Me"—he shrugged, his hands spread open, palms up, in a wide gesture, and said: "Why am I such a fool? Why resist or wait?" He looked around, his eyebrows raised to his imaginary audience, like a comedian—an audience where he himself was every one of the several hundred people staring back at the performer in silent contempt and ridicule. He knew he was thus looking at himself. For his own benefit he exaggerated the action and voice, clowning because of his embarrassment. "I leave it to you, gentlemen, Mac, all," he said aloud; "call me ham if you like but—there's the part! What can one do about it?"

He dropped the role and stood up. He went to the radio and picked up the dollar bill. "Control! Control, Mac," he said. "There's plenty of time." He lifted his coat from the back of a chair. "All afternoon," he added. "Time to go out and plenty of time to get back. Plenty." The Scottie watched him from its basket. He buttoned his coat and went into the kitchen to see if water had been put down for the dog.

On the kitchen table was an envelope addressed to Mrs. Foley. He picked it up and held it to the light. He tore it open and fingered through four five-dollar bills. "*Twenty,* my God," he said. "Why twenty?" It must be Mrs. Foley's pay for the month. She came two afternoons a week to pick up and often at noon to take the dog out. He put the bills in his pocket, wadded the empty envelope into a ball and threw it out the window.

He heard the wadded-up envelope rattle along the fire-escape and he stood a moment longer looking absently out at the blank brick wall opposite. Suddenly he thought of Wick. He would be at the opera now. Helen would be there too, sitting beside him in the great nearly dark house (she's only going because of you). The two of them would be looking at the brilliantly lighted sailing-ship scene that was the first act, and now and again one of them would lean toward the other and whisper something about the performance. Not about him; they wouldn't be talking about him now. Chiefly because he was the only thing on their minds and neither wanted the other to know it. Helen would be wondering if he really wasn't feeling well, or was he off again; and Wick would be wondering if Helen had accepted the excuse. She didn't give a damn for the opera under any conditions and he certainly didn't under these. He would be staring at the stage, half-turned toward Helen to catch her next whispered comment, and think-ing: "If he isn't there when I go back; if he's gone out—" Don felt sorry for the distraction he knew he was causing them, and yet he couldn't help smiling, too. He was taking their minds off the per-formance a hundred times more than if he had been sitting there between them and talking loudly against the music.

On his way out he went into the bathroom to see how he looked. "During the next few days," he said, as he straightened his tie, "I'll probably be looking into this mirror more often than is good for mortal man." He winked. "That's how well I know *my*self. However." Before he left, he looked back at the dog. "Don't you worry, Mac—don't you wuddy—about Mrs. Foley's money. I'll be back in time to hand it to her myself," he said, "in person. Just in case anybody should ask." Then he slammed the door, tried it again to see if the lock had caught, and went down the stairs.

East 55th Street was cool, even for October. He thought of

running back for a topcoat, but time was precious; and besides, his destination and haven lay just around the corner.

When the drink was set before him, he felt better. He did not drink it immediately. Now that he had it, he did not need to. Instead, he permitted himself the luxury of ignoring it for a while; he lit a cigarette, took some envelopes out of his pocket and unfolded and glanced through an old letter, put them away again and began to hum, quietly. Gradually he worked up a subtle and elaborate pretense of ennui: stared at himself in the dark mirror of the bar, as if lost in thought; fingered his glass, turning it round and round or sliding it slowly back and forth in the wet of the counter; shifted from one foot to the other: glanced at a couple of strangers standing farther down the bar and watched them for a moment or two, critical, aloof, and, as he thought, aristocratic; and when he finally did get around to raising the glass to his lips, it was with an air of boredom that said, Oh well, I suppose I might as well drink it, now that I've ordered it.

He thought again of Wick and Helen. Funny relationship. Closer than if they had been lifelong friends; but not because of any real affinity or interest in each other. In fact, each was the kind of person that the other did not care for at all. The only thing that held them together was him, of course. Aside from himself, they had no common meeting ground. And he was able, by his bad behavior no less than his good, to bind them closer than if they had been brother and sister. How they were one, when things were going well with him. How they were united even more, when he was on the loose. If they could see him now. Or perhaps they knew only too well what he was doing at this very moment. Hell, why wouldn't they? It had happened so many times. . . .

Gloria sidled up and put a hand on his shoulder. Imperceptibly he pulled away, careful not to offend her but cold enough so that she wouldn't get any ideas in her head. Gloria was something new here and he didn't like it at all. Why in thunder should a 2nd Avenue bar-and-grill attempt a "hostess," for God's sake?

He didn't like acting snooty about her in front of Sam; and then again he thought it was well that they should be reminded he didn't care for this sort of thing. He was fond of this bar but just the same he was different from most people who came here and they knew it. Gloria was not more than twenty, blonde, not thin, dressed in a brown satin dress that shone like copper. She always asked for a cigarette, so now he placed his pack on the counter with the hope that that would take care of her.

"Hello-o-o," she said. "Where you been? I haven't seen you for days and days." She took a cigarette. "Been away?"

"Yes."

"You look awful nice. That a new suit?"

He didn't answer.

"My, we aren't very chummy today. What's the matter?"

"As a matter of fact," he said, "I was—thinking."

"Okay, that's all right," she said. "I'll come back and have a drink with you later, maybe. Huh?"

"Swell."

She moved down the bar and began talking to the other two men.

His drink was finished and he had not felt it at all. It had been so much water. Funny that he hadn't noticed even the faintest small tingle. He only felt relaxed, for the first time in days—so relaxed that it was almost fatigue. He nodded to Sam and another rye was set before him.

It was true, what he had said about thinking. Ordinarily he enjoyed talking to Sam by the hour—they were old friends; at times he thought of Sam as one of the persons he was fondest of in all the world—but today he didn't feel like talking. He was suddenly very low, all spirit gone. He downed the drink almost at once and asked for another. While Sam opened a new bottle, he looked at his face in the mirror over the bar.

It was an interesting face, no question about it. The mirror was just dark enough so that he seemed to be seeing a stranger rather than himself. Completely objective, he looked at the face in the glass and began to study it so intently that he was almost surprised to see its expression change under his gaze to one of searching concern.

The face showed all of its thirty-three years, but no more. The forehead was good, the eyes dark, big, and deep-set. The nostrils of the longish acquiline nose flared slightly—they were good too; gave the face a keen look, like a thoroughbred. The mustache was just big and black enough; had it been a little larger, he might have been looking into the tragic interesting face of Edgar Allan Poe. The mouth was full and wide, it wore a discontented unhappy expression—interestingly so. He liked the two deep lines that ran down either side of the mouth from just above the nostrils, half-encircling the set bitter half-smile. He liked too the three horizontal lines of his forehead—not really horizontal, for above his right eye they tilted upward to avoid the perpetually raised right-eyebrow, so fixed there by habit that he was never able to bring it down to the level of the other without frowning. He picked up the glass Sam set before him and began to drink.

He remembered a girl who sat behind him in 1st-year Latin class, a talkative girl, the kind who was always wondering what she looked like when she was asleep—things like that. She said to him once, "Faces are interesting, you know it? I was thinking about yours the other day and do you know what I decided? I decided that if someone should ask me what your habitual expression was, I'd say, 'Animation.'" She had paused for the effect, though there was no doubting her honesty. "Even in repose your face looks animated. You always look so alive, and curious— in*quis*itive, I guess I mean." He had been far from embarrassed, of course. When she asked him to describe what her habitual expression was, he had made up something, he didn't know what, already lost in thought for what she had said. Animation, was it.

You could hardly call that face in the mirror "animated, alive." It was set in an expression of studied disillusion which not even the new drink could shake.

He glanced at his watch. Mrs. Foley would be arriving in a quarter of an hour. Time for one more drink—two at the outside. He shoved the glass toward Sam and stared at himself over the bar again.

Mirrors seemed to have taken up a hell of a lot of time in his life. He thought of one now—the mirror in the bathroom, years ago, back home. When he was a kid—fourteen, fifteen—writing a poem every night before he went to sleep, starting and finishing it at one sitting even though it might be two or three o'clock, that bathroom mirror had come to mean more to him than his own bed. Nights when he had finished a poem, what could have been more natural, more necessary and urgent, than to go and look at himself to see if he had changed? Here at this desk, this night, one of life's important moments had occurred. Humbly, almost unaware, certainly innocent, he had sat there and been the instrument by which a poem was transmitted to paper. He was awed and truly humble, for all that he must look in the mirror to see if the experience registered in his face. Often tears came genuinely to his eyes. How had it come about—why should it have been *he*? He asked himself in humility and gratitude. He read the poem in fear and read it again. *Now* it was fine; would it be so tomorrow? He raised his eyes from the scrawled re-written sheets and listened to the night. No sound whatever; and he thought of his brothers sleeping in the adjoining rooms, his mother downstairs. They had slept, all unaware of what had happened in this room, this night, at this desk. Scornful and proud, "Clods" he muttered; but proper appreciation of such a moment was beyond them, of course, even if they should know. He forgot them at once—though he did not forget to the extent of going down the hall at his usual heedless pace. He tiptoed, listening breathless for any sound of stir in the dark bedrooms (too often he had been surprised at three in the morning by a waking brother, who reported at the breakfast table that Don had had his light on all night long; and the recriminations that followed then—the bitter reminders of how he mooned at his desk when he ought to be asleep like a normal boy, the savage scoldings for running up huge light-bills—how shameful these were and humiliating, in view of the poem that justified all this, did they but know). In the bathroom he snapped on the light and confronted himself in the glass. The large childish eyes stared back, eager and searching; the cheeks were flushed, the mouth half-open in suspense. He studied every feature of that alert countenance, so wide awake that it seemed it would never sleep again. Surely there would be some sign, some mark, some tiny line or change denoting a new maturity, perhaps? He scanned the forehead, the mouth, the staring eyes, in vain. The face looked back at him as clear, as heartbreakingly youthful, as before.

He was moved and amused as he recalled that moment— a moment that had been repeated dozens and dozens of times in all his long adolescence. He picked up the glass and drank it to the bottom. A fancy came to him. Suppose the clear vision in the bathroom mirror could fade (as in some trick movie) and be replaced by this image over the bar. Suppose that lad— Suppose time could be all mixed up so that the child of twenty years ago could look into the bathroom mirror and see himself reflected at thirty-three, as he saw himself now. What would he think, that boy? Would he have accepted it—is this what he dreamed of becoming? Would he accept it for a moment? In his emotion and embarrassment he glanced away and signaled to Sam to pour him another.

The men at the end of the bar had gone. Gloria sat at a table in the back, filing her nails. He watched her, indifferent about her now; then fearing that she might see him looking and take it as an invitation to come forward again, he turned back to the bar, automatically picking up the new drink that had been set before him.

Or wait—of *course* he would accept it! It was all crystal clear, like a revelation (suddenly he was feeling brighter, more alert and clear mentally, than he ever had in his life). That kid, could he have seen this face, the man of today, certainly would have accepted it—he would have loved it! The idol of the boy had been Poe and Keats, Byron, Dowson, Chatterton—all the gifted miserable and reckless men who had burned themselves out in tragic brilliance early and with finality. Not for him the normal happy genius living to a ripe old age (genius indeed! How could a genius be happy, normal—above all, long-lived?), acclaimed by all (or acclaimed in his lifetime?), enjoying honor, love, obedience, troops of friends ("I must not look to have"). The romantic boy would have been satisfied, he would have responded with all his ardent youthful soul. There was a poetic justice in those disillusioned eyes and the boy would have known it and nodded in happy recognition.

In the next instant came disgust (self-disgust and scorn; self-reproach for inflating the image of himself out of all proportion to the miserable truth); and in the very next, the brilliant idea. Oh, brilliant! As it swept over him and took possession of his excited brain—so feverishly alert that it seemed his perceptions could, at this moment, grasp any problem in the world—he fidgeted in suspense, shifted from one foot to the other, and made an effort to calm himself. Now wait a moment, just let me order another drink and think this out slowly—it's coming too fast. . . .

A story of that boy and this man—a long short story—a classic of form and content—a *Death in Venice,* artistically only, not in any other way—the title: "In a Glass." What else could it be?—the glass of the title meaning at first the whisky glass he was drinking from, out of which grew the multitude of fancies; then the idea blurring and merging gradually, subtly, with the glass of the mirror till finally the title comes to mean in the reader's mind only the glass over the bar through which the protagonist looks back on his youth. "In a Glass"—it would begin with a man standing in a 2nd Avenue bar on just such an October afternoon as this, just such a man as he, drinking a glass of whisky, several glasses, and looking at his reflection in the mirror over the bar. Thoughts poured in a rush, details, incidents, names, ideas, ideas. At this moment, if he were able to write fast enough, he could set it down in all its final perfection, right down without a change or correction needed later, from the brilliant opening to the last beautiful note of wise and grave irony. The things between—the things! . . . The wrench (the lost lonely abandonment) when his father left home and left him—but anything, practically anything out of childhood, climaxed by the poetry-writing and the episode of the bathroom mirror; then on to Dorothy, the fraternity night-mare, Dorothy again, leaving home, the Village and prohibition, Mrs. Scott, the *Rochambeau* (the *Bremen, LaFayette, Champlain, de Grasse*); the TB years in Davos; the long affair with Anna; the drinking; Juan-les-Pins (the weekend there that lasted two months, the hundred dollars a day); the pawnshops; the drink-ing, the unaccountable things you did, the people you got mixed up with; the summer in Provincetown, the winter on the farm; the books begun and dropped, the unfinished short-stories; the drinking the drinking the drinking; the foolish psychiatrist—the foolish foolish psychiatrist; down to Helen, the good Helen he always knew he would marry and now knew he never would, Helen who was always right, who would sit through *Tristan* this afternoon resisting it, refusing to be carried away or taken in, see-ing it and hearing it straight off for what it was as he would only be able to see it and hear it after several years of irrational idolatry first. . . . Whole sentences sprang to his mind in dazzling succes-sion, perfectly formed, ready to be put down. Where was a pencil, paper? He downed his drink.

The time. Four o'clock. Mrs. Foley would be there now but to hell with that! This was more important. But caution, slow. Good thing there was no paper handy, no chance to begin impulsively what later must be composed—when, tonight maybe, certainly tomorrow—with all the calm and wise control needed for such an undertaking. A *tour de force*? Critics would call it that, they'd be bound to, but what the hell was the matter with a *tour de force* for Christ's sake that the term should have come to be a sneer? Didn't it mean a brilliant performance and is "brilliance" something to snoot at? His mind raced on. But how about "As Through a Glass Darkly"?—or "Through a Glass Darkly"? No, it had been done to death; trite; every lady-writer in the land had used it at one time or another, or if they hadn't, it was a wonder. "In a Glass" was perfect—he saw stacks of copies in bookshop windows, piled in tricky pyramids (he would drop in and address the bookseller with some prepared witticism, like, "I appreciate the compliment you pay my book by piling it up in the window like a staple that should be in every home; but couldn't you add a card saying 'Send in ten wrappers and get a free illustrated life of the author'?"— hell, that was too long for wit, he'd have to cut it down), he glanced over people's shoulders in the subway and smiled to himself as he heard one girl say to another "I can't make head or tail of this"—(she had something if she meant "tale"), he read with amusement an embarrassed letter from his mother regretting the fact that he hadn't published a book she could show the neighbors and why didn't he write something that had "human interest"? With a careful glance about him he picked up his glass, offered a silent rueful toast to human interest, and drank.

Suddenly, sickeningly, the whole thing was so much eyewash. How could he have been seduced, fooled, into dreaming up such a ridiculous piece; in perpetrating, even in his imagination, any-thing so pat, so contrived, so cheap, so phoney, so adolescent, so (crowning offense) sentimental? Euphoria! Faithless muse! What crimes are committed in thy— *There* was a line he might use; and oh, another: the ending!—the ending sprang to his mind clear and true as if he had seen it in print. The hero, after the long pro-cession of motley scenes from his past life (would the line stretch out to th' crack of doom?)—the hero decides to walk out of the bar and somewhere, somehow, that very day—not for himself, of course: for Helen—commit suicide. The tag: "It would give her a lifelong romance." Perfect; but now—oh more perfect still—was the line that came next, the *new* ending: the little simple line set in a paragraph all by itself beneath the other, on the last page:

"But he knew he wouldn't."

How much it said, that line; how much it told about himself. How it disarmed the reader about the hero and still more the author—as if the author had stepped in between the page and the reader and said, "You see? I didn't die, after all. I went home and wrote down what you have just been reading. And Helen—what of her? Did we marry, you ask?" Shrug. "Who can tell? . . ."

"Sam, I'll have one more rye." To celebrate, he said under his breath. To celebrate what?—and a fit of boredom, of ennui so staggering descended upon him with such suddenness that he was scarcely able to stand. He wanted to put his head down on the counter, in the wet and all, and weep: tears, idle tears, I know damned well what they mean—for he was seeing himself with unbearable clarity again and he could beat his fists together and curse this double vision of his that enabled him, forced him, to see too much—though all the while, all the long time he had been at the bar, he knew that to the casual spectator he had changed or moved by not so much as a hair or had a thought more troubling than the price of his drinks. Cloudy the place, who was drinking now with him, in him, inside him, instead of him, he loved and hated himself and that Sam, and groped to think of it again, clearly like before. To live and praise God in blessed mediocrity (Tonio! spiritual brother!), to be *at home* in the world—how with bitter passion he envied that and them, people like Sam here, pouring the rye. Can they imagine the planning of a story like that, the planning alone, much less the writing? Can they imagine how, being able to plan it, being able to master the plan and the writing, can they understand how you would fail—fail merely by failing to write it at all—why, how? The answer was nowhere, the drink was everything. What a blessing the money in his pocket, he must get more, much more for the feast of drink ahead. Ignorant Sam, sweaty man, how far from thy homeland hast thou come, from thy fair Irish county to this dark whisky-smelling mirrored cheap quiet lovely haven! Surely the most beautiful light in all the world was the light on the bricks out there, under the L, the patches of gold edged in black shadow, a street paved with golden bricks truly, with beams of light slanting upward fairer and purer than rays of sun through cathedral glass. Why should Cezanne have painted the blue monotonous hills and fields of France, let him paint *this* for Christ's sake! Or me—let me do it—for he knew now just how it could be done, and downed his drink in an inspired impulse to rush out and spend all his money on painting materials and try. He ordered a drink and drank it and looked again, to fix the scene and the light in his mind: the gold was gone, the rays out, the bricks red and black with neon night.

Gloria was there, her hand on his shoulder. He turned, startled.

"Why don't you come sit down and eat something with me? I'm going to eat now."

"Why? What's the time?"

"Quarter past."

"Five?"

"Six."

"I've got a—dinner engagement. Sorry." In a moment he was gone, in panic to be home before Wick.

At the corner he stopped in the liquor store to buy a pint. He pretended to deliberate a moment, considering the various brands, knowing all the while he would buy the bottle that was just under a dollar as he always did, no matter how much money he had in his pocket; for he had a dread of running out of cash and being cut off from drink and so bought only the cheapest, to make it last. Liquor was all one anyway. He scanned the shelves, self-conscious as always in a liquor store—he could never overcome the idea that he had no right to be there, that the clerks and customers were eyeing him and nodding to each other ("Sure, look who's here, wouldn't you know"), and he envied with a jealous envy those who could come into a liquor store and buy a bottle with the nonchalant detachment of a housewife choosing her morning groceries. He pointed to the brand he wanted and put down a dollar bill.

The Lincoln was in front of the house, the ancient Lincoln that looked as though it might belong to a Beacon Hill dame or a Sugar Hill dinge. He wondered if it meant that his brother was home and then remembered that the garage was to send the car over at about this time. He had to know if Wick was there before going up, had to see that the pint was well concealed in his inside pocket, had to prepare his greeting, his expression, before he walked in. He went in the front door and straight through the hall to the back garden.

The lights were on in the apartment, showing in the two windows of the living room and the window of the one bedroom, his bedroom because he was the older brother (Wick slept on the living room couch). He sat down on a bench in the dark at the back of the garden and looked up. He would wait a few minutes in the freshening air, gathering his strength, cooling off. The night was chill, but he had to open his vest and take off his hat. He mopped his forehead with his handkerchief and took the heavy pint out of his pocket and set it on the bench. Immediately he put it back again, afraid that he might walk away and forget it.

He remembered the time they had first looked at the apartment, standing in the bare flat and looking through the windows at the little garden down in back. There was a high board fence around three sides of it, painted white with large flower designs in yellow and a fantastic huge green vine. His brother had laughed in delight and so had he. "God, such quaint," Wick had said, and he knew that that had decided him: they would take the place because Wick had liked it and it was Wick's money he was living on now. He didn't mind; he was grateful; it was one of those times—a period of several weeks—when he was not drinking at all, when he felt that he would never drink again and said so; and Wick, to help him out, had taken a chance, leased the apartment for them both, and with elaborate gaiety and many plans for the winter (to assure each other that neither had a worry in his head) they had moved in.

How long had it lasted? He couldn't think of that now, mustn't think of it, wouldn't. He sat by the white fence looking up at the lighted windows. Wick would be alone with Mac. They were waiting for him. He buttoned his vest, stood up and shifted the pint to his hip-pocket, then felt to see if it bulged too much. It was all right if he didn't button the jacket. He sat down again. Why the hell hadn't he bought two pints, as he usually did, so that if one was taken away he would have the other? He always planted one in his side pocket, the bulk of it showing conspicuously, and protested with passion and outrage when it was discovered and taken—then retired in a huff to his room, there to produce the other pint from his hip and hide it. Where had he not hidden bottles in his time? In the pocket of his old fur coat in the closet, the coat he never wore; behind books, of course; in galoshes, vases, mattresses.

His brother appeared in the bedroom window. He saw his shadow on the pane, and then the silhouette of his head and shoulders as he sat at the desk, his desk. He trembled with excitement but there was no need for fright. Wick was not looking out. He appeared merely to be sitting there, looking straight ahead at the front of the desk. He couldn't be writing, for his head was erect. What was he doing there, what in thunder was he doing all this while?—for now he realized Wick had been there ten minutes, fifteen, there was no telling how long. The suspense was intolerable. His heart pounded, he ached to open the bottle and take a drink, but he did not dare move—though he knew he was invisible to his brother in the dark of the garden even if he should look out.

He wanted to go in, he wanted now to go up and walk into the apartment and say, "See, here I am, I'm not out, I'm not wandering around God knows where, don't worry, you don't need to worry now"—but he couldn't if his life depended on it. Or he wanted to toss a stone up against the window and shout, "Wick! Here I am, see? Out in the garden, sitting here on this bench, getting the air, please don't worry, this is where I am, you can go on to the farm now, or you can wait a little while longer, just a few minutes more, and I'll go with you." He began to cry.

It was probably a moment he would remember all his life long, with tears; or was he just being maudlin, now, in drink? No, it was a moment of awful clarity, it was too real for that, his heart almost died in ache for his brother and for himself, for the two of them together, and he wept as he had not wept since he was a child. Would nothing stop the weeping? His brother sat there above, so near him, so unaware that all the time he was sitting here below, watching, knowing that Wick was wondering where he was, wondering what to do about him, how to help—go or stay? He could not watch any more. He bent down and put his head on the bench and cried. He buried his face in his crossed arms to smother the sobs. He must stop. I won't look again for minutes, minutes, he'll be gone by then—and with an effort he quieted himself, shifted the bottle to his side pocket, lay over on the bench on his back, with closed eyes, and began to wait. When he looked up again, the windows were dark.

At once, instinctively, automatically, he was wary. He sat up, alert. Was it a trick? Was Wick waiting for him there in the dark, waiting for him to walk in? He smiled. That would be easy to find out. With the caution of a burglar—feeling the excitement, the game of it—he tiptoed craftily across the garden, through the hall and to the front steps. The car was gone.

In high spirits, completely happy now, he went upstairs. The cool evening air of the garden had freshened him and he looked forward to a drink. The moment he switched on the light he looked for the Scottie. The basket was empty. On the living room table there was a note:

> I'm so sorry. Please be careful. I've gone to the farm. I would like to leave Mac for you but I thought you might forget to feed him. If you want anything, call Helen. About Mrs. Foley's money, it should be enough to take care of you till I come back. Do be careful, won't you.

Did Wick know that he was making him feel it just that much more because the entire message contained not so much as a syllable of reproach? Of course he did! But he wasn't going to feel it, wasn't going to allow himself to think of it—I can't; I can't think of that now, he said to himself. He had other problems at the moment: chiefly, money.

It was seven-thirty. Wick had got a late start for the long drive to the farm but he couldn't think of that, now, either. He took the wad of bills from his pocket and counted them. There was more than fifteen dollars. He would get more. He went into the kitchen for a glass, opened the pint and poured a drink.

The problem of money. He knew that if he had money—was suddenly left a lot of money, or found it, or stole it—he would kill himself in a month. Well, why not, what difference did it make, that would be his own affair. If he wanted to drink himself to death, whose business was it but his own? But this way, with his rightful allowance coming to him through his brother, his younger brother at that—driblets handed out to him as if he were a child, not being able to get a suit pressed without finding out first if it was all right with Wick, not being able to tip in restaurants where Wick paid the check, charging everything, never paying cash, getting fifty cents a day for cigarette money—it made him wild to think of it, he would get money and more money, buy as many pints as he liked and still have more money to buy more. How? There were dozens of ways, he had never yet been unable to find a way, even a new way he had never tried before, except when he was physically unable to get up and go out. But he wouldn't fall into that trap again; he'd have it in the house, bottles and bottles—for once be prudent enough to provide himself with a sufficient supply.

After the second drink he was ready. Before he left, he went into the bathroom to see how he looked. He smiled in the glass. He looked all right—in fact he looked wonderful. "But don't forget," he said aloud, "you're skirting danger." He nodded in agreement with his reflection, smiled, winked, and switched off the light. He lifted his topcoat from the rack in the hall and reached for the doorknob. At that moment he heard the two women who lived in the front apartment come up the stairs with their dog. The dog stopped at his door and sniffed, and one of the women said, "Stop that, Sophie. Come here!" The dog ran down the hall and he heard the door to the apartment shut. He listened a moment more, then knew that now he could go out.

Mrs. Wertheim's laundry, in the middle of the block, was closed, but he could see the light on in the back of the shop and Mrs. Wertheim working there, alone, over the ironing board. He rapped on the glass. She looked up from the board, put the iron aside, hesitated, then came forward slowly, uncertain, peering to see who it might be. (This is the Student Raskolnikov.) He tapped again to reassure her. She came up to the glass and shielded her eyes with her hands. He smiled back. When she saw who it was, she nodded with her funny German bow and unlatched the door.

"Guten abend, gnädige Frau," he sang out, speaking loudly as he always did when addressing a foreigner.

"Mr. Birnam, how do you do?"

"I wonder if you can do me a favor, bitte?"

"Okay? What is it?"

"My brother's gone away for the weekend and I find he's taken the checkbook."

"Oh? Do you want a blank check?"

"No, don't bother, danke. Instead could you let me have a little money till Monday? Just for the weekend."

"Let's see—how much?"

"Oh, twenty dollars, bitte schön. That should be enough."

"Oh dear." She smiled, but she frowned too, as if puzzled. "Okay, I guess I can, Mr. Birnam—only, are you sure it's all right?"

"Just till Monday, Mrs. Wertheim."

"I mean," she said—and then seemed to change her mind. "One moment, please. Here, step in." She went to the back of the shop, stood there a moment counting out some bills under the light while he waited in unbearable excitement, and returned. She handed him the bills, shaking her head ever so slightly in a puzzled frown.

He took the money without looking at it and shoved it into his pocket. He smiled cordially at her. "Thank you so much, Mrs. Wertheim," he said. "Mille fois," and he turned back to the street.

In the back of the cab that was rushing him down to the Village he smiled to himself—smiled in triumph. How easy it was. Poor Mrs. Wertheim—she wouldn't have turned him down, of course. He knew Europeans enough to know that. He had played the aristocrat before the peasant—the peasant who never dared refuse the aristocrat anything; who expected nothing less; who felt it an honor to be imposed upon by that privileged charming irresponsible class; who kept himself and his family in lifelong debt to guarantee the aristocracy its birthright; who would have lost *faith,* perhaps, if he and his fascinating kind should settle down and become sober, industrious and productive, like themselves; who smiled indulgently, admiringly, even affectionately, at foibles which, in their own children, would have deserved nothing but a beating. This, for the brilliant moment, was his vision of himself and Mrs. Wertheim now that he had twenty more dollars in his pocket. "Jack's, in Charles Street," he called out, and sat back, pleased with the glimpse of high life he had given the grateful Mrs. Wertheim.

This was absurd, of course; he knew it; the episode had meant no such thing; he knew it even as he daydreamed (Mrs. Wertheim had no use for him whatever, she only did it because of his brother); and he cursed this mocking habit of his which always made him expose his own fancies just as they reached their climax. There was never any pleasure in them beyond the second or two of their inception: they sprang into being, grew, and exploded all in the same moment, leaving him with nothing but a sense of self-distaste for having again played the fool. He didn't mind playing the fool, that would have been all right—he minded knowing it, hated knowing it. It made him seem a kind of dual personality, at once superior and inferior to himself, the drunk and the sober ego. In neither role could he let go, be himself; in neither did he feel in control.

What trick was it now, for instance, that was taking him on to Jack's—when had the drunk suggested that? Or rather, the sober ego?—for he was well aware that when he was drunk he preferred to be and drink alone; only sober did he ever drink or begin drinking with others; and soon, certainly within the hour, he found some pretext to excuse himself from the company (temporarily, of course, he thought as well as they) and disappeared for the rest of the night or the week. Was it some vestige of social sense that took care of this, warning him to drink alone and so minimize the danger of trouble? Did some last scrap of pride intrude on his intoxication to remind him that he was never himself when drunk? He knew he wasn't sober enough now to want to go to Jack's and drink with others at the same bar, even if they were strangers. Why was he doing it, then? And why the Village—why Jack's of all places in New York (he hadn't been there since its fashionable days as a speakeasy)? He was wary, for the moment, as if he suspected a kind of trick; he felt a presentiment of trouble ahead, a premonition and hint of that danger he had warned himself about in the mirror; and then wondered: Was he only imagining this, dramatizing again, having fun?

Jack's had an upstairs as well as a downstairs bar. He walked through on the street level to the stairs at the back. Piano music drifted down the small stairway, and laughter. He ascended and came out into the upstairs bar. There wasn't much of a crowd; perhaps it was still too early. Two young men, looking like football players, stood at the bar. He thought for a moment of standing there too, but instead went over to one of the small tables and sat down on the long bench that ran the length of the room. A waiter came and he ordered a gin-and-vermouth, suddenly sentimental about his favorite bar in Zurich, though he hadn't drunk a gin-vermouth since he came home. The waiter asked if he might take his coat. No, he kept his coat on—with a bored air he said he was only going to stay a few moments. He permitted himself a few amiable words of French. To his surprise, the waiter pursed his lips like Charles Boyer and replied volubly, with such a super-Parisian accent that it sounded obscene—a series of nasty noises in the front of his mouth, as if he were mentally indulging in *fellatio, pedicatio, irrumatio* and *cunnilinctus.* This observation struck him as so comic that he had to turn his head away to hide his smile. Then he looked about the room, feeling apart, remote, above it all. He began to think of himself as a spectator making a kind of field-trip in sociology, and he believed the others, perhaps, might be wondering who he was. Tonight he would be aloof, detached, enjoying his anonymity.

There were couples at some of the tables, a few fellows and girls. He studied them, and studied the football heroes at the bar. Their shoulders were wide and straight, so much like boards (another wonderful notion!) that it looked as if their necks were sticking out of pillories. He watched in turn the bartender, the waiters, the pianist.

A fattish baby-faced young man—Dannie or Billy or Jimmie or Hughie somebody—sat at the tiny piano, talking dirty songs. The men and girls strained to anticipate the double-meanings; and when the off-color line was delivered, they stared at each other as if aghast and laughed hard, harder than the joke warranted, vying with each other in appreciation. There were songs called "The 23rd Street Ferry" and "Peter and the Dyke"; *camping, queen, faggot, meat* were words frequently played upon; the men and girls looked at each other and roared; the two athletes shifted uncertainly at the bar, not getting it; the baby-faced young man half-smiled, half-scowled about the room, his fat fingers rippling over the keys in a monotonous simple accompaniment like a striptease; he himself felt nothing but amused contempt for the cheap sophistication of the place—provincial, nothing short of it; and he ordered another gin-and-Italian.

He was enjoying himself now. He speculated on how he appeared to the others. If anybody was wondering about him or looking at him, they must have decided that here was that rarity, an American who knew how to drink. He drank quietly and alone—an *apéritif* at that. He took his time, and did not bother with others. Obviously he was used to drink, had probably had it all his life, at home—wines at table, liqueurs after dinner, that sort of thing. Drink was no novelty to him—nothing to order straight, or in a highball, gulp down at once so you could order another, get in as many as possible between now and midnight. . . . This was the impression he believed he gave and was consciously giving. With money in his pocket, with several days to go before Wick came home, he had plenty of chance to play the solitary observant gentleman-drinker having a quiet time amusing himself watching other folk carouse, the while he sipped gin-vermouth which, for all they knew, might have been a Dubonnet or a sherry.

A couple came in and sat down at the next table, on the bench beside him, another young man and a girl. He took them in, subtly, not staring, watching his chance to observe them unobserved, as if it were some kind of delightful game of skill. The girl took off her fur and put it on the bench with her handbag, between herself and him, not more than a foot-and-a-half from where he sat. He tried to place the kind of girl she was, mused on where

she came from, what she did. It was a good enough fur—marten.
He looked at the handbag. Brown alligator, with a large copper
clasp, and a metal monogram in one corner: *M. Mc.* The young
man wore a grey tweed suit, an expensive one, so rough and
coarse that it looked as if small twigs were woven into it, chunks
of rope and hemp, pieces of coal—he smiled with pleasure at such
an idea. Isn't that exactly the kind of suit he'd be wearing? he
said to himself—and then smiled again, for of course he wouldn't
have said it if the young man hadn't been wearing that kind of
suit. He was delighted with this observation—it told him that his
mind was working keenly and at the top of its bent, with that
hyper-consciousness that lay just this side of intoxication. Well,
he'd keep it this side, because he was having a good time, enjoying
his own aloofness to the scene around him.

He eyed the handbag again. What was in it? *Lady-trifles,*
probably; *immoment toys;* God what marvelous expressions, what
felicity, who else could have thought of them!—and suddenly, for
an instant, he had a craving to read Shakespeare, rush home and
sit down with *Antony and Cleopatra* and enjoy the feast of language that was, perhaps, the only true pleasure in the world. But
that was irrational, irresponsible: Shakespeare was there, would
always be there, when he wanted him; the thing to do was appoint
a certain period, regularly, perhaps two hours every day, every
evening, why not, he had plenty of time, nothing but time—his
eye went back to the handbag.

M. Mc. Irish or Scotch? She was an attractive girl; black hair,
beautiful fair complexion. Were they sleeping together? Was he
nice to her? They probably didn't begin to appreciate each other
physically, they were too young. The young man would be carried away in his own excitement, she in hers, with no thought of
each other's sensations. Did he know what his body did to her?
Did she forget herself long enough to prize his, did she lay her
head on his stomach, feel his chest and thighs, was he big? The
questions suddenly seemed important, they were all that mat-

tered in the room—important, dangerous and exciting. He felt reckless and elated, larger than life. If she were not there, if the young man were alone, he would advance and find out a thing or two, amused at his own daring, amused at the young man's shock. Or if the young man should go, leaving the girl, if she should look over and see him, let him speak to her, if he should move closer, if they should leave together, go home—how he would teach her what it was to be with a man! It was all one to him, for the moment he was like a god who could serve either at will. The handbag caught his eye and he puzzled about its contents.

He signaled for another gin-vermouth and turned his attention to the room. Odd how he could sit there unobserved by others; he was the only one alive in the place, the only one who *saw*. Their preoccupation with each other, his own solidarity, completeness, self-sufficiency, aloofness, gave him a sense of elevation and excellence that was almost god-like. He smiled with tolerance at the room, and felt so remote and apart that he might have been unseen. He was unseen; for he had had to signal for minutes before he got the attention of the waiter, the bartender had never glanced his way, no, not once since he had sat down, the baby-faced pianist had eyes only for the couples of men and girls, and they for each other. If he should melt into air, dissolve and leave not a rack behind (why had he never looked up what a rack was?), no one would notice. Some time later the waiter would come upon the empty glass at the empty table and wonder when he had gone.

Or if he should lift this handbag, pull it toward him, cover it with the skirt of his coat, who should see? What could be in it, how much money? What would it be like to steal a purse ('tis something, nothing, 'tis mine, 'tis his), how would you feel? Would it be fun, what kind of satisfaction would it give you? A dozen excitements possessed him: he was ridden with curiosity to know what was in the handbag, he could use the money (possibly a fair sum), he wanted to see for his own satisfaction if he could get away with it—commit the perfect crime. Absurd! But on a tiny, on a very small scale that's exactly what it would be. He would return the bag to the owner afterward, having removed and used the cash. Her address was bound to be inside and he would send the bag back in the mail, with a witty, charming anonymous note, signed, perhaps, "Mr X—and sometimes W and Y." Oh, he could use the money (he wondered how much there was, he had to know), but mostly he wanted to see how it would feel to get away with it, he wanted to prove to himself that he could. It would be a new experience, unlike anything he had ever done; certainly that made the risk worthwhile, for how else was a man's life enriched if not by new experience, letting oneself in for all the million possibilities of various existence, trying everything, anything—"live dangerously"? He lost interest in these philosophies, however, as he now bent all his conscious will, all the keenness and alertness of his over-alert brain, to the attempt.

He had never been so sure of himself in his life, so much the master of his every smallest move, gesture, muscle; he was so calm, so thoroughly at ease and at home, that now he meant to prolong the moment as long as possible, savoring its every second to get the most out of it. He would take the bag and then *stay*—linger, not leave at all, not hurry, never move, possibly even order another drink in the assurance and security that no one knew what he was doing, that even if the bag were missed, it would be impossible to think that he had it. One look at him would show them it could never have been he. Preposterous that such a man, well-dressed, composed, a gentleman—he reached the bag with the tip of his fingers and pulled it a few inches his way.

Nobody saw, of course; he pulled it nearer, then signaled the waiter for another gin-vermouth. The waiter came and set it down before him. He watched the waiter's face. There was the bag, resting beside him, touching his coat, under the very eyes of the waiter, yet the man had seen nothing. He picked up the drink by the thin stem of the glass and slowly sipped; sweet and

sharp and thick, a wonderful drink, why did he ever order anything else—but it was too slow, too subtle for his taste, he liked
the immediate effect, the instant warmth, of liquor straight. Still,
this was nice, it was all right for now, the stronger drink could
wait, there were hours and days ahead, he twirled the stem slowly
between his thumb and forefinger, and with the other hand he
lifted the skirt of his coat and covered the bag.

It could go on forever, he could sit here all night, hiding the
bag; he could even put it on the table in front of him and examine
its contents then and there, for all that anyone would notice. How
careless people were, and unobserving—how crafty, subtle, all-
seeing himself. An idea struck him. It might be fun, after he got
out in the street, say half an hour later—it would be fun to come
back, ascend the stairs again, approach the surprised couple and
address them, saying, "Here is your bag, see how easy it was, you
didn't even know it was gone, did you?" The young man would
half rise, the girl would look down at the bench beside her and
exclaim, "Well of all—!" What would be the fun of getting away
with it if you couldn't tell about it, show how clever you were,
how easy it had been? Otherwise it would all be wasted. But he
needed the money too, he wanted it now; and afterward his only
concern would be to get rid of the bag, leave it in some impossible
fabulous place where it would never turn up, never again, in his
or anyone else's life.

The suspense was intoxicating, he was filled with admiration
for his own shrewd, adroit and disarming performance, knowing
that to an observer (but there were none) he gave only the impression of disinterest, thoughtful melancholy, ennui. He pulled the
bag against his hip, adjusted the coat closer about him with a
casual movement, and sipped the drink.

For some minutes after he emptied the glass, he sat there, his
studied expression (wrinkled brow, faint pout, faint tilt of the
head) showing that he played with the idea of ordering another
drink. With an all but imperceptible shrug he made his decision—

called the waiter, examined the check with care, paid with a bored air, tipped well. The waiter thanked him and left. He pulled the bag up under his arm, inside his topcoat, and sat a moment or two longer, stripping the cellophane from a pack of cigarettes, wadding it up, tossing it on the table, selecting a cigarette, tapping it down, lighting it. Reflectively he watched the match burn to his finger tips, then dropped it just in time. He reached for his hat and got up, pushing the table away with a scraping noise. He nodded goodnight to the bartender.

Near the stairs was a poster about some Village dance. He stopped to examine it, as if concerned to see who was the artist. Behind him, a wave of laughter swept the room. He turned and looked back with a philosophical smile at the men and girls convulsed with hilarity over some new double-meaning of the singer at the piano; then turned again and went down the stairs, his hat in his hand.

The bar below was crowded. He walked through the long room toward the street, slowly, regarding the huddled drinkers in a manner detached and aloof. He was the spectator still, unseen—truly he might have been invisible, the figure out of mythology, so unmarked was his passage through the crowded room, his very presence amid all the festivity. Near the end, he stopped and looked at himself in the mirror over the bar through a gap between two men on bar-stools. He smoothed back his hair, then put his hat on and adjusted it carefully. He gave the effect a last approving look and went on.

He saw the big doorman holding open the door for him. He reached into his pocket for a tip. He dropped a dime into the gloved hand, and someone behind him touched his shoulder. He turned. There was the bartender and waiter, the young man and girl from upstairs. His eyebrows went up, his mouth lifted in an enquiring smile. "Give us that bag," one of them said in slow, heavy, even tones—and he noticed that the entire room was quiet, every face at the bar turned toward the door and himself.

"Why certainly," he said, pleasantly, "here it is," and he produced the bag from under his coat and handed it directly to the girl herself with a faint bow.

He would never remember what was said then, who said it, or the order in which it was said. The young man was muttering in threat, the waiter said "Call a cop, Mike's on the corner," the girl said "Never mind, never *mind,* I've got my bag, that's all I wanted, please let him *go,*" the bartender said "If you ever come back here again, if I ever see—" He stood there puzzled in the middle of it all, his polite patient half-smile trying to say for him, What's all the fuss, it's only a joke, I'm sure I didn't realize, truly I wasn't serious, I was only having a little— The doorman put big hands on his shoulders, turned him around, gave him a shove that made his neck snap, and he was in the street.

He recovered and adjusted his coat and hat and walked slowly, leisurely, away, trying not to hear what the doorman called after him, trying not to see the little group of cabbies staring at him in silent contempt. By the time he got to the corner and out of sight, moving as slowly and leisurely as he was able, his legs were shaking so violently he could hardly stand. He thought he would collapse, he wanted to collapse, wanted to give way, fall down, pretend to be very drunk, be picked up and taken care of by someone, a stranger. He thought of Helen in Bleecker Street and recoiled in terror. He stumbled into a cab in Sheridan Square, gave his address, and fell into the dark backseat as if it were his bed, his own bed at home. During the drive uptown, the blessed oblivion of time-out, he became so calm, so deathly relaxed and still, that he was barely able to respond with gratitude as he remembered the nearly-full pint at home. Was this what he had been seeking? He had reached the point where always there was only one thing: drink, and more drink, till amnesty came; and tomorrow, drink again.

PART TWO

The Wife

The windows were blue-white. Was it early morning, or evening? He lay watching the panes between the curtains and wondered if they would whiten into daylight or thicken into dusk. He wondered what time it was, what day. The clock said 6:10 but that told him nothing.

He had awakened fully dressed on the couch in the living room. His feet burned. He reached down and unlaced his shoes and kicked them off. He rose to a sitting position and pulled off his coat and vest, untied his tie and loosened his collar. Automatically his hand groped beside the couch for the pint on the floor. His heart sank as he found it, and found it empty.

Had he been sleeping all night, or all night and all the next day? There was no way of telling till the light changed outside, for better or worse. If it were evening, thank Christ. He could go out and buy another, a dozen more. But if morning— He feared to find out; for if it were morning, dawn, he would be cut off till nine or after and so made to suffer the punishment he always promised himself to avoid. It would be like the dreaded Sunday, always (at these times) the day most abhorred of all the week; for on Sundays the bars did not open till two in the afternoon and the liquor stores did not open at all. Once again he had not been clever enough to provide a supply against this very thing; again he had lost all perspective and forgotten his inescapable desperation of the morning, so much more urgent and demanding than any need of the evening before. Last night it had been merely drink. It was medicine now.

He lifted the empty pint to his mouth. One warm drop

crawled like slow syrup through the neck of the bottle. It lay on his tongue, useless, all but impossible to swallow. He thought of all the mornings (and as he thought of them he knew he was in for another cycle of harrowing mornings) when, at such times as these, he would drag himself into the kitchen and examine the line-up of empty quarts and pints on the floor under the sink, pick them up separately and hold them upside down over a small glass, one by one for minutes at a time, extracting a last sticky drop from one bottle, two drops from another, maybe nothing from a third, and so on through a long patient nerve-wracking process till he had collected enough, perhaps, to cover the bottom of the glass. It was like a rite—the slow drinking of it still more so; and it was never enough.

Though he hated this need of his, hated this dependency on the pick-up, so often impossible to get—hated it for what it did to him till he got it—all the same he had a profound and superior contempt for those who spurned liquor on the morning after, whose stomachs, shaken as they were by the dissipation of the night, turned and retched at the very thought of it. How often he had been dumbfounded—at first incredulous, then contemptuous—to hear someone say, after a night of drinking, "God, take it away, I don't want to smell it, I don't want to *see* it even, take it out of my sight!"—this at the very moment when he wanted and needed it most. How different that reaction was from his own, and how revealing. Clearly it was the difference between the alcoholic and the non-. He was angry to know this, but he knew it; he knew it far better than others; and he kept the knowledge to himself. It would tell them too much about him, tell them he was the drinker who couldn't stop—an abhorrent thing, more shocking to the man who went in for the occasional heavy weekend spree than it ever was to the abstainer. The hair of the dog was no lighthearted joke with him as it was with the others; but he could kid about it with the rest, if need be, hiding his agonized impatience till such time as he was able to sneak a drink or, if offered one as a dare in the presence of others (dare!), quench his thirst with affected bravery amid the shudders of his hungover friends.

Thirst—there was a misnomer. He could honestly say he had never had a thirst for liquor or a craving for drink as such, no, not even in hangover. It wasn't because he was thirsty that he drank, and he didn't drink because he liked the taste (actually whisky was dreadful to the palate; he swallowed at once to get it down as quickly as possible): he drank for what it did to him. As for quenching his thirst, liquor did exactly the opposite. To quench is to slake or to satisfy, to give you enough. Liquor couldn't do that. One drink led inevitably to the next, more demanded more, they became progressively easier and easier, culminating in the desperate need, no longer easy, that shook him on days such as these. His need to breathe was not more urgent.

Today wasn't as bad as that. He could stand it. He had only been drinking one night, this time. Tomorrow or the day after would be a different story, but—now it was hangover, nothing more; and he could stand it till he was able to get another pint. What possessed him now even more than his need for a drink was that inevitable and familiar accompaniment to the first morning-after: remorse (how readily he recognized it; how humbly, from old habit, he accepted it as his just due)—remorse merely for drinking, for having drunk at all, any; but even as he acknowledged the first sickening symptom of anguish and guilt, he knew it was only a tiny twinge or pang to the hounding relentless remorse that would drive him to hell and worse a few days hence.

What had happened yesterday, last night, that he should feel so guilty now? Nothing. It was always the same, regardless of what he had done. He remembered little after he started drinking; but what he recalled up to the time he had gone down to the Village, or up to his call at Mrs. Wertheim's laundry, was enough. Merely to have started again, when he was only just safely out of the other bat, was enough now to make him sick with despair and regret. Why hadn't he waited—why hadn't he waited *one more day*? Just one! He had been coming out of a bad week as it was; he had been off liquor since Monday; one more day would have finished it, made him whole once more, with no need to drink till the next cycle came around. If he had been able to hold off through yesterday, today he would have been normal again; and he knew himself and his habits well enough to know that that would have lasted some days, held possibly even two or three weeks, for he was a periodic drinker, with intervals of sobriety between. At the same time, he knew himself well enough also to know that once started, he had to go through it to the end, there was no stopping now, he could not prevent the downward curve to the final state of danger, destruction, or collapse. Short of being locked up, nothing could help him now till it had played itself out, safely or otherwise. The old Demon of Ennui had given him the shove, the Old Enemy had tricked him into starting all over again before he had recovered from the previous drunk, before he was well out of it at all. They were dangerously close together, those two binges—dangerously overlapping. This new one was bound to leave him worse off than the other, because he was hardly strong enough, as it was, to begin again. How had it happened—at what moment had it started—why? The barometer had been set for a spell of riot, true enough; but in all honesty, no matter how much he wanted to believe it, he couldn't lay the blame on a phrase in a book. If it hadn't been that, it would have been something else. Left unguarded by Wick, determined to avoid the long weekend that was to help him, he would have found the thing to set him off, regardless.

Spell of riot, Raskolnikov, indeed! How could his intelligence permit him to blow himself up to such exaggerated proportions, so great by contrast to the miserable fact of his piddling little spree that he was ashamed now of all the heroic fancies in which he had indulged himself yesterday. He had pictured himself as the sensitive gifted man going to the dogs with practically noble abandon, seeking destruction with gallant and charming and even amused resignation. Balls! He was a drunk, that's all; a soak and a dip; and the dangers that he skirted were picayune, no more threatening or perilous than the twigs and leaves which the night-flying bat, like the drunk, avoids so skillfully, with such ridiculous and unnecessary ingenuity, darting about in the darkness reckless but safe, always safe, detecting with its sensitive wings the slightest stir of air against the obstacle or tiny danger in its path. Such a creature was he, no more heroic, skirting traps of thread, landing always safely at home at the end of his reckless little tour, with nothing to fear but this unreasonable unshakable remorse—remorse for having done nothing worse than to go out at all. Such self-reproach, without foundation, would be inexplicable to another. A friend could learn all the details of the night before, if he could remember and tell them, and think nothing of it—be surprised, even, at his groundless concern. Only he himself knew the significance of that guilt. It had recurred too many times to be meaningless.

He knew the question was not: Why had he deliberately missed the appointment with his brother, why had he done what he did yesterday, why was he in this fix now; but: Why did he *ever* do it, why was he *always* doing it over and over again, why was he forever fetching up at just such an impasse as this, just such despair, depression, remorse? The remorse was the key to his despair, as it probably was to his salvation, should he ever be able to take hold of that key and use it. If he wanted to drink himself to death it was nobody's affair but his own; his life was *his* life to throw away, if that's what he wanted; but—was that what he wanted? If so, why did he suffer remorse? Obviously there was the will in him to destroy himself; part of him was bent on self-destruction—he'd be the last to deny it. But obviously, too, part was not; part held back and expressed its disapproval in remorse and shame. Why hadn't the foolish psychiatrist ever been able to get hold of *that* part, done something with it, made something of it, brought it into full being till it topped and outweighed the other? But the foolish psychiatrist knew so much less about it than the poet, the poet who said to another doctor, *Canst thou not minister to a mind diseased. . . . Raze out the written troubles of the brain?,* the poet who answered, *Therein the patient must minister to himself. . . .*

The windows were lighter now, the blue was white, it was morning. With a sinking heart he realized that the day was to start out like the dreaded Sunday after all. He was in for at least two hours of this, two more hours of waiting for the bar or the liquor store to open; for remorse or no, he meant to go on with it, the thing was in him now and must be finished, Wick was away for the long weekend, he'd be alone till Tuesday, he'd have his long weekend, here. A golden opportunity to go on his tear without interference, provided Helen didn't catch up with him or intercept him, provided he kept out of people's way, kept to himself and avoided seeing anyone he knew. For six days—for five more—he could move through the city at will, as he often had in the past, going here and there about the town like a ghost, unknown, unnoticed, like a man moving in a kind of time-out. A solo flight (flight indeed), unheeded by anyone because no one knew who he was (whoever stopped the anonymous drunk?); a flight that would last just long enough, for in his present weakened condition he knew that six days would be about the limit of his endurance. No three-week bender this time, ending up in Chicago, Philadelphia, the Fall River boat, a filthy room in a 9th Avenue hotel—God knows where. Tuesday morning Wick would be back and he'd be ready to call it quits by then. Wick wouldn't return before: he knew too well what he'd be coming back to, he knew he couldn't stop what had started, it was best to stay away and let the thing play itself out, pretending in the meanwhile that nothing was going on in the city or at least shutting it from his mind entirely. By deliberately not thinking of it Wick had learned not even to worry: if he worried, he would begin by worrying about fires, about whom Don might be having in the apartment, about the loss of his personal effects, about his brother's danger, arrest, death—and to do that was to suffer too much. Don knew that at this moment Wick was up and waiting for Mr. or Mrs. Hansen to get his breakfast on the coal range at the farm—or he was already out feeding Mac, or playing with him on the lawn, or throwing sticks in the water for him to swim out to—while he sat here, hanging onto himself, waiting for the liquor store to open, waiting to get started again on the bout that Wick would not allow himself to think of, thank heaven, for five more days. And waiting, knowing that the remorse would pass and high spirits return with the first drink of the day, he deliberately reviewed and explored that remorse, as if self-abasement were a kind of expiation, as if this were his last chance at self-search, as if the promised drinks were justified provided he faced the facts and knew in advance what he was in for.

He supposed he was only one of several million persons of his generation who had grown up and, somewhere around thirty, made the upsetting discovery that life wasn't going to pan out the way you'd always expected it would; and why this realization should have thrown him and not them—or not too many of them—was something he couldn't fathom. Life offered none of those prizes you'd been looking forward to since adolescence (he less than others, but looking forward to them all the same, if only out of curiosity). Adulthood came through with none of the pledges you'd been led somehow to believe in; the future still remained the future—illusion: a non-existent period or a constantly-receding promise, hinting fulfillment yet forever withholding the rewards. All the things that had never happened yet were never going to happen after all. It was a mug's game and there ought to be a law. But there wasn't any law, there was no rhyme or reason; and with the sour-grapes attitude of "Why the hell *should* there be"—which is as near as you ever came to sophistication—you retired within yourself and compensated for the disappointments by drink, by subsisting on daydreams, by living in a private world of your own making (hell or heaven, what did it matter?), by accomplishing or becoming in fancy what you could never bring about in fact.

The foolish and tricking fancies of yesterday afternoon, for instance. "In a Glass"—who would ever want to read a novel about a punk and a drunk! Everybody knew a couple or a dozen; they were not to be taken seriously; nuisances and trouble-makers, nothing more; like queers and fairies, people were belly-sick of them; whatever ailed them, that was *their* funeral; who cared?—life presented a thousand things more important to be written about than misfits and failures. "Don Birnam: A Hero Without a Novel." "My Life; or, Words To That Effect." "Total Recall: An Anthology." "I Don't Know Why I'm Telling You All This"—oh he'd have a circus dreaming up titles but that's as far as he'd ever get and a good thing too. Like all his attempts at fiction it would be as personal as a letter—painful to those who knew him, of no interest to those who didn't; precious or self-pitying in spots, in others too clever for its own good; so packed with Shakespeare that it looked as if he worked with a concordance in his lap; so narcissistic that its final effect would be that of the mirrored room which gives back the same image times without count, or the old Post Toastie box of his boyhood with the fascinat-ing picture of a woman and child holding a Post Toastie box with a picture of a woman and child holding a Post Toastie box with a picture of a woman and child holding— But it was silly to consider the book at all or to think of it for a moment. He only wanted to be The Artist, anyhow, with no thought of the meaning or content of the work which would win him such a title—just as he wanted to be (and often fancied himself, especially in drink) an actor without ever thinking of going on the stage, a pianist without having taken a music lesson in his life, a husband and father without marrying.

All he remembered of yesterday was the afternoon or at most the early evening, but that was enough. He had never intended going to the farm from the moment the idea came up. Shameful to think of it now! At some point he had decided to stay behind; he'd manage it, somehow; he'd get out of it, he'd just not be there. He had used the matinée, the not going, as a way out; and it had worked, as he knew it would work from the beginning, in spite of all Wick's tiresome pleading to come along too. "We've had the tickets such a long while"—he could hear Wick now, and he felt a pang of pity as he thought of the futility of Wick's ever trying to plan anything with him. You always got left. Wick (or anyone) could never bank on his being "all right" when the date came around. Worse than that, he had become a liar and dodger; there was no depending on him for the immediate afternoon, much less for dates ahead; he wasn't to be believed; not a word he said was to be taken seriously; but everybody went on pretending, others as well as himself, that this wasn't true; that maybe this time it would be different; that Don would certainly, now if never, keep his promise, make good his word, meet the date or the debt. Instead of the fellow everyone had always been so fond of— friendly, social, good company, bright, lively—he had developed into a crafty sly masquerader, artful and elusive, presenting a front so different from his real self that they pretended to believe out of sheer embarrassment, as much to save his face as their own. During all that long and repetitious dialogue yesterday, when they sounded the old refrain they had sounded over and over, so many times before that it was like a ritual, Wick hadn't once said, out loud, what was really on his mind: "I don't believe you." That would have been more painful to him than to Don; but only because he couldn't bear to hear Don's hurt protestations on top of the rest of it.

Talking German to Mrs. Wertheim—aaah! To Mrs. Wertheim, who spoke American better than he did. And calling her gnädige Frau! She was too much of a person to smile—*she* saved his face too, covered up for him, pretended as one pretends with a child that their fancies are real, oh yes, quite genuine and real. She was the aristocrat, not he; and he felt sick shame as he recalled,

now, his fanciful daydream about how he had given the bedaz-
zled Mrs. Wertheim a tantalizing glimpse of reckless glamorous
high life. What a fool and an ass he had made of himself—and
there was one more avenue of escape closed, one more source
he had cut himself off from, a source of loan he could never go
back to again. One more person to shun in the street, one more
shop to go by with face averted, one more *bête noire* added to
the growing neighborhood collection of persons he must not see
again.

And now he would live in dread, of course, of that moment,
a week or so hence, when Wick would come into the flat, the
laundry bill in his hand, and say almost with tears: "Don, why
did you have to go to her of all people, what will she think, why
didn't you go to Helen or anyone, anyone else?" It was a moment
to dread because there was no possible way out of it: simulating
innocence was no good; hanging your head was worse; the disarming open admission was long since out. It was one more thing
he could and would, in the mornings to come, mornings such as
this, build up an anxiety about. Slight it seemed; but by the time
Wick approached, came nearer and nearer, it would have grown
by then to one of those many real terrors from which he must
somehow, someway, escape.

"Two-and-Twenty-Misfortunes" the family often called him,
after the character in Chekov. Well, it was a family joke, and fun
(to them); but he got a bit tired of hearing it just as he got a bit tired
of those two-and-twenty misfortunes themselves. Why wouldn't
he be? They began further back than he could remember (so he
was forever being told), they had come to be expected by everyone in the family (Don wasn't running true to form, something
was amiss, if he came through an experience without damage);
so that by the time the fraternity shock sent him reeling, the two-
and-twenty seemed but a preliminary warm-up. All the woeful
errors of childhood and adolescence came to their crashing climax at seventeen. They gathered themselves for a real workout in

the passionate hero-worship of an upperclassman during his very first month at college, a worship that led, like a fatal infatuation, to scandal and public disgrace, because no one had understood or got the story straight and no one had wanted to understand, least of all the upperclassman who emerged somehow as a hero, now, to the others—why, he would never know. . . . He had survived (didn't one always?). The experience had left him reeling for a couple of years, sent him reeling back home with the resolve never again to leave the security and safety of his hometown where everybody knew him and had always known him; but after that couple of years, the shock had paled and receded in the back of his mind till he was able to tell himself that the only thing he regretted was that he had left behind and lost forever his precious marked copy of *Macbeth* that day he was ushered out of the Kappa U house for good and all. . . . That's what he was able to tell himself; but when he left home and tried his wings again, he knew only too well that he lived unconsciously in perpetual dread of one day meeting up face to face with one of those thirty-six erstwhile brothers, perpetual fear of running into any of the thousand other students to whom he was guilty if they believed he was guilty. It was a dread that he fully understood, but which carried so many other fears in its wake that he had never been able to free himself of anxieties since his seventeenth year.

These were not the fancied fears that had become fashionable, lately, among his class and his generation. Quick to spot the fake in others as in himself, he had only contempt for those fondly-cherished phobias which drove their nourishers to dangerous distraction when they heard whip-poor-wills, which prevented them from sitting in crowded theaters or entering subways, which kept them forever in the country or forever in the city, which forbade them eating anything but ice cream ever, which allowed them to hear only a very little bit of fine music at one time (a whole symphony at a sitting was more than one could bear and to hell with the composer's design), and which culminated in what their cre-

ators shyly-proudly spoke of as their "weekend psychoses," meaning nothing more than boredom and irritation at having to spend
two days at home with their wives and children. These carefully
nurtured aberrations were supposed to signify a refinement and
sensitivity superior to the temperament (or lack of it) of maddeningly well-balanced mates; in reality, they provided a compensa-
tion and screen to frustration, inferiority, and failure.

He was a fine one to speak of failure, of course. From childhood his record had been one of opportunities missed (on purpose?), excited but half-hearted attempts at finding the right niche
(with always the next niche a better one), moves to a new city or
new state or even new country where certainly things would be
better or at least different, returns home to renew himself, to find
again the native stimuli that never existed, to seek the old roots.
Excuses, excuses, literary at that. He had repeatedly and purposely
destroyed every opportunity that ever came his way, and this pattern went as far back as he could remember. His history of defeat
was so consistent that he could almost point with pride to the fact
that his Algebra teacher had snarled at him savagely, before the
whole class, "Don Birnam, I wouldn't recommend you to sweep
a sidewalk!"—and these same words, syllable for syllable, were
spoken at him in clipped impeccable speech twenty years later by
the editor of a broadcasting company, a superior Britisher who
obviously never had a moment of qualm or self-doubt in his life.
Both pronouncements had been received almost with satisfaction;
they relieved him of further effort in either field. It was as though
he could say to himself, or to the world: "You see?" and shrug.

He could never get used to the fact that he was grown up,
in years at least, living in an adult world. When the barber said,
"Razor all right, Sir?" he had to think for a minute. What was
it men said when asked about the razor? And when he said it
("Razor's fine, fine" or whatever it was) he felt a fraud. Out of the
corner of his eye, over the vast bib, he looked at the man in the
next chair. Did *he* feel foolish at being accorded these formalities,

these symbols of respect? Was he ill at ease in the role of solid and substantial man, obliged to run true to form, behave like all the others, reply in kind, no matter how much his mind wandered on private or past excursions? But that mind certainly didn't wander; there sat no perennial eavesdropper and wanderer and wonderer; the calm eyes looked neither to right nor to left; the man was as incurious and uninquisitive about Don as he was about himself.

If he had put childhood behind him at all, it had been with a lingering glance backward, and regret. He had never looked forward to the long-pants, like other boys. He remembered his mortal embarrassment, almost shame (as if he had suddenly been exposed naked), when his mother announced, "Don's shaving now." It was a joke to everyone; they laughed. Other boys were only too proud of the first shave and boasted of the razor before they ever used one; but he—he was reminded that the razor meant he was growing body-hair elsewhere than on his lip, and he bitterly, privately, resented this evidence that childhood was slipping by.

Where, along the way, had he missed the great chance to take the difficult but rewarding step from boyhood into manhood, the natural hazard that others took as a matter of course, without even knowing; and would he ever have such an opportunity again? Yes, he believed he would; but perhaps it meant going down to the bottom first, the very bottom; and then again, perhaps he might not recognize the opportunity if it should return. But somewhere he had missed the boat (was his own realization of this any good, any help?). Somewhere along the line had come a moment when he had looked the other way, willfully and on purpose, reluctant to part from the pleasant ways of childhood. When, at what time, had he deliberately ignored the responsibility and opportunity that beckoned him? Oh, he could put his finger on a dozen such moments, but no one of them was big enough in itself to have colored and crippled his whole life from that time forward.

Some were more revealing than others; one he would never forget. A note had been passed across several aisles, a note from his friend Melvin. He knew what it said without unfolding it, these came every afternoon, from him or from Mel, worded the same; but he unfolded it as always and wrote "Okay" under the message: "How about going over to the church-sheds this afternoon after school and having fun?" The *having fun* was supposed to veil (and did, since no one intercepted the notes) what went on between them in the carriage-sheds back of the Presbyterian Church, several afternoons a week, in the backseat of an abandoned carriage that hadn't been used for years—used for anything but this. The phrase was their phrase to describe, for their own private use, what they had lately found to be the most exciting thing in life. And later, amid the dry acrid semen-like smell of the sheds, the two of them shivering and groaning in the dark backseat of the dust-foul buggy, what prompted him then one afternoon to ask (with that prescience that was native to him): "What are you thinking of?"—meaning, What are you picturing? meaning, What scene do you conjure up to aid the act? meaning, Who? And when the panting answer came: "Gertrude Hort. I'm laying my face on her little bare belly"—what instinct then, as prescient as the other, made him hold back, be still, keep to himself the suddenly surprising fact that it was no one like Gertrude Hort with whom he dallied in imaginary amorous play? The realization made him stop. He looked up unseeingly at the jiggling fringe of the buggy, feeling already strange and alone and different. He was lost in startling thought. Melvin stopped too. "What's the matter?" But what could he answer? He suddenly knew what he hadn't dreamed of before, Mel was way ahead of him, miles and years—so far ahead that he could certainly never bring himself now to tell Melvin it was his father he had been thinking of, Mel's own father who, when he took a bath, always had Mel come in and wash his back. This fact had been related casually a week or so ago, and the scene, somehow exciting (but why? Because there was no father at home?) had stuck in his mind.

Realizations such as this and others, over a long period of years, had placed him—unprotesting on his part—in the position of child (he knew it even better than they did), the child and hero-worshipper to practically everybody he ever met older than himself. Thus it had been easy to give himself up to the foolish psychiatrist, more wholeheartedly, perhaps, than probably any other patient the man had ever had—easy and interesting and pleasant and just what he wanted, at the time. He looked forward to the daily visits, one hour every morning, six days a week, for more than five months altogether. His interest waned after a while, of course, but at first it had been exciting, he had some wonderful things to tell and was eager to tell them, things that he knew would add to and enrich the doctor's own lore—just as it was always exciting to make a new friend because it meant a new listener; a good while would elapse before he had used up all the frank entertaining and amazing stories about himself; these would sustain the friendship for some time—though he well knew that his interest in the friend and the friendship would dissipate when the stories began to run out. He could almost gauge the length of such a relationship by how much or how little he had revealed of his past.

So it had been with the foolish psychiatrist. But it was more than this that had caused the failure. After a very few weeks, three at the most, he discovered he knew more about the subject, more about pathology, certainly more about himself and what made him tick, than the doctor. What the doctor knew he knew academically, according to rule and case. His own varied experiences in life had taught him nothing about himself and therefore others. These things did not count. Only the grammar and syntax of psychiatry applied. The great catalogue of behavioristics was so complex and complete that everyone fitted in somewhere, a place and a tag could be found for each, regardless of the fact that the elusive bundle of contradictions (like the bundle of nerves) sat there across the desk, whole traits not checking or fitting at all, some of them even canceling out and voiding what did fit and check when considered alone. The human being was lost sight of—certainly the surest way to offend; for the human and the personal was the only thing that counted with Don ever.

And even that was not the cause of their failure. It was ultimately due to that very father-and-child nature of their association which, at the start, had augured so well for success. The doctor carried this relationship to such lengths, refusing finally to allow the patient even to think for himself, that he rebelled. He took to cheating on the doctor, holding out on him, disappearing, drinking and then keeping the secret to himself—a thing he had always been willing and even anxious to confide before. One morning he was presented with a little document which the doctor had drawn up and which he now asked the patient to sign:

April 13th 1936

I hereby acknowledge that I am a pretty good guy when I am sober but that when I am tight I am not responsible for what I do or say. I know that I must be very bad when I am tight from what my best friends tell me. In order therefore not to become a nuisance when I am tight I should like to make the following agreement.

If I feel the urge to drink, and am able to control this urge enough to go home and in the presence of my brother or doctor drink 6 bottles of beer, I agree that I shall then remain in my house two days. If, on the other hand I am not able to control myself in this manner and I feel myself forced to drink whiskey or more than two beers without consulting my doctor, I agree that I must spend seven days the first time this experience happens, 8 days the second

time, nine days the 3rd time, etc. in my house. I must spend
the full time arranged for in my house except for two hours
from 10:45 to 12:45 during which time I shall visit my doctor and get fresh air.

Furthermore I agree that if under the influence of alcohol I fail to cooperate in this agreement I must be forced
to cooperate by any measures my doctor finds necessary. I
wish this agreement to hold until I and my doctor decide it
should be dissolved.

It had been dissolved then and there (and the swell fee with
it). Childish he was, but not that childish—nor so foolish as the
foolish psychiatrist. He could certainly not agree to such an agreement. The object, of course, was to make the ultimate punishment
for each successive misstep so severe that a mighty taboo would
be built up about misstepping at all. But punishment would do no
good, no matter how severe. He knew better than to sign such a
document because he knew he couldn't keep the promise, and he
wouldn't sign it and then not keep it. It was simply a case, again,
of knowing himself better than the doctor. He would make ver-
bal promises fifty times over and break them right and left, but
he would never actually swear to a thing and then sign his name
to it unless he meant to abide by it; and he knew that to abide
by this was impossible. He might mean it now and not mean it
tomorrow; and knowing this was so, he couldn't honestly put his
name to such a pledge. Yes, it was honesty, of a sort; but it was
also a wariness and apprehension of being trapped. It gave his
brother as well as the doctor too great a weapon. To sign and then
fail would be to lay himself open to such charges of trickery and
deceit as had never been brought against him yet. Apart from his
refusal to use the key to the applejack closet, his denial of this
document was about the only thing he could cite to his credit in
the past half-dozen years.

That winter at the farm a strange thing had happened, revealing something about his nature that surprised even himself. The applejack closet, off the caretakers' bedroom next to his own, became the object of his constant watch. He hung about his room and literally laid in wait for the door to be left ajar or unlocked. Several times a morning, again in the afternoon, when Mr. and Mrs. Hansen were downstairs in the kitchen or somewhere about the farm, he would tiptoe into their bedroom, listening anxiously for a step in the hall, try the door, find it locked, and tiptoe out again. They knew what was going on, of course, and he knew that they knew, but no one ever mentioned it. They knew because of what was in the closet and because they knew him. Their bedroom closet was the place where the applejack was kept, several kegs of it; the Hansens each had a key, and were careful to lock the door after they had been in to take some clothes out or hang something away; they kept their keys about their persons always—he had never even seen them, but he knew only too well that such keys existed. Only twice that winter had the door been carelessly left unlocked, and in the space of a few minutes he had got in and siphoned off six or seven pints of the strong brandy-like applejack and hidden them in secret places about his room. When the row began between the Hansens as to which of them had left the closet-door unlocked, he was already drunk. . . . But a day came when he was handed the key on a silver platter, as it were. He had been away, spending the Easter holidays with Wick in New York. Almost the first thing he noticed on getting back to the farm was that one of the keys was missing. Several times a day he heard Mrs. Hansen shouting for her husband: she wanted to get into the closet; and Mr. Hansen would have to drop what he was doing, fish out his key, curse her for her carelessness, and yell after her as she departed for the upstairs, "You bring it right back again, too!" He could not help smiling over these scenes because he knew he was the cause of them, but he pretended not to notice the confusion, the unnecessary running back and forth, the shouting, and the anger. Some nights later, intending to read in bed, he got out his camel's-hair bed-jacket and put it on. He noticed a bulge in the left pocket. He reached in and found a wad of used Kleenex—in his absence Mrs. Hansen had been wearing his jacket. And there too was the key. . . . He did not leave the farm, then, till June; but in all that time he did not use the key, either. Why, he could not have said; except, perhaps, that it would have been too easy. Saturday nights when Mr. and Mrs. Hansen went in town to the movies, he could have used the key at his leisure and siphoned off every pint of applejack in the place—he could have; but he could not. It wouldn't have left a trace of guilt behind, it would have been taking such an easy advantage. He'd sooner have broken the door down, got at the liquor that way; and once, when they were away on such an evening, he even went so far as to get a ladder from the barn, raise it to the little window of the closet, climb in and help himself. When the Hansens returned from town and found the ladder against the house, they knew without going to his room that he was drunk. . . . Though he couldn't bring himself to use it, he had no intention of giving up the key. They had lost it; very well, let them pay for it. He even enjoyed, now, the scenes this caused between them (always out of his presence and supposedly beyond his hearing): the fits of temper, the distracted running up and downstairs, the times without number Mrs. Hansen started for the closet and then remembered that she'd have to go all the way out to the chicken-coop and find her husband before she could get in. Reading in his room he would listen to all this. He would hear Mrs. Hansen throw open the window of her bedroom and call "Jake! I want to get in the closet!" Mr. Hansen could be heard hollering from way across the field: "Come and get it then! *You* lost it!" Neither now mentioned the object by name, they didn't need to, it was only too much on all their minds. . . . No, he had no intention of giving it up till the day he left. That morning, he planned to tell them when he was at breakfast. As the moment approached, he began to get so nervous that his hands shook—he couldn't have said why. His throat was parched and he had twice to run upstairs to the bathroom, as if he had been taken with a kind of stage-fright. The tension and suspense of all the long weeks leading up to this moment had become almost too much for him, but he intended to go through with it all the same. He called the Hansens in from the kitchen. He swallowed some coffee, then drew the key from his pocket and laid it on the tablecloth. They stared at him, Mr. Hansen with mouth open. He put his hands in his lap under the table and clasped them together to keep them from shaking. "Now listen," he said, "I've never used this key once since I've had it. Never once. I've had it since Easter. I found it in the pocket of my bed-jacket." Mr. Hansen hit the ceiling in a rage; but Mrs. Hansen, to his relief, turned her head away to hide a smile. . . .

This kind of honor had baffled the foolish psychiatrist, as it had baffled many another before, from his mother on. But could it, by any stretch of ethics, be called honor at all? Or was it honor so honest that it transcended the human, so human that it had not been characterized by the convenient words in the catalogue? They were both at sea to understand; but the one didn't care: the story itself was the thing, not the explanation; and the other withdrew still further from the baffling bundle of contradictions that spoke so articulately for itself, at once so completely objective (and just as completely subjective) that he had nothing and everything to work with. It was an embarrassment of riches that vanished as it appeared. The material at hand slipped through his fingers even as he held out his palm—and came up behind his back to hit him over the head. At such times Don waited politely for the other to recover himself, his mind already delving further back into the past in search of another episode to entertain and instruct them both.

Why was the patient here at all, what did the doctor have to offer, what was the nature of the trouble and what was the cure? Why did they never get at the root of the matter, the thing that drove him to do what he did, the thing that drove him to drink?

But what was the good of the knowledge?—since no one, certainly not himself, knew the origin or nature of the secret pain which impelled him blindly, if by such roundabout ways, to self-destruction: the fears which he could never bring himself to face and which receded into blank when he got the drinks under his belt. You could name them and they were still not named. Face them and they vanished—to sneak back during an unguarded moment and hit *you* over the head, too, knocking you out completely. The never accomplishing anything, the continual failure, the failing even to try, the disgust of friends and family, the loss of reputation—the only loss ever, the one robbery. *Who steals my purse steals trash. . . . But he that filches from me my good name*— And who was doing that for him, who but himself?

He sat up. In an instant he was off the bed. He all but crouched, as if a voice had thundered at him and startled his already jangling nerves. *Who steals my purse*— Fear hit him, not merely (now) the thought of fear or remembrance of fear. The foggy memory that clouded the events of the evening before, the events he had not even troubled himself to think of, suddenly cleared.

He had to get out of here. He looked at the clock and found it was twenty minutes to eight. Bars opened at eight, if the bartender was on time. And could sell liquor from eight o'clock on, if the guy was on time. Liquor stores didn't open till nine but to hell with that now. Twenty minutes to go. He began to walk around the apartment, went into the bedroom and kitchen, came back and put on his shoes, hurried to the bathroom to button his collar and pull up his tie again. But why hurry. Twenty minutes took a hell of a while, he could do a million things in twenty minutes, chances are an hour later it would still be twenty to eight.

He sat down, breathing heavily. What in Christ's name was he ever going to do now? To visit Jack's for the entire rest of his life, of course, was simply out of the question; but that didn't matter, either. He didn't need to go to Jack's. But how could he ever pass through Charles Street again, how could he go anywhere near

Sheridan Square or even down to the Village—ever? But that didn't matter, either. He didn't need to go to the Village. He could stay uptown for the rest of his days. Could? He'd have to.

Suppose he should meet somebody who had been at Jack's last night. Suppose somebody he knew had been there and he hadn't noticed—and the other one had. What about M. Mc. and her tweed friend. The people at the bar downstairs. The plank-shouldered football players. Dannie or Billy or Jimmie or Hughie. The taxi-drivers out in front. He might meet them, he might run into any one of them some day, maybe they even knew someone he knew. It was not beyond the bounds of possibility, it was a small world. Hadn't it been beyond possibility, beyond thought, that he—yes, even he—would ever sink so low as to steal a woman's purse? Would anybody ever have believed that? Would he himself? The stealing or the attempt to steal was bad enough; the being caught was worse. To expose yourself as a common thief before a whole bar full of people—

He went into the bathroom again, loosened his collar and tie, and began to shave. *One* thing they could never say about him: he was never not neat. He never let himself go to that extent. He still had some pride and self-respect left. But what good did it do him? Control was gradually slipping away. Who knew what he might not do next? I've got to watch myself, I've certainly got to *watch* myself; no telling what undreamed-of fantastic thing he might catch himself doing next. Catch himself? If he could only be sure of that! But last night it had gone so far that others had caught him first.

There was no sense in going down now and cooling your heels in front of a bar that hadn't opened yet. Stand there leaning against the door, looking at the clock inside, while other people hurried past you to work. He hadn't sunk that low, either. Or maybe this clock here this God-damned Dutchman's little clock was slow. He went into the bedroom and sat down at the desk and picked up the 'phone and dialed ME-7-1212. He listened breathless to the breathless voice, with the oddly questioning lift at the end: "When yew hear the sig-nal, the tie-yum will be seven-fifty-fie-yuv and thrrree-quar-ters." He did not wait for the signal, he said "Thank you" automatically and hung up. Fool! he said as he went for his coat. Why the hell did I thank her, she can't hear me. . . .

He found his coat and vest lying in a heap on the floor at the end of the couch. He went through the pockets. He fished out all the money and spread it on the table and counted it. My God there was twenty-six dollars and something. Talk about windfalls. Today of all days!

He did not go to Sam's place. Not because Gloria would be there (because she wouldn't, she didn't come till noon). But he wanted to start off someplace else, today. Maybe Sam's later. He went to a little bar-and-grill just below 55th and thank Christ the bartender was on time.

"Rye, please."

The bartender looked at him. "Double?"

He checked an impulse to draw himself up. "No!" Where had the guy got *that* idea? He ought to be put in his place. Just because you came around at eight-something in the morning, did that necessarily mean—? They were open for business, weren't they? Well, then?

He ignored the drink for a minute or two. He picked up a *News* that was lying on the counter, folded back at the editorial page. He scanned The Inquiring Fotographer column: "Do you sleep raw at night or do you wear pajamas?" He glanced at a cartoon called The Family—somebody's idea of an aristocratic middle-aged couple discussing politics in language never heard on land or sea. He reached for the glass, looked at it critically a moment, then drank.

He ordered another and faced the mirror. There was no sense in working himself into a fright, all because of something that had happened last night when he wasn't responsible, wasn't himself—something that hadn't turned out disastrously, after all. Not as bad as it might have. But it was a warning, a danger-signal, one of the sharpest he had yet met up with. In spite of his trying to rationalize the whole episode of last night and his fear today, a sinking sensation plunged down through his breast again and again, his body began to get hot all over, his palms sweated: it was shame.

He drank the second drink in one swallow, and a third, and in a moment or two he felt better. Now he could begin to take it easier, why not, he had the whole day ahead of him, several days, there was money in his pocket, plenty money—really, come to think of it, he hadn't a care in the world. Absurd silly cheating little glasses; thick; all run to fat, as it were. All bottom. You could probably pour the contents into a thimble. Surely a dozen of these wouldn't be the equivalent of the kind he drank from at home.

On the mantel over the bar, tilted against the mirror, was a yellow card advertising the double-feature at the Select next door. Greta Garbo in *Camille,* and some other movie. It was like a sum-mons, for God's sake. He had seen the picture three times dur-ing the week it opened on Broadway, a month or so ago. All of a sudden (but no, it was too early, it would have to wait) he had to see again that strange fabled face, hear the voice that sent shivers down his spine when it uttered even the inconsequential little sen-tence (the finger-tips suddenly raised to the mouth as if to cover the rueful smile): "It's my birthday." Or the rapid impatient way, half-defiant, half-regretful, it ran off the words about money: "And I've never been very particular where it came from, as you very well know." And oh the scene where the Baron was leaving for Russia—how she said "Goodbye. . . . goodbye" like a little song. ("Come with me!" The shake of the head and the smile, then; and the answer: "But Russia is so co-o-old—you wouldn't want me to get ill again, would you," not meaning this was the reason she couldn't go, not even pretending to mean it.) He knew the performance by heart, as one knows a loved piece of music:

every inflexion, every stress and emphasis, every faultless phrase, every small revelation of satisfying but provocative beauty. There was a way to spend the afternoon!—The bartender slid the bottle across the counter and this time he poured the drink himself.

Of course they had let him go last night—of course they had! They didn't want any trouble with the police, did they? Isn't that what always happened when something like that occurred in a bar? They let the fellow get away with it, let him get as far as the door, and then nabbed him. They didn't want to accuse him while he was at the table, not while he was still on the premises, inside and upstairs. That would mean a row, maybe, and calling the police, and probably frightening or upsetting everybody in the place and ruining business for the night. The customers would think it was a raid, like the old days. No, the thing to do was let him get as far as the very entrance, take the purse away from him there, and then kick him out. Nobody wanted to press charges anyhow—what was the good? Boot him into the street and be done with him.

Quickly he picked up the bottle and poured another drink, then set it down again with a great show of relaxation. The bartender glanced at him out of the corner of his eye every few minutes, or turned his back and watched him in the mirror. It was plain that he couldn't figure him out. Well, what of it, he couldn't figure himself out, sometimes. Not often but sometimes.

How the cab-drivers had watched the whole business in silence. Looked at him without a word as he straightened his coat and walked off. If they had only laughed or something. He couldn't have taken one of those cabs for anything in the world. Faced the driver through a long drive uptown. Well, not had to face him, exactly. But sitting in silence in the backseat would have been worse, while the driver sat just as silent up front. Could he have maybe kidded the driver about his name, called him by his first name as it was revealed on the lighted card between the seats? And when they arrived, getting out, having to hand the driver his money, listen whether he said Thank you or not. Christ he couldn't think of that now, mustn't, wouldn't. He felt the need to talk.

"Are you a News fan?"

"What?"

"I see a News on the bar here."

"Some drunk left it last night."

A crack. But he wasn't going to be thrown off, not by that. "What's the matter, don't you like the News?"

"It's all right."

"I always read 'How He Proposed.' I dearly love 'How He Proposed.'"

The bartender picked up a tumbler and began polishing.

"Oh, and 'Embarrassing Moments.' Ever notice how they're always about some poor dope of a stenographer with delusions of grandeur? She puts on the dog about her wonderful wardrobe or husband's fine job or something, and of course always gets caught."

"Never noticed."

"How can they write such stuff about themselves. Signed and everything. They don't seem to mind a bit."

"Ayuh?"

"Maybe it's the two dollars."

"Ayuh."

He looked searchingly at the bartender. "What's the matter, you tired or something?"

"I'm busy, Jack."

It had been the waiter upstairs, the waiter with the Charles Boyer accent. He must have seen it all along. From the beginning. But how could he? The waiter had never shown by the slightest sign that he knew what was going on—any more than *he* showed it. He knew he couldn't have been smoother, cagier, more the master of his every smallest move—as only the drunk can be who is just drunk enough, just enough to know exactly

what he is doing, with a clarity denied the sober. Oh, and not
know, too. That was the humiliating and the dangerous part of
it. Drunk enough to know what *he* was doing but not the others. Concentrating so closely on himself, studying his own performance so intensely, that he lost track of everybody else, forgot
they were able to see too—able to see him and what he was up to
in a way he couldn't see at all. Why hadn't they *told* him (as he
would have done for another), why hadn't somebody tipped him
off that he was going too far, why hadn't someone been decent
enough to come over to his table and say "Careful there, friend,
you're headed for trouble, we see you"? But no, they had all sat by
or sat back and let it happen, waited for it to happen—sure, why
not, it wasn't happening to them!

It was silly staying on in this stinking place, the bartender was
a suspicious crab, it was nine o'clock, the liquor store would be
open by now. He paid and left.

He stood in the middle of the wide clean liquor store and
deliberated. A quart would be enough for now; he'd be out again
later, probably half a dozen times. Scotch for a change. He named
the brand, stopped himself just as he was about to say "Don't
bother to wrap it," and put the money on the counter. Funny how
you could say it when buying a tube of tooth-paste or a box of
Shredded Wheat or anything else under the sun. But naturally
you didn't care whether or not the clerk would think you were too
anxious to get at the tooth-paste or Shredded Wheat the moment
you got home—which naturally the clerk wouldn't think to begin
with. . . .

The purchase made, the fruits are to ensue. . . . How could he
ever communicate to anyone the sense of luxury he felt as he came
into the flat with the Scotch under his arm? The day was his, the
drink, the whole place. And no one knew where he was and what
he was doing. He opened the lid of the gramophone, released the
switch, and set going the record that was on. He got a clean glass
from the kitchen, tore off the paper bag and the foil wrapping of

the bottle, and poured himself a decent drink. He carried it to the big chair in the corner and sat down.

Schnabel was hammering out the Rondo of the *Waldstein*. As the music increased in volume and acceleration, as the new drink warmed his stomach, he lay back in the big chair and deliberately and consciously went into his favorite daydream, planning and plotting it out as if it were a delightful treat he had long promised himself and one of these days meant to get around to.

It was a dream he could re-live forever and had already enjoyed many dozens of times. He came out on the stage of Carnegie Hall, smiled, bowed, sat down at the piano, and awaited the assignment. He did not wear white tie, tails, and a stiff-bosom. He was in grey flannels, comfortable sport-shoes, soft sleeveless sweater, and a white shirt. No jacket or vest, no tie. He glanced about the packed expectant house and wondered indifferently how many would stay to the finish, long after midnight. Most of them, probably; the evening had been announced in the paper for weeks, the house had long since been sold out, music circles talked of little else, everybody wanted to be in on this unique and extraordinary event. . . . The little group of critics were still in a huddle down front, just beyond the footlights. They had arrived long before anyone else (they were supposed to have gathered at six, he believed), they buzzed among themselves and conferred and whispered, exchanged notes and sneered at each other's taste, got cross with one another, looked up things in books, finally came to a grudging agreement around nine-fifteen, and handed the finished list to a waiting typist. Then one of them climbed up onto the stage, turned about to face the auditorium, raised his hand and cleared his throat. "Ladies and gentlemen. As you know—" The vast restless mumble of the house died down. "As you know," he began again, "we are gathered here tonight to witness how a great artist shall meet, if he can, a challenge unique in musical history. If he wins, the feat and the victory shall ring forever throughout

Euterpe's storied halls. Mr. Birnam has yet no idea what his program tonight is to be. He will not know until I read from this list
which my colleagues and I have only just completed." He waved
the little paper. "I beg your indulgence and forgiveness for being a
bit tardy, but we were at some pains to agree on just which works
of which masters Mr. Birnam was to play to us. From Poulenc
back to Scarlatti"—(Did he mean Alessandro the father, Don
wondered, or Domenico the son?)—"from Buxtehude down to
Copland, the literature of the pianoforte offers a range so rich that
our task was, you may well imagine, most difficult indeed. To say
nothing of Mr. *Bir*nam's task, I might add"—and he waited for
the appreciative laughter and applause which obligingly swept
the house. "Not to try your generous patience any further, then,
perhaps I should announce the opening number without more
ado. And of course, each succeeding work, as the program pro-
gresses, will be similarly announced—but only just be*fore* it is to
be played." He turned. "Mr. Birnam, are you ready, Sir?" Mr.
Birnam nodded. "Very well: Sonata Number 12, in F Major, by
Wolfgang Amadeus Mozart." Mr. Birnam permitted himself a
small smile and said, barely aloud: "Köchel *Verzeichnis* 331." The
critic murmured "Oh yes, yes of course; I meant to add—" He
plucked in confusion at the black ribbon of his pince-nez, hurried
back over the footlights, and Mr. Birnam began. . . .

The Rondo was finished. He put the record back in the album
and got out the 1st Movement. He set it on the revolving disk
and went to his chair again. A dream indeed. Comic, to be sure;
ridiculous, childish; but—most musical, most melancholy. . . .

He couldn't make up his mind, then, who he wanted to play.
In the middle of a Debussy prelude he dragged out the album
of Medtner, and before he got the first record out of its envelope
he remembered a Schubert *adagio* that was certainly, God, the
greatest moment in all music. But it wasn't when he played it.
Somehow it seemed oddly trite, oddly undeveloped, not rich in

any way, not remotely satisfying like the one and only Beethoven. He went back to the Schnabel albums of the great Thirty-Two and turned the volume-button up full.

Let the ladies in the front apartment pound on the wall and complain of the noise (noise!), let their dog Sophie bark her silly head off, this was Music! Just when was it Beethoven had gone deaf—before, or after, this particular opus-number? He reached for the Grove Dictionary and became absorbed at once in the description of the great Rasoumovsky household. Lord what a subject for a book. Or a play; a great play! Suddenly he was very hungry.

Christ why wouldn't he be? Wasn't it noon? The little eight-day traveling clock and the generous Dutchman said it was. No wonder. Besides, as far as he could remember, he hadn't eaten a thing all day yesterday, after his breakfast with Wick. Ordinarily he never thought of food when he was drinking. Now it was different; he hadn't been drinking enough, yet; he wasn't tight at all, not really; how could he be, if he was thinking of food? His stomach was beginning to need it. Why not? If he knew himself, he certainly didn't eat last night at Jack's, certainly didn't order anything to eat there. Jack's—

He grabbed up his hat and coat. He'd go out and get himself a sandwich or two at the delicatessen, bring them back here and finish the bottle after he ate. There was a good pint left. Yes, he ought to do that. The food would help counteract the drink, keep him fit and upright for the rest of the day, fortify him enough to carry on and enjoy the whole afternoon and night. He carefully counted his money all over again, and went out.

It was a wonderful day, oh wonderful! Cool and clear, my lord you could see way to the rivers at both ends of the street, October was certainly the best damned month of the year no question about it. Especially early in the month, right now, this very week, today! He almost felt like dropping in on somebody he knew, finding out how they were. Oh-oh, forget that. He knew better than to make any calls, even on the telephone. What the hell was he trying to do, spoil everything? let everybody know he was on the loose again? invite them to step in and ruin the whole week-end? Let them leave him alone! He was all right, perfectly able to handle himself, behaving just like anybody else, he meant to stay this way too, wasn't he on his way to buy food for Christ sake? Could they ask for any better assurance than that? Did he ever buy food when he was drinking? Certainly not, they knew that as well as he did, he was sober as a Lackawanna judge.

He knew better than to go to the good delicatessen at 56th. He still owed Mr. Schultz ten dollars he'd borrowed in the summer. Or did he? Maybe Wick had paid it back; anyway he couldn't remember. No use taking a chance. He turned south to go to the one at 54th.

He passed the Select. My God, Garbo! In *Camille* no less. This was luck. He stopped and looked at the stills tacked up on a board outside. There was the one on her knees before M. Duval (but not on her knees to him!); there was the one in the theater-box, smiling under raised opera-glasses as she first found Armand in the crowd below; and of course there was the unforgettable picture of Marguerite in death, the fabulous face looking already cold, white, more poetic and elusive than ever. What a performance that had been. Amid all the vulgarity of that garish noisy movie, how she had stood out, so right in every move and gesture, in every inflexion and emphasis of the thrilling voice (that last long scene, whispered throughout), in every wonderful expression of the wonderful face. Strange and moving the indescribable rueful melancholy she cast over the entire film—the acting art at its very purest, surely. He slid his quarter under the glass window of the box office and went in.

"Smoking?"

"Upstairs."

He went up the ramp into a dark smelly corridor but he scarcely noticed the smell. He was thinking of the time he had first read in the paper that Garbo was to do *Camille* and how he had said to himself: "God damn it, why do they have to put her in *Camille* of all things! Hasn't it been done to death by every throbbing female who ever fancied herself an actress?" And how, when he finally saw it some weeks ago, he saw how she had made it completely her own, played the hackneyed role as if it had never been played before—and as far as he was concerned, that was the end of the Camilles: it had been done for good and all as it could never be done again. He turned at the end of the corridor and came out into the upstairs balcony.

He groped his way to a seat near the front. He still couldn't see but nothing was familiar—there was no music, none of the familiar dialogue he knew so well, nor the voice. He stared at the screen. Two men in drab cotton jumpers sat at a wooden table peeling potatoes. They couldn't talk because a man with a rifle stood behind them, but one was trying to indicate to the other that a note had been dropped somewhere among the potato peelings.

Damn it to hell, a prison picture, a gangster movie or something. Double-feature? Why hadn't he found that out before he came in, then made sure which one was on? Wouldn't that happen, just as he was all set to enjoy Garbo? He hated prison movies and he knew only too damned well why. Every time he saw a movie about a prison, a guy behind bars, the death cell, he knew that one day he was going to be right there, in that same spot. Melodrama!—but he couldn't shake the feeling nevertheless. He fidgeted throughout such films, looked away for whole sequences, tried to think of other things, and very often had to get up and leave.

The scene had changed. A crowd of people, mostly women, waiting for big iron gates to open. Visiting day. An attendant approached, cranked up the gates, and the crowd surged in.

Now the camera concentrated on a surly good-looking girl. She was shown walking along a corridor toward the narrow entrance to the visitors' room. She wore a beret and a polo coat, both hands in her pockets. Her face was expressionless. Two guards watched her coming toward them. One glanced at the other. Suddenly, just as she came up to the door, a loud stinging bell rang out in a frenzy of alarm. The girl stopped dead in her tracks, still expressionless. One of the guards smiled, turned off a tiny switch in the wall, and the bell ceased. "Okay," he said, holding out his hand, "give us the rod." She looked up at him without expression. "You've just passed through the metal-detector beam," he said quietly; "we know you've got a gun on you." Without a word she reached in her pocket and drew out a small automatic. She handed it to the guard. "Okay, you can go in now." And expressionless still, she passed on in.

He was getting uneasier by the minute. He knew he had reason to fear. The foolish psychiatrist had once told him something that stuck in his mind and would probably stick there forever and ever (not that he ever thought of it, except times like now): The alcoholic, to get liquor, will do everything that the drug-addict will do to get drugs, everything but one: and that is murder. Cut off from drink, he'll lie to get it, beg, plead, wheedle, borrow, steal, rob—all the crimes in the catalogue. But he won't kill for it. That's the difference between the drunk and the drug-addict. But the *only* one.

Maybe.

Was he supposed to have found consolation and comfort in this dictum? He didn't. The foolish psychiatrist had been too often wrong. Besides, *he* knew the alcoholic from the inside. He knew (not the other) to what lengths the drinker will go to get that desperately needed drink the morning after. Or that is (and this was worse) he *didn't* know to what lengths he would go. If he knew, he could say then how right or how wrong the foolish psychiatrist had been, how safe he himself was, and what chances he had of not ending up in just such a place as this on the screen, the screen that he couldn't look at, now, no not another minute. He slumped down in his chair, put his hand over his eyes, and tried to doze off. Maybe he could sleep until the opening music of *Camille,* the *Traviata* theme, told him Garbo was on. . . .

A burst of machine-guns knocked him nearly out of his seat. Jesus Christ what was going on—where the hell was he! He gripped the two arms of his chair and stared.

The screen was exploding in noise. Bells rang, sirens screamed to a pitch never heard before, the night was blasted with gun-fire. *Dut-dut-dut-dut-dut-dut.* Searchlights swept the dark yard back and forth, moved along the walls, finally found the two potato-peelers where they crouched against the gate like snarling animals, frozen in the glare.

Had he been asleep? How long? There was a large illuminated clock at the right of the screen advertising some neighborhood jeweler; it was two-fifteen. Lord this couldn't last much longer, Garbo would be on any minute. But suddenly he couldn't wait, either. Not even if this was the final sequence of the film. One of the men now lay face down in the dirt, the other clutched his side and writhed and grinned in pain. He grabbed up his hat and left.

He stopped in at the bar next door and bought a drink.

"Hi, Jack," the bartender said.

Oh sure. This was the one he'd been in before. The guy must be feeling better, he actually spoke. To hell with him. He drank the drink and looked around.

The *News* was still on the counter. Somebody had been reading the Broadway column. He read it too. "Eileen Dorrit, who has a lake named after her in Argentina, is about to leave the Follies chorus at the behest of her mother. . . . What prominent Park Avenue matron is about to change her couturiere because she doesn't like her face—or because Mr. B. does?. . ." A hell of a way to earn a living and if the guy must use French why the hell doesn't he learn how to spell it?

This was no place to hang around in. What did it offer? Sam's was better. Sam was better too. He paid and left.

Sam was a philosopher but he didn't feel like talking philosophy today. He wanted to see Gloria. "Where's Gloria?"

"Ladies' room."

"God, I didn't know this place *had* a ladies' room."

"Why not? What'll it be? Rye?"

"And White Rock. Some ice."

"My, that isn't like you, Mr. Birnam. You always take it straight."

"I feel like spreading it out a little today."

Sam was a nice guy but he'd never forget how mad he got once. He had been desperate for a drink and hadn't a nickel. He thought he'd try something new, something he'd never tried before. He came in here and ordered a drink, stood around as casually as he could, and drank it. Took his time so it would look all right. Then he ordered another. Sam served him, of course, and poured him still another, then several others, for more than an hour. They chatted pleasantly about one thing and another, Don all the time wondering how Sam was going to take it. He didn't feel like making up some story like "Well, what do you know, look here, I haven't got my wallet with me, I just changed my clothes an hour ago and must have forgotten it." That was too damned mean, somehow; it left Sam obliged to believe him. Finally he said, right in the middle of one of Sam's stories that he wasn't paying any attention to, "Listen, Sam. I can't pay you today." Sam looked at him as if he didn't quite hear right. "I haven't any money on me. I'll come in and pay you tomorrow. Or anyway as soon as I can." Then Sam began. Gave him a long song-&-dance about Christ almighty didn't you know that you can't do that, the bar business was stricter than cash-&-carry, it had to be, now what in Christ's name was *he* going to do, why the hell did you order drinks you didn't have the money to pay for, a fine kind of trick to play on a guy, what was the boss going to say, sure you were sorry but did that make it right, did that replace the money he'd have to pay now out of his own pocket?... Don hadn't gone

back to Sam's for a good while, after that; but when he did, and
paid, everything was all right. Except from then on, Don always
made a point of paying after the first drink, just to show Sam he
had it. He bought another drink now and paid for it.

Gloria was being a hell of a time in the ladies' room. Probably fixing her face and hair all over again. He was beginning to
get impatient for her. He studied Sam across the bar. Funny how
some people ran so true to type. If you cast Sam as a bartender in
a play, the knowing critic would say, "Come now, that's going too
far, being too obvious, why don't you use a little imagination?"
Sam was so Irish-looking that he looked like a cartoon. Only
thing wrong about him was his name. He ought to have been
called Mike, or Paddy. Hey, who wasn't using imagination now?

Now he was feeling just swell. *This* was the way to be. Relaxed
and calm and warm inside, warm toward all the world. Thoroughly at home and at ease in yourself. What a boon liquor could
be when you used it right. He was being the very soul of propri-
ety; temperate, controlled, very gentlemanlike in fact. The drinks
were hardly affecting him at all. He could even speed things up
a little. Might as well get *some* lift out of the afternoon, specially
when you'd had such a slow start. He told Sam to pour him
another.

Sam must have seen he was in money. He slid the bottle across
the bar to let him help himself.

Gloria came out, her copper-satin dress shining in the dark
back part of the room. She looked as pretty as a picture. Her
orange-colored hair was as lively and vivid as her dress; she was
color itself; yet with all that, there was something pathetic about
her. Infinitely touching. Child of nature, so unnatural. . . . "Gloria! Good afternoon!"

She came up to the bar. "Oh. I'm *okay* today. Is that it?"

"What do you mean 'today'? You're one hundred per cent
with me, you know that. Always were. Let me buy you a drink."

"Maybe I need it."

"Have it then."

"Usual, Sam."

Sam mixed whatever it was and immediately tried to show, by his preoccupation, that from now on he would be having no part of the conversation, he wouldn't even hear a thing that was said.

"What's the matter, Gloria? Blue funk? Brown study? Pink elephants?"

"Say, you know I don't drink. Not like you I mean."

"Why Gloria. You're actually cross."

"Don't mind me. I just—" She picked up the drink Sam set before her, probably ginger ale, and slowly sipped. "I don't know."

"*I* know."

"What?"

"Love."

"Don't give me that."

"What's he like, Gloria? Big and strong? Good-looking as all hell?"

"Oh stop. Please. I don't feel like it today."

Suddenly he was terribly sorry for her; and suddenly, too, he felt he was rather drunk. And he didn't give a good God-damn, either. It was swell. His mind was beginning to pick up and he wasn't bored not any way you look at it. It must have come on him all of a sudden but it was damned good. He liked it. He felt hellishly sorry for Gloria, poor kid.

"I don't like you shutting me out in the cold like this."

"I can't explain it, Mr. Birnam, so what's the use of talking about it. It don't make sense when I do."

"But I'm interested. Truly."

She looked up at him for a full moment to see if he meant it. He raised his eyebrows questioningly and steadily returned her steady gaze.

She turned back to her drink. "It's home. I'm thinking of leaving."

"Why?"

"Oh, I don't know. I guess I'm not very hospitable there. My father—"

Hell, this wasn't very interesting. But he'd finish this drink and maybe have one more and then go back to the flat where he could really enjoy himself. Take in a few bottles and maybe just stay there the whole rest of the weekend. Meanwhile it wouldn't hurt him to listen to Gloria for a few minutes. He'd asked for it.

"I certainly'd think twice, Gloria. Or even thrice. Home isn't something you can find just any day of the week. They don't grow on every bush. Jeeper's, Sam, you're certainly taking your time."

Sam handed him the new drink without a word.

"I know," Gloria said, "but if you don't feel you belong any more?"

"I know what I'm talking about when I talk about homes."

"Are you married?"

"What do you think?"

"Well," she said, "I don't know."

He looked at her a moment before making up his mind. "I'm married, yes." He picked up his drink and swished the ice slowly around in the glass. "I'm married all right, no fear," he added with a sigh. He glanced up at the mirror over the bar and at once seemed to become lost in thought.

"What's the matter," Gloria said.

"Nothing."

"Why are you looking like that?"

"You asked me if I was married, didn't you?"

"Yes."

"Well, I told you." He downed the drink and pushed the empty glass across the bar toward Sam.

Gloria waited. When the new drink had been set before him, she said, "Tell me about it."

He took a deep breath and expelled it with the words: "I'm married and I have two little boys. Anything else you want to know?"

"Is she pretty?"

He struck a note of heavy irony. "Lovely. Lovely, Gloria. She's so lovely she isn't human."

"What's her name?"

"Theodora. But she's called Teddy."

"Teddy. That's cute."

"Yes, isn't it. God."

"I'd love to see her. I knew you'd have an awful pretty wife, Mr. Birnam."

"I have. I have that."

"Does she dress nice?"

"Very. It's her chief interest in life."

"More than you?"

"Are you kidding?"

Gloria slid a cigarette from his pack. "Where do you live?"

"We have a little house, just a two-by-four really, in Sutton Place. And then a place in Greenwich."

"Greenwich Village?"

"God don't talk to me about Greenwich Village. Stinking slum. Greenwich Connecticut."

"I never was there."

"God."

"Why do you say God all the time?"

"Because that's the way I feel."

Gloria considered a moment. "A farm?"

He permitted himself a small rueful laugh. "A farm. Christ I wish it were. That would be something useful, at least." He took a drink. "No, it's no farm, dear. It's just a great God-damned moratorium of a place—mausoleum of a place, fronting the Sound. Private beach, stables, gardens. Hell, what's the use. Let's change the subject for Christ's sake."

"Are you that rich?"

"My wife is."

"Oh."

"What do you mean, oh?"

"Is that the trouble? She has the money?"

"You're just being romantic now, Gloria dear. Money doesn't necessarily mean trouble. She's always had it. I've always had it too, for that matter. And there are lots worse things in the world than money, Gloria. Lots. Frigidity, for example."

"What's that?"

"Leave it lay. Don't get me started. Hey, what are we talking about this for, anyway? I thought we were going to have fun?"

"I'm interested, that's all."

"Well, I'm not."

"Pardon me, Mr. Birnam. I didn't mean to intrude."

He downed his drink and then started to pay, as if he were about to leave. "Before you get married"—he waved a finger at her—"be mighty sure, Gloria, that your wife isn't frigid." He heard himself, and laughed. "Hell, I was forgetting. You'll be marrying a man anyway—I hope. And they're never frigid."

"What's that word mean?"

"I will a round unvarnisht tale deliver—"

"But what does it mean?"

"Frigid? It's one of nature's little tricks of revenge, dear. One of woman's tricks. It's all terribly terribly nice and proper, and keeps the lady a lady. Oh, always a lady. And makes a bloody monkey out of the poor sap who happened to marry her—because he loved her. If monkey was the worst of it, the story would merely be comic." He sighed. "As it is, I could a tale unfold whose lightest word— Well, never mind."

"It's a rotten shame."

"What is."

"That you're not happily married. Teddy—I mean, your wife—ought to be ashamed of herself. A nice man like you—"

"Oh-h-h no-o-o!" he said, his voice shuddering humorously. "I'm not nice, Gloria. Not a bit of it. I'm no better than I should be, like the cat in th' adage. But I *could* have been a nice guy, if— given a chance. If given half a chance. . . ."

"By who? Your family?"

"By my wife. My dear beautiful lovely frigid wife. Now look. Are you going to drink with me, or are we going to waste the whole afternoon with wild and whirling words."

"I never know when you're kidding and when you're not, Mr. Birnam."

He smiled quizzically. "Neither do I, Gloria. Neither do I. Now what about it. Drink?"

"Sure, I'll have another. The usual, Sam," she said, and turned back to Don. "I bet you been taking me for a terrible ride, though."

"Really? That's not kind. What makes you think so?"

"The way you kid all the time."

"And if I kid at any mortal thing, 'tis that I may not weep."

"You see? You are now."

"I promise not to crack another crack. No, not even a smile."

Plainly, she was interested in him. "I like you to laugh, but I want," she said, "I want to believe what you say."

"You don't mind if I keep on drinking, do you?"

"You said you had two little boys."

"My jewels."

"Tell me about them."

"Well, I have two little boys. They're wild as Indians and smart as whips."

"Funny, a minute ago you were all in the dumps."

"I'm resilient, Gloria. Mercurial. Volatile."

"What are their names?"

"Who."

"Your little boys."

"Oh. Malcolm and Donaldbain."

"Funny name."

"Donald?"

"Oh."

"Bright as buttons."

"How old are they?"

"Four and six. Just like that. That's planning, dear, in *spite* of the frigidity. That's one time I got my oar in. Or two times."

"Are they dark like you?"

"Blond, both of them. Just like their blonde lovely frigid mother. A pity, isn't it? Christ what I am standing here with an empty glass for? Sam what the hell are you doing? Here!"

"I wish you wouldn't talk like that."

"I want a drink!"

"Why is it a pity? Don't you like them to look like their mother?"

"God *I* don't care. I'm only too thankful they aren't girls. Because if they were, and if I thought they were going to grow up and put some poor devil through hell, the way—" He broke off, unable to go on, and picked up the glass.

"Are you crazy about them?"

"Gloria, I love those two boys this side idolatry. Now if you don't mind, I'd rather not talk any more about it."

"I know. Okay."

He stared at his face in the glass. "Gloria," he said, without turning toward her, "I'll tell you something." He lowered his voice. "And this is something I've never confided to a living soul till now, Gloria."

"Don't say something you'll be sorry for, Mr. Birnam. It don't make any difference."

"God, I won't. Maybe I'm even glad to find release, get it off my chest. Gloria look. My wife is a lovely woman, and she's a good woman, understand? A good woman. Do you know what that means? Do you know what a good woman is? They're hell on wheels. They're simply not for men. Not for a man like me they aren't."

"What's there about that? I mean, I don't get it."

"Wait a minute, let me finish. My wife, she'd— Yes, honestly. She'd rather have me be unfaithful to her, habitually—rather I'd sleep with one of the chambermaids even—than go to bed with her." Gloria had colored, but he pretended not to notice. "She tries every trick known to woman to keep me out of her bed. Feigns headaches, reads, falls asleep the minute she hits the hay, has the curse practically every day in the month—" He stopped, aware that Gloria had turned from him and was staring down at her glass.

"You ought not to talk like that, Mr. Birnam," she said, almost sadly. "It isn't nice."

"My dear girl." He put his hand tenderly on her arm. "I'm sorry. Forgive me. Did I offend?" Suddenly he felt all affectionate and warm toward Gloria. "Look Gloria. Have a drink with me now to show that you forgive me."

"There's nothing to forgive," she said quietly, "it's all right."

"Have a drink anyway. Sam!" He turned to her. "I forgot myself. I was forgetting you were only a child—that you didn't understand the talk of a man."

Amazing then, touching too, the way Gloria responded, the way she seemed to open up to him, under the warmth of his words. "You're a terribly nice person, Mr. Birnam," she said very soberly. "I want you to *be* nice."

He could have wept, of course. It was one hell of a long while since anybody'd said anything remotely like that—to him. Gloria plainly meant it. The words were so simple there couldn't be any thought of trying to fool him. He told her he was touched and grateful. Perhaps he could *be* a nice person, for Gloria. He had an inspiration and suddenly became very happy.

"Gloria listen. What time are you off tonight?"

"Why?"

"I was wondering if you'd do me a great favor and go out with me. Please say you will."

"Where?"

"Anywhere." He wouldn't make the mistake of suggesting some place like the Coq Rouge or LaRue's where Gloria would only be miserable. He'd let her pick the place and then play up to her idea of the evening. "You say where. Wherever you'd like to go."

"I don't know if I could."

He could see she was eager to accept, but holding back. Certainly she must know by now he wasn't pulling her leg. He'd never been more sincere in his life than he was this minute. "You'd make me a very happy man, Gloria."

"I'd have to ask the boss."

"Do. Will you? Right now?"

"Yes." She flushed, smiling. "Wait a sec, I'll be right back."

She left him and went to the rear of the room where the proprietor sat alone at a table reading the evening paper. As she bent over his shoulder and began speaking, he saw the man turn and look up at him with a puzzled frown on his forehead. He bent his attention on his own reflection in the mirror while Gloria continued to talk with the boss.

A wonderful idea—Wick would certainly approve of this! He couldn't wait to tell Wick—Wick wouldn't mind any of it in the least. He was doing the girl a kindness, being nice to someone else for a change. For once he wasn't on the receiving end. He wanted genuinely to put himself in the role of benefactor and gentleman and give Gloria as good a time as he possibly could.

Apart from all that: what an experience it would be; almost a study. He was curious to know what the evening would be like, what kind of place she would want to go to, the things she would say, the things she would find pleasure in. He would try to fill all that Gloria longed for and looked up to in her idea of the ideal escort, which tonight would be him. Think what he himself might learn before the evening was out, about places he'd never seen the inside of (Danceland?), about young aspiring girls of her class to whom a date of this kind (and a gentleman at that) was as near to romance—so they thought, perhaps—as it would ever be given them to come. He would be careful and watchful to get the most out of it himself, to add to his own experience and knowledge—not drink too much, only enough to make the evening a pleasant social one for Gloria. He would be careful, too, to act the gentleman only insofar as Gloria understood the term. He must not embarrass her by ordering things she had never heard of, translating the French if there was any, taking a taxi when a bus or walking would do. With Gloria at his side he'd remember not to say "Please" and "Thank You" to the waiter; he'd join in the fun with people he didn't know, if that was what she wanted; buy her a gardenia or an orchid, a lavender orchid of course, but not a camellia. Certainly he would not wear his dinner-jacket. . . . All this, Wick would understand. Wick wouldn't mind his drinking at all, under these circumstances. He'd approve, even commend him for it. The evening promised to be a wonderful, a happy experience, something he would enjoy telling Wick all about later and hearing Wick's approval of the whole thing.

Gloria was back at his elbow. "Is eight o'clock too late?" she said, almost under her breath. "I can go."

"Gloria, that's wonderful!"

"You don't mind waiting till eight?"

"Hell no."

Her face fell. "Now don't talk like that, Mr. Birnam, or I don't want to go."

"Excuse me, Gloria, I'm just so glad, I guess. I forgot my manners. Where would you like to dine?"

She loved the word. Tentatively she suggested her idea. "Would—would The New Yorker roof be too much?"

"I think we could manage it very nicely. I'll 'phone for a table."

"They have a floor-show, you know. Ice and everything."

"It sounds wonderful."

"You've never been there?"

"Not yet. And you know? I've always wanted to go."

"It'll be the first time for you, too!"

"Let's see." He glanced at the clock. "Suppose I go home and take a tub and maybe get a bite to eat—"

"Don't eat too much!"

"I won't. Then call for you here at sharp eight."

She touched his sleeve. "Listen. Do you care? I'll have to wear this old thing I've got on."

He glanced down at the brown satin dress. "Why, you look perfect!"

"There wouldn't be time to go all the way home and change. Not when I don't get off till eight."

"What's the matter with it? You look all dressed up, Gloria, just as you are. And I'll buy you a flower and you'll look even more so."

"You're awfully nice to me, Mr. Birnam. I told you you were a terribly nice person."

"Now none of that or *I* won't go. Sam, here!" He tossed a ten-dollar-bill on the bar and Sam made the change and counted it out to him. "Goodbye, Gloria. I'm so glad you're going to do this for me."

"For you. What about me?"

"We'll talk about you later. 'Bye. I'll be here on the dot."

When he walked out into the street, he realized he was suddenly very tight. Why wouldn't he be? He'd had at least six or seven in Sam's bar alone. He supposed the stimulus of conversation with Gloria had kept his wits in order, but now he felt everything beginning to sag and blur and drop. What he needed was a good drink, a stiff one, a straight one, to bring him around.

There was an empty bottle from yesterday on the living room table and a quart more than half full. He tossed the empty pint into the leather wastebasket. It landed in the bottom with a loud *kunk*. He poured half a glass of Scotch into the sticky tumbler that had been standing there since noon. He carried it to the big chair and settled himself for a comfortable slow drink. He shook out a cigarette and fished in his pockets for a match. He came up with a paper folder advertising "JACK'S—in Charles Street— WHERE GOOD FELLOWS GET TOGETHER. Close Cover Before Striking Match." He drained the glass almost at a swallow and read the advertisement again.

If it wasn't one thing it was another, and it never mattered which. Always something to run away from, no matter what, no matter why, as though you'd been born with a consciousness of guilt and would find that thing to feel guilty about regardless. Feel? Be.

He ought to stay away from the Village. Knew better, after what happened once in 10th Street. Ought to stay away from bars, for that matter, but certainly Village bars. A few years ago, when Rudolph's was still a speakeasy, he had been drinking alone at the crowded bar one Saturday night. He wasn't tight, not yet. He was saving that for later—had a quart of gin at home, looked forward to making a night of it in his chair, and that's where he was headed for after a few preliminary drinks here. As he started to leave, someone touched him on the shoulder.

"Have one with me before you go."

He turned. It was the fellow who had been standing next to him since he came in, but this was the first he had really noticed him. He was a young man about his own age and class, dressed very much the same as he was. Good suit; presentable; decent manners. He was shy, but friendly. He looked a little worried; also faintly belligerent; the frown challenged Don not to misunderstand the impulse which prompted the invitation. Don got it at once; and as he recognized, like a veteran before a neophyte, the stage of drinking the other had reached—the confidential, the confiding stage—he began to feel superior, amused, tolerant, generous, and warmly friendly himself. "Why, thank you very much," he said with a smile. "And then perhaps you'll have one with me." They exchanged names and ordered drinks. Amid the babble of the bar Don missed the last name; but it didn't matter, the first was Brad.

"You probably wonder why I did that," Brad said.

"No I don't, at all." Don smiled to reassure him.

"I'm staying up late tonight and I feel like talking to some-body."

"I understand." Oh, he understood. How many times indeed, under just such circumstances, in just such places, had he been in on conversations of just this sort. That familiar opening line: it was the prelude to who knew what confidences—boring, very likely; nothing to confide about; intimate but unrevealing and finally elusive or even resentful. Oh well, he could afford to listen awhile and ask the necessary colorless questions to give the guy relief. On many an occasion he himself had wanted a stranger's ear, and got it. Now he gave his own.

"I've got to 'phone Chicago at midnight and it's rather on my mind."

"Oh?" Don fiddled with his glass, knowing it would all come out in due time.

"My father had an operation in Chicago today. I can't 'phone till twelve to find out how it went." Brad addressed his highball. "I'm very fond of my Dad. He's a minister." He glanced sharply at Don. "But he's a good guy!"

Don smiled to himself. God knows *I* can see how a man could be a minister and still be a good guy, if that's what's worrying you. "I'm sure he is," he said. Then, in case Brad got the idea he was thinking different, he asked, to show his interest, "Does he have a church in Chicago?"

"No. Philadelphia."

"Oh? I went to school in Philadelphia."

"Did you," Brad said. "So did I."

"The U of P?"

"Yes."

"Isn't that funny. Because so did I." Normally Don gave a wide berth to Pennsylvania guys, but tonight, somehow, it didn't matter. This one was a little tight, and he could steer the conversation where and how he pleased, or, if things got close, pull out whenever he liked. For once, he was in the driver's seat, because—as always happened when drinking with someone else—the tighter the other got, the soberer and clearer he became.

Acquainted now, with something found in common, Brad grew a little shyer. "What Class were you?"

"'24."

"Well for God sake. So was I."

Nothing so remarkable about that, to either of them. They merely exclaimed out of politeness. It had been a big class, of course. Couple of thousand. Not at all unusual that they'd never met or had been there at the same time. Don could and should have left it at that. Ordinarily would have. And knew that ordinarily he would have. But now he was engaged by the idea, interested, and tempted to go into it further. "I suppose, if we cast about long enough," he said, "we'd turn up some mutual friend."

"I suppose so."

He named the first one that came into his head—and him because of who he was and what he had meant to him. "Ever know Johnny Barker?"

"Johnny Barker! Why, Johnny Barker was my best friend!"

Now wait a minute. This was going too fast and cockeyed. Take it easy here, don't make any mistakes, somebody's apparently made one already. For how could Johnny Barker have been his best friend when he was your best friend. But you couldn't say that, of course. He said, "Now, that's very odd. I knew Johnny very well. For a while, there, we were inseparable. And I knew all the fellows he knew, or—or thought I did. But I—I don't remember you."

"Funny, I was just thinking the same thing about you, as a matter of fact. Because Johnny and I were pals all through college. In fact we were fraternity brothers."

"Johnny *Bar*ker?"

"Certainly."

Don picked up his glass and looked at the whisky. "You mean you were Kappa U?"

"Johnny and I both. What were you?"

Cockeyed wasn't the word. He felt he was being made an absolute fool of—by whom or what, he didn't know. That was the trouble, he couldn't tell. Not by Brad. Brad obviously meant what he said, thought he was speaking the truth. Not by the drink, either. He wasn't tight. He had never been soberer in his life. But all this had no basis in reality whatever. Here were facts different from what he knew to be the facts. He knew this guy had no connection with Kappa U whatever, not the Chapter and house and gang he had known, not when *he* went to school. He could almost suspect a trick or a trap but for the fact that it was he himself who had first mentioned the U of P or brought up the name of Johnny Barker. It was dangerous ground, the more so because it didn't make sense. The further into it he got, the more fantastic it became. Like when you first experience an earthquake and foundations cease to be foundations at all. Was he completely crazy? Was he hearing right? But he had to go on with it. Some devilish compulsion insisted that he find out and be put on the right track. Or the wrong track, even. But *any* track.

"Now listen, fella," he said, very calmly. "I don't doubt your word at all, so don't get me wrong. But there's something screwy about all this."

"Why?"

"Well, now look. I knew all those boys very well, the Kappa U pledges. True, I was only there one year, but I knew the whole freshman crowd, all twelve of them. Joe Bruce, Hans von Wille, Arch Gilbert, Potter Smith—"

"Yes, and Shrimp Taylor, Russ Gerard—"

"That's right," Don said. "I knew all of them. I—I lunched at the house, often. But I don't remember you in the outfit."

"Oh, I get it. You only knew them as pledges, in freshman year. Well, I wasn't taken in till May. They kicked a guy out just before Easter Week and that made a place for me."

Like all other moments of crisis, of course, the incident had never ended. It sent its reverberations down to this very second, to this very place, and all but shook the glass from his hand. Was the incident finally closed? But in a sense, it was only happening now, for the first time. Out of the past, across miles and years, the accusing finger of the Senior Council pointed at him over the bar. He raised the highball and drank as calmly as if they had been talking about the weather. "Who was the guy," he heard himself saying, "—and what did they kick him out for?"

"I don't remember his name. Not sure that I ever heard it, because the fellows didn't talk about it much. But it seems he had a crush on Tracey Burke and Tracey got fed up. He showed the Senior Council a letter the kid wrote. Hero-worship stuff, but pretty passionate. Well, they couldn't have that sort of thing in a fraternity, so they kicked him out. Lucky for me, of course. I'd always wanted to be a Kappa U but they were full up, till this happened. Remember Tracey Burke? Upperclassman."

It was outrageous. Outrageous. (Was there a stronger word? Were words ever strong enough?) Oh, not the story, not the incident itself. He had been over that so many times it had ceased to be anything but inane. But outrageous that this should and could happen tonight, or ever. Out of all the how many millions of people in the world, outrageous that this one should have come here, to this bar, at this time, and engaged him in conversation. What could he do about it? Tell Brad *I'm the guy who made the place for you*—which was one way of putting it? No, he couldn't do that. It wouldn't be fair to scare him half to death; Brad wasn't to blame. What he could do and did do was go home and drink himself blind in five minutes, just as he was going to do now. He could and did (but he'd never do that again) ring up the Kappa U house in the middle of the night and ask some sleepy freshman if anybody knew where Johnny Barker '24 could be located. Why? Because he had to know if Johnny ever believed the story and what he thought about it now after all these years. But as far as Johnny was concerned, when he finally did get hold of him, it was just some drunk calling up from New York; and he said, bored and sleepy as the sleepy freshman: "Write me about it sometime."

He got up from the big chair and filled the glass half full again and then half again. Remember Tracey Burke? Thank God he was drunk now and one more would finish the job. He went back to the chair, determined this time to drink more slowly and feel himself go and appreciate the going. "Outrageous." Ridiculous word. But some words were strong enough. One was. Tracey's word and the way he had said it. He swallowed some of the Scotch. But the raw stuff, hot and cutting, would gag him if he lingered over it. Not daring to taste or pause, he finished the rest at a gulp. He let the glass fall to the carpet and lay back in the chair, in sudden sleep.

Somewhile later (he did not know what time and was too foggy to think or look) he awoke. For a moment he sat staring at the brightly lighted room. Every lamp in the place was on. He got up, shaking with chill and cold, and turned them all off but one. He was so tired he could gladly die. All he thought of and longed for was a sleep forever. He emptied the bottle into the sticky glass, filling it almost to the top. He shut his eyes and drank it down, leaning against the table for support; then, coughing and sputter-ing, his throat and stomach afire, he staggered over to the couch and fell at once into sound sleep again.

PART THREE

The Joke

A telephone was ringing somewhere. He opened his eyes. Where was he. Home? His mother's? Oh. Here.

He listened to the 'phone. It rang six or seven times and then stopped. He closed his eyes, relieved.

It began to ring again. It rang out from the bedroom, stinging him like some nasty metallic kind of gnat, impossible to fight off. Whoever it was had thought maybe they'd got the wrong number, maybe, and tried again. He had no intention of answering it so that didn't matter, but he was fully awake now and that did.

The telephone finally stopped ringing and then didn't ring any more. He looked at the clock. It was half-past nine. The room was filled with light, a kind of glare reflected from the bright sun on the back of the apartment building across the garden. He turned his head on the pillow and looked around to see where the bottle was and found it. Oh there it was, all right. On the table. A great big quart. Large as life and twice as empty.

Was he ever going to learn? Ever be wise and smart and sober enough one night, or one day, to see that he had something put by for tomorrow? Did he always have to drink it all up? Was he going to keep on forever and ever being trapped for a fool, by no one but himself?

He got up to see if it was really empty but really empty, he meant of the last little sip. It was. Trust him. Trust the drunken hog of the night before. And the stupid fool. *Never put off till tomorrow what you can drink today,* that's me. As he stood at the table, he realized how weak he was. This was hangover. But the real thing. Thank God he was dressed, he wouldn't have the dressing to go through, the fumbling with buttons, the insoluble puzzle that would be the shoelaces. He trembled like a high-strung terrier—shook all over with little fine tremors, a minute palsy. Not so damned minute, either. *Now* what was he going to do?

Anyhow the liquor store would be open. Clerks couldn't be that late. This wasn't going to be one of those terrifying torturing Sundays. What day was it? He guessed it was Saturday. Guessed? He wasn't that far gone, hadn't lost track to that extent, it was Saturday. He was probably dirty as a pig and needed a shave but it didn't matter now, not the half-block he'd have to go and the couple minutes he'd be there. But could he make it? His heart pounded, he was all out of breath for some reason. Sighing like a furnace. And with each sigh his heart hit just a little harder. He broke out in a sweat at the very thought of the stairs.

God damned fool what the hell was the matter with his brain if any. What was the good of these telephones that rang you out of the only peace you ever knew if you couldn't get back at them by ringing up somebody else, the liquor store for instance. We Deliver. He could never get over the fact that liquor stores were listed in the Classified for what they were—just like that. Christ they'd be listing dope-peddlers next. DOPE—*See* NARCOTICS.

He picked up his jacket and vest to find the money first. He wanted to get it counted out and ready before the guy came in. He couldn't have him standing there in the open door watching him while he fumbled through his pockets with shaking hands, shaking still more because somebody was looking at him. He dragged the coat and vest over to the chair, sat down, and went through the pockets.

Then he put the coat down because the money must be in his pants. Nothing in the coat and vest at all. He turned on one hip and felt in his right pocket, then on the other and felt in his left. Then he began to feel panic.

He stood up. He thrust both hands deep into his side pockets. He reached back and searched the two hip pockets. He fingered in the little watch-pocket. He grabbed up the vest and went through all four pockets. He took the coat and felt in the side pockets and the little change-pocket inside the right pocket. He turned the coat back and ran his hand into the deep inside pocket where he found a few old letters but no money at all. Not five cents.

He carried the coat and vest over to the couch, sat down, and went through the whole routine again. He wasn't that much of an idiot, he knew he had money somewhere, there had been more than twenty-five dollars yesterday. Could it really be possible that he had spent it? What the hell had he done last night? Where was that bloody money? Who had it now?

To his certain knowledge he hadn't had anybody up to the apartment so nobody had stolen it. But what good did that do him? How certain was that certain knowledge? How far did it go, what did it cover and include? A few events during the early part of yesterday, and from then on—blank. About all he remembered was some prison movie with wailing sirens and machine-guns. The drinks, sure; he remembered them; here and there; chiefly Sam's. But he had certainly never spent twenty-five dollars at Sam's. You couldn't spend twenty-five dollars at Sam's no matter how hard you tried. And God knows he ought to know. He'd tried if anybody ever had.

He couldn't just go ahead and call up the liquor store now. Say send up this-and-that and then tell the guy when he came that you'd pay later. That's something he had never done yet and he didn't know that he ever would. He didn't know; he might some day; how was he to know? He might even do that and then out of impulse or inspiration or panic grab the package from the guy at the door, give him a shove, and slam the door in his face. He'd a lot rather do that than pull some song-and-dance about how he was suddenly unaccountably fresh out of cash but was expecting some any minute by Western Union. He couldn't crawl to that extent yet. But why think of that now? In the meantime he hadn't quite lost his wits, had he? He'd find some other way. The day he couldn't find a new way he might as well be dead.

Well this was hardly a new way but what of it, it always worked. He went into the bedroom and began packing up his Remington portable: got the dusty case out from under the desk, set the machine inside, hit the spacer a few times till it was centered and would fit, and closed the cover.

The times this poor old typewriter had been in the pawn-shop. And why not? Was it any better than his suits, some of his good English suits, or his good top-coats? They'd been in and out of hock a dozen times and it hadn't hurt them any. It hurt him more than it hurt them. Three-fifty for a suit from Hogg & Sons in Hanover Square or five for a top-coat by Gabarsky in Zurich was certainly a neat irony, but an irony you could only appreciate and laugh at and not give a damn about after you had the drinks under your Brooks belt that wouldn't bring a nickel.

The telephone rang and he nearly jumped a mile. He picked up the typewriter, left the room at once, and closed the door behind him. He set the typewriter on the floor of the little foyer and went into the bathroom to see how he looked.

He'd have to shave. He couldn't go out like this. To the liquor store on the corner was all right but not as far as the pawnshop he always went to between 58th and 59th. He took off his tie, tucked the collar of his shirt under, and began to shave.

His hands shook but he managed. Staring at his face in the glass, seeing how the sweat stood out on his forehead, he knew he was in for a day of it if he didn't get that bottle. One of those days. One of those nightmare days he was headed for anyhow but God not today, he couldn't take it today. But what was he weeping and sniveling about? The typewriter wasn't *that* old, it was always good for five bucks.

Who had that been on the telephone. Oh sure. Helen probably. She was calling him up to see what he was going to do over the weekend, why didn't he come down to dinner tonight, or tomorrow, or both? Sorry. He had his weekend all planned, thank you. Right here. Or would have as soon as he got that money.

What had become of the money. Maybe he better go look again. No, he wasn't going to drive himself crazy doing that. He'd looked. Could he have given it away, thrown it away, lost it? No fear, not when money meant as much to you as it did when you were in this condition. At such times nobody in the world could hang onto it better than he could. There was a thought. Had he hidden it—been so cautious and cagey that he thought he ought to hide it? It could have happened, he had done such things before, in his fear that the money was going to be taken from him; but he hadn't been that drunk last night, and besides: nobody had been around to hide it from. Wick was in the country.

Helen of course was trying to check up on him. That matinée business hadn't fooled her a bit, the not feeling up to it. He knew these innocent invitations to dinner. She didn't want to feed him, hell! She wanted to give him the once-over. She only wanted to see if he was able to show up, see what he looked like, see if his hands were shaking. He knew those little Saturday- and Sunday-night suppers in Bleecker Street, so charming and cosy and *intime*—so God damned *intime* that you weren't even left alone long enough to sneak a drink out of the hall-closet where she kept the liquor (and kept it is right). You almost didn't dare go to the bathroom. If you did she found some pretext for coming into the hall to see if it was the bathroom door you had opened and not the door to the closet next to it. And then the several hours more of sitting there in the so charming little living room while she sewed and you died, died for a drink, soaking wet with sweat, keeping up a conversation you didn't even know the gist of, waiting for a chance to glance at your watch without being noticed, trying to decide if ten o'clock was all right or would it put ideas in her head, then beating it for the nearest bar—not the one across the street, because Helen would be at the window, but the one around the corner where she couldn't see.

98 THE LOST WEEKEND

He put the razor and brush away and slammed the cabinet door. The noise made him jump. Christ he must be in lousy shape. He was. Suddenly he felt he couldn't move another step or even stand. He drank a glass of water and managed to get back to the big chair in the living room.

He sat there panting. Maybe if he sat awhile his heart would go down. Something had to happen pretty soon, he had to feel better, he couldn't stand this. But Rabinowitz or whoever he was certainly wasn't going to call up and say "Have you got a type-writer you want to pawn today? I'll send a boy over." Could he have made the bedroom to answer the 'phone?

It was exhaustion. Physically he had reached bottom. Bottom, hell! There *was* no bottom as long as you still had the desire the urge the intention the need. Your heart and lungs still functioned—after a fashion; your eyes were wide open, you could hear and think; what more did you want. These were faculties. To be used. He got up. But it was no use. He stood there weaving, faint and sick. He sat down again. Could you possibly make 58th Street? If your life depended on it? Carrying a typewriter besides? Not only make it but get back again? And on top of all that: the traffic that would scare you out of your wits, the noise and the uproar of the too-lively city, the sound and fury that frightened the living daylights out of you. Frightened you almost as much as the thought of the afternoon ahead, here, alone, without anything.

The very thought of it was sickening. He closed his eyes, sank back to relax a moment, to shake it, if he could; and unaccountably, an irrelevant episode slid into place in his memory. A married friend of theirs called him and Wick up one day, asked them if they would please save their theater-stubs from then on. Did they have any old stubs in their suit pockets now, by any chance? Oh it was silly to explain, but—you see, his three-year-old daughter had found a hat-check somewhere and for some reason or other—you know how those things are—was crazy about it. She called it her "ticket." She carried it around in the pocket of her bathrobe at supper-time, always looked for it after her bath, and went around showing it to people who came in to dinner. But the other day the maid washed the bathrobe and threw Mary's "ticket" away. It seemed to mean a lot to her—you know how those things are (Did you know? Would you ever?)—and he just wondered if Don or Wick happened to have an old stub or two till he and his wife got around to going to a theater again. . . . The father's attitude on the telephone, his pretense of making light of the whole thing in order to hide his genuine concern—it was all too sweet for words, oh just too cute, what an ass fathers made of themselves (his anger rose), what an ass children made of their fathers. . . .

If there was a fire he'd get out of here all right. Or would he. He'd be able to get up and get out of here and down those stairs and into the street if there was a fire. Wouldn't he? He listened as if for an alarm, but all he could think of was the stinging frenzied bell shattering the darkness of the movie as the surly expressionless girl walked through the metal-detector beam, the bell that later took over the whole screen and theater during the prison-break. If such a bell really rang he'd be up and out of here in no time, wouldn't he, collapse or no collapse. Or if there was a bottle of whisky to be had after your little exchange with Mr. Rabinowitz. He got up.

He found his hat and his coat and vest and got to the bathroom mirror to see how he looked. Would anybody think anything if they looked at him? Did he show it much? He tried to believe that as far as they could see he looked all right; but he knew how he looked, how he felt inside, how it showed in his face (showed in his walk, the very motion of his legs), how he wouldn't be able to look anyone in the eye, how he'd have to avoid all eyes looking at him, how he couldn't trust himself to say two words to anybody till after he got the liquor or he'd go to pieces. If he hung onto himself hard, shut out everything else—his exhaustion, his fear, the city itself—it could be done. Could? It had. Often and often before. He picked up the typewriter in the foyer and went down the stairs.

Thank God it was cool. Cold even. It would help keep him going as far as 58th and back. He hadn't worn a top-coat on purpose, because he knew that by the time he reached the corner, only half a block away, he would be sweating like a man in a fever-cabinet. So he sweated now. He made the corner and turned north into the swarming clanging shouting hell that was 2nd Avenue on a Saturday morning.

He passed the liquor store without a glance (it could wait, he'd be back); the A & P where Mr. Wallace stood in the window and tried to wave to him, without a glance; the bar-and-grill of his friend Sam, without a glance; the delicatessen where he once owed and maybe still owed Mr. Schultz ten dollars, without a glance; passed all these places without noticing on purpose, because if he took his eyes off the objective before him he would sink to the sidewalk. The three dimly gold balls hung out over the street far ahead, three and a half blocks away, on his side of the street; but as long as he fixed them with his eye and doggedly put one foot in front of the other (taking deep breaths to still, if he could, the pounding heart), he knew they were drawing nearer. Overhead the L roared like tons of coal rushing down iron chutes.

At 56th he paused at the crosswalk. His nerves were so jumpy he didn't dare trust his senses. He looked again and again at the traffic-light to make sure before leaving the safety of the curb, and even then wasn't sure. He stepped down into the street, then quickly back up on the curb again. He was far from blind, he couldn't ask anybody to take him across. He couldn't have spoken to anybody to ask. He started again, and horns shrilled anger at him, brakes slammed on with a screech of rubber.

How many times on mornings such as this, mornings in other cities as well as New York, had he taken such walks. Mornings when he truly didn't know if he was going to give way in a faint

after the next step, much less before he reached his destination—
liquor store, pawnshop, bar, bed. Mornings of preposterous inexplicable panic because somebody was going to intercept his glance
in an unguarded moment and look him squarely in the eye. Walking along the Esplanade in Boston, he saw a man emerge from
a comfort-station and begin coming his way. The man was still
some distance off but the two were going to meet and pass each
other, there was no way out, how was he going to be able to go
through with it, get by and past? If the man caught his eye, looked
at him, spoke to him, he would fall down. He fixed his gaze on the
Charles River bridge far off and walked on in a blind and dumb
daze, his teeth tight shut, his hands clenched stiffly at his sides. . . .
Starting out along Commercial Street in Provincetown to find
one of the Portuguese fishermen and buy a pint of the grappa-like
drink they called *prune,* what a haven the little alleys that ran off
to the right, away from the sea, alleys in which he could idle or rest
a moment till the approaching stranger or strangers, on their way
into P-town, had gone by. . . . Here there was no escape from the
crowd of looking strangers; you stared straight ahead and went on;
and if you did not see them looking, perhaps they were not.

He smelled the oily pickly fishy smells of delicatessens. He
passed the little antique shops of charming, chipped, expensive
junk; in each, a faultlessly dressed immaculate young man idled
in the window, watching the street. The chain-stores were so
much like the chain-stores back home, with exactly the same red
or yellow fronts of his home town, that he did not dare think of
them. A man stood in his way and he turned to look at a window
display of refined wedding-invitations, the Commercial & Soci-
ety Print. Every few feet there was a bar—cottagey, some; others
saloony like the old days. The sidewalks were thick with women
with Scotties and dachshunds and women with kids.

He turned into the entrance of Rabinowitz's and bumped into
an iron gate. He stood back and looked up. An iron sliding-gate
had been drawn and locked across the entrance to the shop.

He gazed at the windows stacked high with luggage and fishing-rods, baseball gloves, watches and jewelry, guitars. He looked at the locked gate. Was somebody dead? He turned north again.

A cruel and fiendish trick but somewhere along the way there would be another. The Avenue was lousy with pawnshops. He squinted far ahead into the distance; and sure enough, several blocks off, three golden balls hung over the sidewalk on the other side of the street. He started out, and at once ran into the inferno that was 59th.

Trucks with coughing klaxons speeded up, here, to make the grade to the bridge, the vast resounding grinding structure of the Queensboro bridge. The traffic was incoherent bedlam. Trolleys danged and clanged up the slope. Overhead the L exploded periodically with the supernatural rush and roar of a rocket-train out of the comics. His eyes fixed on his goal, he passed through it all like a sleepwalker in a nightmare, shaken by every insane noise but with one increasing purpose in his reeling mind: to reach the end of the dream and wake up.

He staggered up the slight rise of ground to 60th Street and into a sidewalk world again of vegetable and fruit markets like pushcarts; bakeries, florists, funeral parlors, stores for rent, tinsmiths and paint shops and thrift shops. The smells. The sights. The dyed-hair and wigs; the poor; the nigger-pink-and-green playsuits; the hatless bald men carrying groceries home; the blind musicians; the broad broad women, the million bandanaed women, the million pregnant women. The noise. And in the intervals between trains passing overhead, the sound of the L on 3rd Avenue a block away, like the faraway thunder of surf.

What fiend ever gave the name portable to a portable. It was a dead weight that dragged you down, held you back, it pulled your arm out of the shoulder-socket, it fixed you fast to one spot in the sidewalk. It was a solid block of lead, but lead that would become pure gold if only you could drag it far enough. The sweat was running down his back in little trickles, he felt it drop from his armpits inside his shirt, his feet burned as if the sidewalks were hot lava.

The three golden balls were above his head. The entrance to the shop (not so good a one as Mr. Rabinowitz's but a pawnshop all the same, with a cash-register in the rear) was shuttered with a grey iron gate, fixed with a padlock. He gave the place no more than a sidelong glance, fearful that somebody would see him looking, see that he had been thwarted, think "Sure, some drunk caught short, out to hock something so he can start over again." He affected indifference; smiled to himself as if he were amused; he had only paused anyhow to see what these funny places looked like. Almost casually he shifted the handle of the typewriter to his left hand and went on.

Down each street to the right he caught glimpses of trees and lovely house-fronts, charming façades of grey or tan or pink or black, some with little white iron balconies: the tenement homes of the rich. He turned from these vistas and squinted into the distance ahead. He found what he was looking for. Perhaps five blocks away, maybe four—you couldn't tell.

The vast dark-red structure set in the whole block of 65th and 66th—Cable & Power Station No. 1. It looked like the fort in the bay of Naples, looked older and more permanent than anything he'd ever seen in New York, built to remain long after the last pawnshop had been closed forever. Kids had covered the base of the walls with chalk, communicating to one another and to the adult indifferent world the gossip, imprecations, and yearnings of their kind. "Richard Adams loves Sandra Gold." "F--- you!" "Miss Ellison of P.S. 82 is going to die next week—you watch!" He passed these by and left them behind.

Passed the wide doors of garages where fine cars gleamed and glowed inside in the dark; passed the diners and restaurants; the American flags and the red-white-&-blue bunting; the vacant shops; the barbers and hairdressers; the drugstores; the vision of the future that was the New York Hospital down 68th and 69th Streets; the radio repair and electricians; the laundries, the tailors, the furriers, the cleaners and dyers; the bars (taverns, cafés, grills, casinos); the pushcarts, the bowling alleys, the trunk shops; the brau halls, the cider stubes, the lieder clubs, the turnvereins and singvereins; the one-arm joints; the movie dumps.

He wondered if there was anywhere in all this pushing mob one like himself. Did he too pass along with the awful calm desperation that lies just this side of the breaking-point? The unhuman control of the somnambulist? Would he too jump out of his skin or let go his bowels or drop in a sweaty heap on the sidewalk if someone approached to ask him a direction? Was he unnoticed too? Or spied upon, trailed, spotted every minute, watched but not watched over by someone in the crowd, who followed along behind, waiting for the collapse? But he did not collapse, he would walk like this till Doomsday if necessary, they were not going to see him fall. His whole frame shook as the L trains pounded overhead. It was like walking directly underneath a gigantic bowling-alley, with the bowls constantly thundering and the pins crashing together with ear-splitting *craacks* as the trains braked at the platforms.

He was reminded dully of a scene in *The Big Parade* years ago (was everything in fiction or in film more real to him than fact?) in which the American troops were shown advancing across a wooded slope into battle: walking slowly doggedly on, their guns in their hands, their grim faces set: plodding straight ahead in a kind of frightful and relentless monotony, undeterred by bursting shrapnel, smoke, gas, tank-fire, or their own dead. . . . He did not push his way through the crowds. He stumbled on, but carefully, moving clumsily but accurately for a gap or an opening, drawing himself up and turning sideways to avoid being pushed or bumped by the mountainous mothers; by the roller-skating terrors of brats; the carriages with the flushed sleeping babies; the busily chatting little girls, arms entwined, wandering absently along as if in an open field of daisies; the pathetic little stringy-haired girls in glasses or braces; the healthy sexy aggressive little girls with red fingernails; the deep-throated boys; the men in polo shirts with bobbing breasts; the young sad snappish fathers; the cops; the darting, screaming, gawping or melancholy kids; the Germans, the Jews; the young women in satin dresses and black watered-silk; the fat women with high shoes; the old old-world women with faraway eyes; the skinny chalk-white women; the waddling broad enormous women like vats of flesh. An Italian woman suddenly dashed away from a pushcart, grabbed his arm and screamed in his ear, screamed in shattering dactyls: "*Mis*ter he's *chea*ting me *Mis*ter he's *chea*ting me *you* help me *you* help me *you* help me!" He recoiled in panic and stumbled off.

The grey iron gate was drawn across the entrance to the pawnshop. (He was Hans Castorp lost in the blinding suffocating snowstorm in the mountains back of the Berghof, returning after a bewildered circuit to the hay-hut or shepherd's shelter he had passed before, describing some great silly arc that turned back to where it had its beginning, like the long weekend itself.) He fingered the small lock absently a moment, showing no trace of his growing rage. Who was insane? Not he! Pawnshops were open on Saturday, he wasn't that crazy! *Sure* Saturday was their Sabbath but catch a Jew closing his shop on the best day for business in the week!

He gazed through the glass. Nothing in this world could look more pathetic than fishing-rods on 2nd Avenue. Dozens of them hung in the window, forming a fringe across the front. Back of and through the fringe could be seen violins, mandolins, banjos, guitars, zithers, musical instruments of all kinds. A gaudy hammered-silver cocktail-set, its monogram partly effaced (M. Mc.?), stood among the baseball gloves and the catchers' masks. There was a portable typewriter plastered with the peeling souvenirs of European travel. An enormous accordion spilled itself out in the corner of the window like an exhausted Jack-in-the-box. Dozens of glittering watches hung on little white cards. Hundreds of other white cards displayed the glass and flash of diamond rings. A mink lay curled up like a mink asleep on the round disk of a small ancient phonograph whose horn had been removed to bring it up-to-date. He raised his head and his own melancholy face gazed back at him from an old-fashioned shaving-mirror, exactly like the mirror of his father's that still stood on the bathroom shelf back home in his mother's house. His fingers were on fire from the burning pull of the leather strap in his hand. How near was the next one?. . .

The street to the left was strung with flags and electric-light bulbs for some neighborhood fair or religious holiday. A shoeless drunk lay half-in half-out of a stairway; mothers and children stepped over and around him, unnoticing. The second-story windows across the way bulged with leaning women, dirty curtains, stained bedding, men in underwear reading tabloids. The cruising cabs were like mobile individual gardens of red and yellow lights. An ambulance careened in and out of the L pillars, its dang-danging bell scarcely heard in the grinding roar from above. He studied the distance ahead for three golden balls, and an idiotic story came into his mind. . . .

A story from the 4th- or 5th-Grade Reader—a little boy in the late afternoon, in the early evening, at sundown, had strayed too far from home. He wandered over the neighboring yet foreign hills. On a hill in the distance he saw a house with golden windows: the lowering sun struck the house and fired the panes with gold. He descended into a little valley and climbed up to the house; and the house had panes of glass no more gold than his own drab house at home. But there, in the distance again, was another house with golden windows, and again he started out; and again the golden windows changed to colorless glass as he came near. But still another, on another hill—and so on; till finally he saw that his own house, far on the horizon, had windows of gold such as none of the others had had. Back he hurried;

and found them, alas, plain glass as always; but he was home, and happy, and safe. . . .

Idiotic and insulting and why in Christ's name did he have to think of such a thing now! He was drenched with sweat, panting for breath, but so resolved, now more than ever in his desperation, to find that pawnshop open (they couldn't *all* have a death in the family) that he did not even feel the hot ache in his calves and his back.

The cigars, the glass shops, the hamburger joints, the cafeterias, the newsstands, the dishes in bushel baskets, dishes for sale; the Ruppert brewery stretching from 92nd to 93rd, looking timeless and European, like something you checked in the Baedeker and went around to see; the hardware, the framers, the upholsterers, the haberdashers, the key shops (Keys Made), the moving and trucking, the Soda & Candy, the dairies; the stockings set up on the sidewalks (the tables and tables of boxes and boxes of stockings); the chi-chi horror of the flea-markets; the milk-bars, the orange-juice stands, the weighing-machines, the gaping smelly dead fish; the 5 & 10's, the linoleum and bedding, the cut-rates, the remnants; the Slavic faces, the Negroes, the beautiful Spaniards, the cross-legged idle bums, the cats, the kittens, the barking dogs; the furniture stores, the shoe stores, the pork stores, the stores to let; the analytical laboratories, the trusses and suspensories, the abdominal supporters, the surgical belts, the contraceptives, the sick-room supplies; the watch-repairing, the barber-poles, the million fire-escapes; the smells; the noise of the L like an avalanche of 4th-of-July torpedoes; the jewelry shops, the Chinese-American food, the sheet-metal places, the sport-shoes; the photo studios shedding lambent lavender livid lunar light on gorgeous wop-weddings; the konditerei, the pizzeria, the confiseries; the liquor stores; the closed pawnshops; the interminable glimpses of the Triboro bridge down every street to the right. . . .

Now wait a minute now wait a minute take it easy here's one without a gate.

He approached cautiously. He found himself breathing so hard he was sure the panting must be audible. He looked around on all sides to see if he was noticed, then went into the entrance-way between the two show-windows, the entrance free of a gate. He touched the knob and turned it and rattled it and found it was locked. He stood back to get his breath.

He tried the door again. He leaned against it and pushed. He rapped on the glass, pounded the frame. He raised a hand to his eyes and peered in. He saw the banjos, the knives, the guns, the suits, the furs—he saw the cashier's cage at the back where the money was. He pressed his nose and forehead to the glass, staring. No one looked out at him but a bright dummy in a Tuxedo with a red cummerbund. A raw electric light burned overhead.

He fell against the door as if in collapse.

Two little men in their Sunday-best, with derbies, leaned from a dark stairway next to the shop. "What's the metter with you," one of them called in a loud rapid whisper, "what do you want?"

His face broke up into wry wrinkles as if he were going to cry. Somehow he managed to control a helpless rage. He fought for breath, afraid that he would break into a wail if he didn't hang on hard. He yanked at the doorknob (the glass shook and rattled) and gave way: "Why aren't you open, what's going on, why are you all *closed!*"

The two glanced at each other, incredulous, and then one darted his head farther out of the dark stairway and snarled, "What's the metter with you, it's Yom Kippur!"

He was stunned. Were they joking? He looked up, not comprehending; and when the man said "Go away!" he shied off, frightened, and turned back as if he had not meant to stop there at all, as if he had got the wrong place. He resumed his way, understanding only that he must walk back, now, go home. Who could have played such a joke as this—and what was the point of it, anyway, what was the point, he didn't get it, he'd never be able to get it. The strap-handle cut into his palm and he shifted it to his finger-tips, which at once began to burn. He fixed his eyes far down into the distance of the far swarming avenue and started out. He came to the first street-crossing on the way back and looked cautiously up to see the red or green light before stepping off from the curb. He saw instead the sign marking the street, and now he got it.

He paused, stupefied, and the sweat seeped out under his hat-band and ran down all sides of his head—he felt it trickle warm and slow behind his ears. It was 120th Street. But the joke was beyond laughter—or it called for laughter so huge and ribald it was beyond mirth; so loud you couldn't hear it; abhuman. He stood on the corner in a daze and marveled that he had been able to come so far. All this distance. . . . Sixty-five city blocks. . . . He marveled at it, remembering his exhaustion and panic as he turned the corner at 55th Street and started the journey up 2nd Avenue.

He supposed it was comic after all, but comic on a scale so vast there was no basis for human comprehension—it was only awful and stunning. Re-living the torment of those first few blocks (remembering how, at 59th, he couldn't go another step, and did; recalling his fright at every street-crossing; seeing again in his mind's eye how far the next pawnbroker's sign had been, hanging far up the street; how much farther the next), he would never have believed he could have made it. Not all this distance. Soaked with the sweat of that inhuman effort, he stood in the uproar of the traffic almost in smiling wonder and marveled at his feat. People rushed by and around him, clanging trolleys lurched and ground on, klaxons screeched, trucks bounced with a roar on the pavement, overhead the L exploded like a series of land-mines. *What's the metter with you?*—

A joke, of course it was only a joke, they were joking, surely the man had joked, Yom Kippur was always good for a joke, it was just another one of those Jewish jokes; but at a time like this— How could they joke at a time like this? He stood feverish, faint, his eyes bright and absent, and the typewriter pulling his arm from its socket was like iron drawn to some giant magnet buried deep in the center of the earth, a weight of acid that would burn its way down to China, dragging him with it. He was lost in a delirium of exhaustion, spent and consumed to the uttermost, dead on his feet; till suddenly the joke came again to his mind in all its final meaning: how was he going to get back.

Not all that distance. Not that many miles. What was it—twenty city-blocks to the mile? Or was it ten? Oh no, no, twenty was bad enough, inhuman enough, impossible enough—impossible without the enough, impossible period, not possible. It could not be done, it could not. A nickel was all that was needed, a nickel for carfare, but you might as well dream of a drink as dream of a nickel. You couldn't have one or the other, you couldn't ask. There was no one in this world you could face at that moment to ask. You couldn't get back, that was simply all there was to it. But you couldn't lie down on the street-corner either, you couldn't lean against the pole here and gradually slide down till you rested comfortably on the sidewalk, you couldn't do that, you weren't a bum yet not yet, you'd never get a drink that way, nobody was going to walk up and hand you a drink, no not even if you were dying, and you were dying. . . .

Swaying there on the roaring corner, he went into a trance of time that took him at once many miles many years away. For some reason his mother came to his mind, out of the bedlam of noise and the street, and he welcomed the thought of her and thought of her. He leaned against the pole in a kind of daydream for a moment (but only a moment) and thought of her. The too-substantial pageant faded and there was his mother. It was as if she spoke to him; or more, were there and not speaking. There too was he, back in time, a child. He lay on his side in the porch-hammock, curled up in the pleasant chill of a rainy spring afternoon, a sweater thrown over his shoulders, his arms hugging each other across his chest. Some illness, fleeting as it was imaginary, kept him from school for the afternoon, and his mother half suspected the deception and half played-up to it also—for what reason he never knew, when he did these things, unless it was too much trouble to argue or unless she liked the idea too. She came out once and angrily threw the sweater across his shoulders, murmuring something about catching his death; and later he heard her come to the front window a couple of times to see if he was still covered. He thought of the kids in the schoolroom looking at his empty desk, and he wondered if the teacher was wondering if he was all right. He felt sorry for her concern and loved her for it. He wondered too what they were all doing at the moment and missed them all very much, lovingly, every one. At rare intervals a car raced down the quiet street, its tires tearing through the mud and the wet. Between-times the rain was the only sound in the town. He lay hunched up, pretending to sleep, enjoying the luxurious sense of time-out, feeling the comfortable presence of his mother moving from time to time inside the house, listening to the lovely sound of the rain washing down through the heavy vines of the porch and bubbling and tumbling from the eaves, loving the whole timeless grey delightful careless day. Careless, without a care, not a care in the world, a marvelous dream. The L roared overhead like a bursting dam, but all he heard was the telephone ringing in the living room, his mother's heavy step as she came from the kitchen to answer it, the familiar creak of the wicker-chair as she sat down, and her low rich good voice as she answered Hello? He unfolded himself to listen who it might be, and all the noise of New York poured back upon him. . . .

Not much more than half an hour later, very little more than thirty minutes, he dropped the typewriter on the bathroom floor (the case split open from the fall) and tore off his coat and his tie and his shirt and all his soaking clothes. He was working in a rush, in a panic, frantic to achieve his objective before total collapse overtook him. Working against time and exhaustion— beating breakdown, as it were, to the punch—he had fled down

1st Avenue in headlong blind staggering flight (not as fast as he believed it to be, but fast) and so got home. 1st Avenue had been a crazy lucky inspiration: the surroundings and background would be different, the same route not have to be retraced, the time go faster. Of the whole journey back he remembered not one single detail, he registered none of it, he had seen nothing, he had not even traversed it, so to speak, fleeing blind in a kind of vacuum, a deliberate self-imposed self-willed delirium—for if he had stopped to realize his condition, stopped to see the distance yet to go or even the street-signs ticking off his considerable prog- ress, he would have fallen. He was only dimly aware that it was an incredible performance. He had not had the strength to get to 59th Street, he did not have the strength for the journey back from 120th, but he had done it all the same, by—by summon- ing something more than strength? by heeding something more than fear? It was drink that did it, he could not have done it if it had not been for drink—the lack of it and the need for it—and he might have been spared some of the torment if only he had had sense enough to remind himself of this when so often those waves of sickness and exhaustion seemed sure to drop him. With the promise of drink at the end of the journey, somehow, some- way (he'd find that way yet, he always had), there was nothing he could not have gone through. He sprang into the too-cold shower and washed away the sweat.

In a few seconds he was dressed again in dry clean clothes— dressed enough to run down and borrow ten dollars from Mr. Wallace at the A & P, enough to run into the liquor store for a quart and bound up the stairs again with the bottle in his hand, tear off the wrapping, open it, pour, all in the space of five min- utes. Listening to the sound of the liquor spilling into the glass, thinking of the ordeal he had been through during the past few hours, how long it had taken, how much it had cost in mental agony and physical sweat, his spirits rose. He held the glass in his shaking hand and almost did not need it. Why didn't I do this in the first place? he asked himself with a surprised smile. He had not even thought of Mr. Wallace till after he got back. Think what I could have saved myself. It was almost amusing! If he had been normal this morning, not befogged and benumbed with fatigue and shattering hangover, he would have thought at once of this easier quicker way. What a story that little jaunt would make someday, in the right company. How he would laugh and they would laugh. Don Birnam's Rhine-Journey. Great! He drank.

Or if he had been normal at all during any part of that long ordeal, if he had not had to summon all of his concentration, all of his energy, merely to set one foot in front of the other at every step, merely to keep his balance and so keep on, he would have realized before he had gone five blocks that something was amiss besides himself. One pawnshop closed, or two—three at the most—would have told him that nothing was in league against him beyond the season, the holiday, the New Year of the Jews. It would not happen again in a lifetime, such a coincidence never happened to anyone, but it would happen to him and it did and it had. That would be the hard thing to explain when he told the anecdote (anecdote!). People would think he had made it up, had picked Yom Kippur to make the story a good one. In any case they wouldn't care so long as it *was* a good one—any more than they would care to learn or hear of the real, the uncomfortable, the cruel and painful details behind the joke. These would only embarrass them, these they would believe even less than the hard-to-believe fact of the coincidence. And why should they—didn't he look like anybody else, wasn't he neat and clean, respectable? Did things like that happen to people like him or them—were they, or he, Bowery bums?

The new drink warmed his stomach, warmed all his whole tired frame, his arms even, his aching legs, and he felt a rising sense of well-being, heightened and hot, such as he had not felt, it seemed, for months. Well, truth is stranger than fiction, you could say—and just to prove it, just to make the story completely preposterous, you could throw in that little detail of the frantic wop (and don't forget the dactyls) who clutched at your arm and scared the daylights out of you by shrieking "*Mis*ter! he's *chea*ting me!" Who would believe that? Nobody. And wasn't it just as well? Wasn't it even more fun—weren't you liked even more—if they sort of got the teasing impression that maybe the story was true and maybe it wasn't?—if you left it up to them, like the author's point in *The Guardsman*? They would look at you with a faint tilted smile, one eye partly closed, trying to dope out if you were pulling their leg. You would look back—

He poured another drink, a full tumbler, and went into the bathroom to see how he would look back. Dead-pan, that was it; eyebrows raised a little; frank eyes wide open; followed, perhaps, by just the suggestion of a sigh suppressed (as if the memory were, for the moment, too painful); and then—then the slow disarming ultimate winning smile to take the edge off everyone's discomfort and make you loved again. In the glass of the cabinet he saw the sweaty clothes lying on the tiled floor and kicked them under the washbowl out of the way.

Everyone's? Whose? Who, for instance? Loved by whom? Who would he ever be telling the story to in the first place, where would he ever be welcome with such a story or any story, who ever gathered around for him to charm them with amusing anecdotes believable or not, when was he ever the center of any kind of gathering, any group at all, even of two or three—who had anything to do with him nowadays except his brother and Helen? True, he was the center, the talked-of one, when the three of them were together, but the talked-of and center for reasons quite different from those he'd been dreaming of now—and indeed the foolish psychiatrist had said his only importance was his nuisance-value; the only way he made himself felt was to cause anxiety in others; failing to achieve prominence in any other way, he achieved it by becoming a worry; he'd probably stop drinking entirely if people stopped talking and worrying. The patient is

trying to wheedle attention and comfort from his betters by flinging his infantile narcissism in their faces. Words, words, words.
The patient is using a technique of hysteria to exploit his illness
for epinosic gain. What a ridiculous notion, what did *he* know
about it, what did they, what did anyone—how did *they* know
why you did what you did, when no one knew the things that
drove you, not even yourself? He turned in disgust and saw the
typewriter and its split case (the schizoid portable) against the
wall of the tub. But the Nightmare of the Avenues was a fading
nightmare now, something that had not happened—or had happened only in his imagination as an episode with which to regale
companions he would never have. With nearly seven dollars in
his pocket, with a full quart on the living room table, a half-full
glass in his hand, he had no need of 2nd Avenue now.

The glass was empty, the quart by no means full; and some
moments later there was scarcely more than a pint. He looked at
the bottle in sudden alarm. The alarm gave way as suddenly to a
feeling of delight and self-congratulation. Jesus *Christ* was he for
once going to have sense enough not to be caught short? He had
the money, he still had his faculties and the strength, he was a
long way yet from passing-out, still further from the greater need
later—well, good for him! He sprang up.

That money. Did he still have it? Maybe he ought to carry his
money around tightly wadded in each fist, strung together with a
string running up inside his sleeves and across the shoulders, like
the homemade mittens he used to wear to school. He smiled at
such a delightful idea. But the money. As he pulled it out of his
pocket safe and sound, he wondered again what had become of
all that money he had had yesterday, last night. Certainly he had
never spent it all. He wouldn't be as good as he was today, if he
had. To hell with it! It didn't matter now, not with these bills in
his hand—these bills that were as good as any others, as good as a
million, as good as enough-to-drink (for once) and more.

Provided he got there and got back. He would. He was feeling fine, great; a little unsteady, perhaps, but strong enough, and bright as hell. The things he felt, thought! His mind seemed to rise clear of his body, be larger than himself, see everything. It was intoxication (hell, he knew that), but it was also that old god-like superiority again, a superiority conscious of itself but superior just the same. Larger than life; with always the comforting assurance that just over the crest lay wonderful Lethe, Lethe that would absorb the plunge back again, erase the waning ecstasy, wipe out Helen and Wick and all the frowning un-understanding world. Larger than life. Of course! *that's* why he drank! But who could hope to understand that—who but the guy who did it himself?

This time he would make a better impression in the liquor store, just in case they had wondered a little at his haste, or had any misgivings. He would put on a tie, he'd wear a jacket and even a vest—hat too. He whistled about the flat as he prepared himself; and just as he left the door, he looked back at the half-empty whiskey bottle. He pointed with an elaborate gesture, like a matador, like a showy radio-director indicating a cue. "You stay there!" he said in low, dark, super-menacing tones. "Don't disappear; don't hide or evaporate! I'll be right back."

At the top of the stairs he heard people on the landing below. He looked over the rail and saw the two ladies and their dog Sophie who lived in the front apartment. As they started up the last flight, loaded with bundles, they saw him looking down. They stepped back as he stepped back. "No, come along," he said, "I'll wait."

"No no, that's quite all right, Mr. Birnam, *you* come down."

He took off his hat and nodded gallantly. "Aprés vous. I'll wait, there's no hurry."

"Do come down, Mr. Birnam," one of the ladies said again. "We have all these packages and things—and there's Sophie."

"Very well," he said. "Thank you." He started down, smiling, his hat in his hand.

He found himself falling. A wonderful feeling, easy, light,

pleasantly chilling in the stomach. Easy, easy the way you landed unhurt at the bottom, laughing at yourself, feeling absolutely no pain—'twas as easy as lying.

The dog barked, the two ladies squealed. "Oh Mr. Birnam! Are you hurt—oh!" They dropped their packages, bent over him.

He picked himself up, smiling. "Not a bit, not a bit, I— I didn't even fall!"

"Didn't fall, good gracious!"

"I mean," he said, "it was almost as if I didn't fall at all, the way it felt. They say if you fall relaxed— Hello, little Sophie."

The two ladies exchanged glances. "Mr. Birnam, are you sure you're all right?"

"Quite, I'm not hurt a bit, don't trouble yourself. Goodbye. Sorry to cause such a fuss. Goodbye, Sophie!" He walked lightly along the landing and turned for the second flight.

Flight is good. His silly foot missed as before—it was easy, delightful. . . . He heard the women squeal again and saw with a smile the newel-post rising like a growing expanding up-swinging hammer to strike.

PART FOUR

The Dream

Like a fish of the deep rising to the surface of bright air and sun, he swam up to consciousness out of a dead blank into a whiter world than he had ever seen. The daylight was blinding. He heard voices very near at hand, as if just behind his ear, talking together quietly in a business-like way against a background medley of babblings and shrieks, moans and mutterings. He was lying prone and someone was working on his back—fingers probed at his spine. He flopped over, like a fish out of water, and found himself in a low bed, little more than a mattress, so low that the two men who worked over him were kneeling on the edge.

As surprised as he, they looked at him in impersonal silence, and then recovered themselves.

"Just a moment, take it easy, turn over again, please," one of them said; and the other: "Take it easy, baby."

They must have anticipated what he was going to say because here he was saying it—saying it all in a rush as if he hadn't heard or as if he were too exasperated, angered, and offended to take it easy. "What's going on here, where am I, what are you doing to me!"

"Just lie back again, it'll only take a second," the first man said; and the second murmured the classic "It won't hurt a bit" as he himself cried out the still-more-classic "Where am I" again.

"You're in the hospital."

"What for!"

"Take it easy, baby."

"*What* hospital?"

"The alcoholic ward."

He didn't get this, not any of it. He had awakened fighting-mad, or at least bitterly offended and indignant because he couldn't figure out where he was, because he was being taken advantage of, because he didn't know who these two men were and what right had *they* to touch him? Now he heard the bedlam going on in the background and he was outraged at this further intrusion on his peace. "What's all that racket!"

"The others."

"Other *what*?"

"Patients. Now just turn over and relax, it won't take a moment."

"What do you think you're doing! Who are you!"

"We want to draw off a little of the spinal fluid. Relieve the pressure on the brain."

"Spinal tap, baby."

He suddenly understood. "Oh *no* you're not!" He drew up his knees against his chest, and as he did so his head exploded in pain above his eyes.

Both men straightened and stood back from the bed. One of them put his hands on his hips. The other's already were.

He saw now the syringe and needle and also saw the two men more or less clearly for the first time. One was small, bald-ish, pleasant-looking, in his middle forties. Probably the doctor, though he looked more like a professor or teacher. The other was a big strapping fellow around thirty, broad and well-built but far from muscular. With a frame like a hammer-thrower, he was yet soft, just this side of fat. He stood looking down with a half-smile on his face, and the impression he gave was that of an enormous sleepy tomcat, indifferent, self-sufficient, yet predatory.

"What's the matter, what are you afraid of," the teacherish man said.

"I'm not afraid of anything!"

"Then why won't you let us do it?"

"Because I won't have it! You're not going to do that to me!"

"A spinal tap won't hurt you any. We do it all the time."

"Not on *me* you don't!" He had a horror of the spinal puncture because when it had been used in the TB sanatorium as a means of anesthesia some years ago, a friend of his had been paralyzed by it; not temporarily, which had been the idea, but permanently.

"You must listen to reason. You have too much alcohol in your system. This will help clear your brain, take some of the pressure off. Do you understand?"

"*Sure* I understand, what do you think I am!"

"Besides that, you have a fractured skull."

"Fractured *skull!*"

"A slight fracture, between the right temple and eye."

"I don't believe you!" His splitting head denied this disbelief but he didn't believe it all the same.

"The X-ray showed it very clearly. It's not serious, however. There's no real concussion."

"But where did I get—"

"Don't ask us, baby," the bigger man said, smiling. "That's what you came in with."

"How did I get here? *I* didn't ask to be—"

"You were brought in by the ambulance. Now let's go ahead with this. It's the best thing for you. It'll make you feel a lot better."

"I feel all right, right now!" He didn't. His head was bursting with pain, but—hadn't it often, didn't it always, on such mornings as this?

"You refuse?" the professor-like man said.

"I certainly do! You're not going to do that to me!"

The small man turned to the other and spoke as if Don weren't there at all, or as if he didn't understand English. "I guess there's nothing to do then, Bim. We can't give it to him without his consent, now that he's conscious. The patient seems to be in his right mind, capable of deciding for himself."

"Try him, Doctor."

The doctor turned back to Don. "What's your name?"

"Don Birnam," he answered, almost haughty.

"Where do you live?"

"Three-one-one East Fifty-Fifth."

"Manhattan?"

"Certainly!"

"What do you do?"

"Do? I—well, I'm not doing anything, at the moment."

"Unemployed?"

"He didn't look unemployed to me," the other said with a smile. "Not from the clothes he was wearing."

Don automatically looked down at himself. He had on a short white gown that barely reached to the knees; made of a heavy cloth as stiff and rough as canvas. It was tied in the back: he could feel the thick knot, now, between his shoulder blades. He was outraged at the spectacle he must present of himself, outraged that the man should smile. But the smiler was not smiling at him, he noticed; it was just a habit, a fixed expression of the sleepy cat-like face.

"What year is it?" the doctor went on.

"Why are you asking me these fool questions!"

"What year is it?"

"Nineteen thirty-six!"

"What month?"

"October."

"What day is today?"

Oh-oh. This is something he couldn't be sure of.

"What day is it?"

"I—I'm sorry, I guess I don't know. Monday or Tuesday, maybe, but I—" God if it were Tuesday he had to be back home, had to be safely back and in bed and finished with the weekend before Wick came in. He had to get out of here and quick.

"What's your name?"

"I *told* you. Don Birnam."

"Where do you live?"

"Three-one-one East Fifty-Fifth. Man*hat*tan!"

"Three-eleven?"

"Three-one-one, I said! That's three-eleven in *any* language, isn't it? Or it was when *I* went to school."

The doctor turned again to the other. "Okay, Bim. Give him some paraldehyde and let him go. Ten grains. I'll be in the women's ward." He started down the room.

Don suddenly couldn't let him go like that. "Doctor!" he called out. "Wait a minute!"

The doctor went on without turning back.

The big fellow was looking down at him, squinting faintly. "What did you want?"

"What day is it?"

"Sunday."

"Oh." He sank back, relieved.

"You were brought in here yesterday afternoon."

"Really in an ambulance?"

"I'll say. You were out like a lamp. You've got an awful black eye."

Instinctively Don raised his hand and touched the eye with his fingers.

"Too bad. Such nice eyes, too. Really awful nice." The voice had no fiber or resonance at all. It was the audible but whispered intimacy of one who spoke from a pillow in the dead of night. "Want to see what you look like?" From a pocket in his jacket he drew out a small round mirror and held it between thumb and forefinger.

Don pulled away. "No thank you."

"What's the matter?"

"Nothing."

"What's the matter, baby?"

In anger, Don glanced up again. But he was in no position to be angry. He had to bear with this until he got out of here, or at

least until he got his clothes. "Are you a doctor?" he said, to say
something.

"No."

"Orderly?"

"No."

"What."

"Nurse." He smiled. Then, barely audible: "Is that all right?"

"All right what?"

"All right with you." He smiled as if he were privately
amused—a little wryly but still amused—at some secret slight
joke of his own. Nothing to laugh about; just sort of muse over,
continually.

Don was too uncomfortable to face him. "What's the other
guy," he said, looking away.

"That's Doctor Stevens. Did you like him?"

"Listen. Didn't he say I could go?"

"Okay, baby. Hold your water. I'll go get it."

"My clothes?"

"Your paraldehyde. You'll love it." He moved silently away.

When he was at a safe distance, Don turned on the mattress to
watch him go. He moved down the ward with a noiseless casual
tread as if in carpet-slippers on his way to his own bathroom at
home, indescribably nonchalant and at ease. It was infuriating.
But you didn't have to watch him, did you? He lay on the mattress face down, refusing to look further.

Though he couldn't believe the business about the fractured
skull, he began to realize the spot he was in. The alcoholic ward.
So here he was at last. Inevitably he would wind up in this place
and the only wonder was that he hadn't been here before. This
was your natural home and you might as well take it. Take it and
lie low and wait for your chance to get out again—and then forever afterward watch your step. But it wasn't happening, either—
not any of it. You had a bad head but you certainly didn't feel the
pain you knew you had, didn't shake (no more than usual), didn't

sweat (no more than usual). It was all so unreal that you weren't even suffering; you were merely biding your time, in a time-out. He began to look about him.

It was a long high-ceilinged room with a concrete floor bare of anything but beds, most of them so low they were little more than pallets. Only three or four were of normal height, and these were boarded up at the sides like babies' cribs. The idea, he supposed, was to keep you from falling out; or, in the case of the low beds, from hurting yourself if you did fall.

On the mattress next to his, a man who looked like some kind of crank messiah (but only because of the gaunt and hollow face) lay staring at the ceiling. He had a three- or four-days' growth of beard, his cheeks were sunken, his eyes large and sad. His white legs stuck out below the pathetically short gown like a cadaver in the morgue. He might have been dead, but that his entire frame—all over, all of it at once—quivered. It shook with tiny tremors, regular, precise, constant, as if a fine motor operated somewhere beneath him, in the mattress itself.

Farther off, a middle-aged Negro babbled God knows what at the top of his lungs, and no one paid enough notice to find out what he was complaining about. In the bed across the way another Negro got up on his knees, lifted his gown, and urinated on the floor. No one seemed to notice or mind that, either, least of all the intelligent-looking man who leaned against the wall a few feet away in a stiff faded robe held together by a safety-pin, looking about as casually as he could and being very careful to avoid every returning glance. His self-consciousness was painful to see. Don felt that the man had been looking at him, but by the time he noticed the fellow, he had shifted his gaze an inch or two to the left. You couldn't have caught his eye if you'd tried. Other men in faded robes or short gowns open at the back moved restlessly up and down the aisle or went in and out of the two rooms at the end where most of the shouting seemed to be coming from. There was a strong smell of disinfectant and dirty feet.

It wasn't possible that he was here or that he had come to this place in an ambulance, clang-clanging through the streets like the ambulances in the movies or like the one he had seen yesterday tearing in and out among the pillars of the L. You couldn't ride in one of those things and not know it. But you had. You had been rushed zig-zagging through the city streets while an interne sat at your side taking your pulse or your temperature and bracing himself for the turns. But how had you got into it in the first place? Where had you been picked up—by whom? What or who had given you a fractured skull—if you had one? All he remembered was the bottle left behind on the living room table.

The nurse Bim appeared again, moving down the ward like a cat. He was even cat-like in color: tawny; neither blond nor brunet. From a little distance he smiled at Don and raised his eyebrows, and his head waggled from side to side ever so slightly. There was something contemptuous about his every motion, a carelessness or insolence which yet solicited attention—and got it, Don realized. Damn his eyes, why did you have to notice, why did you look at all? But this kind of coquetry was so bold and mocking that you couldn't take it seriously, you shouldn't allow yourself to become exasperated. Maybe the guy was clowning.

He sauntered up to Don's bed and handed him a small thick glass half-full of a colorless liquid. "Here's your drink, baby. You can pretend it's gin. Doesn't it look like it?"

"Set it down, will you please?" Because of his shaking hand he didn't trust himself to take the glass under the other's gaze.

But the nurse, God damn him, always seemed to be two jumps ahead of your own thought. "Go ahead, I won't look."

"What's it for?"

"Your head and your nerves. It will clear you up. No, don't smell it, just take it." He pretended to look away and Don picked up the little glass and downed the stuff in one swallow.

It was the foulest tasting liquid he had ever had in his mouth and that was going some; bitterer than anything he'd ever heard of (he'd be tasting and smelling it for weeks); but almost instantly, miraculously, the throbbing in his head died down, his heart quieted, his hands stopped trembling. He felt suddenly clear and normal; all trace of hangover and fright were gone. He couldn't believe it. He looked up at the nurse in surprise. "What was the name of that stuff?"

"Paraldehyde."

"What?"

"Paraldehyde."

He had heard perfectly, but he wanted the name said again, wanted to fix it in his mind forever, wished he had some way of writing it down so that he would never never forget it.

The nurse sat down beside him. "Feel better, baby?" The words were a vibrationless hum, intimate and secret-sounding as the voice of Marlene Dietrich. You had no defense against him. You couldn't even snub the guy.

But the perpetual slight smile bothered him even more than the voice. "What's so funny?"

"Nothing. I was just wondering."

"What?"

"Ever been here before?"

"No."

"You sure?"

"Yes."

"Maybe you're right. I would have remembered you. Anybody ever tell you that you look like Ronald Colman?"

If you only had sense enough to *laugh,* or kid back!

"Little younger, but the same eyes and puzzled forehead. Nice."

"Listen. I've taken that drink. Now what about—"

"Want to bet something?"

"No."

"I'll bet this isn't your last time." He put his hand on Don's knee—completely impersonal, oddly enough—and nodded toward the man Don had noticed before, leaning against the wall. "See that one over there? He won't look at us but he's listening to every word. He's a repeater, that one. I'll bet I've seen him six times this year, and it's only October. Advertising man. Lovely fellow, too."

Don studied the empty glass, in his embarrassment. "What about my clothes."

"What's all the rush? It's only noon. Sunday at that, don't forget. You can't get a drink till afternoon."

There he was again, knowing your thought. "Listen. Can't I get my clothes? The doctor said—I heard him say—"

"Now now. Just relax, baby. I'll get them for you if you're in such a sweat." He got up from the mattress and sauntered off through the ward.

Paraldehyde. Was that the word—had he got it right? God this could maybe turn out to be the discovery of your life. As long as there was such a thing as paraldehyde in the world—

Doctor Stevens came into the ward again. He was accompanied by an older man in a business suit. They stood in the middle of the room talking together and looking about. The doctor pointed out first one patient and then another, not troubling to lower his voice. "Now that one over there—" And even as the alarmed patient began to respond in excited fearful apprehension, the two men slowly turned their backs and began to regard and discuss another. They might have been visiting a picture-gallery, or admiring impersonally the various blooms and plants in a hothouse.

They came forward and stood between his mattress and the one next to it. "Now this fellow"—indicating the staring messiah—"came in last night. He says he'd had only one glass of beer."

As the gaunt skinny man awoke to the fact that he was under study, the invisible motor somewhere within the mattress speeded up at once, accelerating the tremors that rippled throughout the whole body. Sweat began to stand out above the apprehensive eager eyes, eager to please, eager to prove he was master of himself. The sweat broke and ran down his face as the doctor addressed him.

"How many did you have," the doctor said in a loud voice, as if speaking to some one hard of hearing.

"One, Doctor. Just one."

"One what?"

"Just one bottle of beer, Doctor."

"What's your name?"

"Yes, Doctor."

"What's your name?"

"John Haspeth."

"How do you spell it?"

"Haspeth, Doctor."

"How do you spell it?"

"John Haspeth." The front of the gown, across his chest, was already dark with sweat.

"You can see," the doctor said, "how he's beginning to perspire. The whole bed will be soaked in a minute or two. That's because we're talking to him, of course. And notice the feet and legs—well, the whole body, for that matter. The tremors are getting worse. He'll be shaking himself right off that mattress onto the floor if we stand here long enough. It's the effort at concentration, plus self-consciousness. If we turned our backs, the shaking would die down very quickly."

The patient watched and listened with passionate anxious concern, hanging on every word, and the tremors quickened even more as the doctor addressed him again.

"What do you do, John?"

"I'm a painter, Doctor."

"House-painter?"

"Signs. I paint signs."

"Where do you live?"

"Yes, Doctor."

"What day is it?"

"Day?"

"What day is it?"

"Wednesday, Doctor."

"What month?"

"Yes, Doctor."

"What's the month, what month is it?"

He raised his hand to his mouth but it kept hitting his chin, so he lowered it again and clutched the sides of the mattress to still the shaking. Then, as if a tardy answer would spell ruin, he gasped, breathlessly: "January."

"What year?"

"Year, Doctor?"

"What's the year? Is it Nineteen-thirty-four, Thirty-five, -six, -seven?"

"Thirty-six, Doctor." The shaking had become violent now. The hands and arms pumped up and down, the legs danced like a puppet's, the entire trunk jumped and bounced on the bed.

The two men watched this in silence for a moment, regarding the struggle almost without interest. "How many drinks did you have?" the doctor went on.

The patient hugged his shoulders to quiet himself. "Just one, Doctor—I only had one. Just one glass."

"I thought you said bottle."

"Oh no, Doctor. Just one. Only one small jigger."

"Jigger of beer?"

"Whisky, Doctor. Only one little glass."

"Okay." The doctor turned to speak to his friend.

"Doctor! Doctor!" the patient called out. "Won't you give me something?"

"No no, not now. You can have all you want of those things in the hall. They're in the jar on the desk. Go help yourself. You know where they are. Take as many as you like."

"What does he want?" the man in the business-suit said.

"Medication. A sedative. I tell him he can help himself to the salt-tablets. We encourage that as much as possible. No sedatives in the daytime. We try to maintain or restore the normal sleep-cycle, you see—make them stay awake during the day. Put them to sleep now and they'll be raising hell all night. That fellow over there took a running jump at the wall around three-thirty this morning and got a terrible shaking-up. Thought it was the ocean and wanted to jump in. That wouldn't have happened in the day-time. Delirium is a disease of the night."

As the two men moved down the ward to the rooms at the end, the staring messiah began gradually to subside in his pool of sweat, a grey oval stain that ringed him completely on the bed.

Delirium is a disease of the night. God what an expression. Beautiful as a line of verse, something to remember and put down sometime—remember in quite a different way and for quite a different reason than he meant to remember *paraldehyde.* . . . Besides, it was a good thing to know. Could you bank on it?

Here was the nurse Bim with the clothes. He came along the aisle with a little bouncing step carrying the clothes wadded in a ball against his chest, with his arms around them and his hands folded in front. He set them down on the mattress and undid the rope that tied them together. The clothes rolled out in a messy heap on the bed.

"There they are, baby."

"Where do I dress?"

"Right here." He moved away with a smile, leaned against the wall, folded his arms, and began to watch—casual, indiffer-ent, disinterested; but somehow it was intolerable. Nobody in the world could have been more at home anywhere, more at ease, than he was at home and at ease in this place and in himself. It simply wasn't normal to be that nonchalant.

Don fished in the pile till he found his shorts. Burning with self-consciousness, he swung his legs over the edge of the mattress, and shifted and wriggled till he got his shorts on, under the gown. As he began awkwardly to dress, then, an idiotic picture came into his mind: Pola Negri sitting across the table from a lecherous Prussian officer in some ancient film, and a camera-trick in which the dress seemed to fade away, revealing her naked, as if to indicate that Noah Beery had undressed her with his eyes.

He heard the purring voice. "Three-one-one, did you say?"

He glanced up sharply, to show his anger. It was no use. But the question gave him an idea—under the circumstances, a shameless one. Shameless to take this advantage. "Bim, listen. Is it possible to get some of that paraldehyde?"

The nurse shook his head. "The doctor said one dram. You had yours."

"Look. Couldn't you get me a little more? Sneak me some? I mean, to take home. In a little bottle or something?"

"Can't be done. But I'll tell you what."

"What?"

"I could bring some over sometime."

"No thank you."

"Are you in the book, baby?"

"No thank you, I said! Forget it." He found his shoes and put them on. When he stood up, he felt in his pockets for money. There wasn't a bill. In a vest-pocket he found four nickels, that was all. He wasn't surprised—nothing about money could surprise him any more. Apparently he was supposed to go on losing it and losing it and losing it every time he got his hands on some. He looked around for his hat. "Where's my hat?"

"Are you sure you had a hat?"

"Of course I had a hat!"

"They didn't give me a hat with your clothes, but I'll go see again."

Don watched him go, the frame and build of a truck-driver sauntering along softly, insolently, like a dancer. He sat back helplessly on the bed and helplessly gazed after the receding offending figure of Bim, accepting him at last, and knowing why. . . .

Here was the daydream turned inside-out; a projection, in reverse, of the wishful and yearning fancy; the back of the picture, the part always turned to the wall. The flower of the ingrown seed he had in him was here shown in unhealthy bloom, *ad terrorem* and *ad nauseam*. It was aspiration in its raw and naked state, aspiration un-ennobled, a lapse of nature as bizarre and undeniable as the figures of his imagined life were deniable, bizarre, beyond reach. All that he wanted to become and, in his fanciful world, became, was here represented in throwback. He himself stood midway between the ideal and this—as far from one as from the other. But oh, too—oh, too!—as far from the other as from the one. If he was uncomfortable in Bim's stifling presence, did he not also have reason to be comforted? Or was midway, nothing—nothing at all?

Thank Christ he'd be out of here in a minute. He had never belonged here even for the few hours they'd put him away. He couldn't identify himself with the place or with the guy sitting here on his bed waiting for his hat. It isn't me, it isn't happening to me. He looked about the room again, as a spectator.

A young woman had come into the ward, apparently to call on a patient who was ready to go home. The patient sat on the bed waiting for his clothes and the young woman sat in a chair. They were talking together. Don saw the young man quicken with interest and enthusiasm the longer he talked; and though he couldn't hear a word that was said, he knew what the young man was saying—the plans that were being made, he'd get a job, maybe they'd go to the country, all he needed now was a good job, he felt like it now, he'd learned his lesson, this could never happen again, not possibly, wasn't it a good thing it had happened really, maybe he'd needed just this to wake him up, he even welcomed the experience, didn't regret it at all, the way he felt now he'd never touch the stuff again in his life, and he was going to *stay* that way too, she could watch and see, he'd get that job and she wouldn't have to go through a thing like this again, ever again, or he either. . . .

The girl nodded, like Helen.

Doctor Stevens and his guest came back through the ward. They stopped at the end of Don's bed.

"Now, this one came in with a slight fracture of the skull. He'd fallen, evidently—they're always falling—and struck his head between the right temple and eye. No real damage, just a crack. But there are a good many broken blood-vessels, which accounts for the violent discoloration. The nerves just under the surface are probably damaged too. He may have a slight area of numbness there for some time to come, possibly even for the rest of his life. I noticed when I probed, he didn't seem to feel it at all. Here, touch it."

Don tried to look away but he could not. If Wick could see him now, if his mother, if Helen, they would die of shame. He didn't. What was happening to him was, in a sense, not happening at all, because nobody knew about it—least of all the man who bent over the anonymous patient and touched the right temple with his finger.

"Do you feel that?"

He couldn't answer, he merely shook his head.

"He's probably been drinking for days," the doctor said. "The blood showed quite a high content of alcohol. We tried to give him a spinal tap but he wouldn't take it. He came to at that point and refused. Obviously he's a man of intelligence and in full possession of his faculties, for the present. So there's nothing to do but let him go. He's all right. Did the nurse give you the paraldehyde?"

He nodded. The other man studied him abstractedly, apparently deep in thought. It wasn't Don he was seeing, it wasn't anybody. Don returned the gaze. But there was no recognition, no exchange in it at all.

"Do you feel better since you took it?"

He nodded again.

"I thought you said, Doctor," the man in the business suit said, "that you didn't give them sedatives in the daytime."

"Oh, this one is ready to go home and we want him to be able to get there. We don't want him to collapse in the street."

"And then what will happen? Will he start all over again?"

"Possibly. They usually do. But that's something beyond our control. Most of them come back again and again. Not so much this kind of patient—they can usually afford the private hospitals or sanitariums—as the others. We can't help them or cure them, not here. This is merely a clearing-house. Our only business is to help them get on their feet and out of here as soon as possible."

"I see. The poor keep coming back. The rich go away to the private places and get a cure."

"There isn't any cure, besides just stopping. And how many of them can do that? They don't want to, you see. When they feel bad like this fellow here, they think they want to stop, but they don't, really. They can't bring themselves to admit they're alcoholics, or that liquor's got them licked. They believe they can take it or leave it alone—so they take it. If they do stop, out of fear or whatever, they go at once into such a state of euphoria and well-being that they become over-confident. They're rid of drink, and feel sure enough of themselves to be able to start again, promising they'll take one, or at the most two, and—well, then it becomes the same old story all over again. Too bad, too. You and I don't realize it, because liquor doesn't mean to us what it does to them." The doctor turned to Don. "Why don't you go home? You can, you know."

"I'm waiting for my hat."

The men glanced at each other and laughed, and then moved off.

He could have kicked himself for saying that. It made him, somehow, so utterly ludicrous and laughable that he was ashamed for the first time that morning. Oh, Christ, what difference did it make? Nobody knew he was here, and nobody here knew or cared who he was. But he was ashamed all the same. He got up and stepped to the small barred window near the end of his bed. He looked out and down. Cars and busses were going by, people moved along the sidewalk. Who of those down there knew who was up here, what was going on in this room, what was going on inside the men in this room? How many times had he himself driven down this street, past this very building where he stood looking down, and never even looked at the place, never dreamed that one day— Never dreamed it because those things just didn't happen. Not to the kind of person he was, the kind of people he knew. . . .

"They say you didn't have a hat."

He turned and there was Bim.

"You weren't wearing one when you came in, they say."

"I wasn't?"

"That's what they tell me, baby."

He moved away from the wall. Surprisingly, he walked well enough. He felt weak, but not too unsteady. The paraldehyde still held, if that's what it was that was doing it. It had to hold till he got home. "Will you show me, now, how to get out?"

"Okay, let me take your arm."

"I don't need it. Thanks."

They started down the ward, Don keeping his eyes straight ahead, unable to meet the derisive, yearning, or fearful glances he felt from all sides.

"You've got to stop at the desk and sign something."

"What?"

"A paper. You release the hospital from all responsibility. That's because you wouldn't take the treatment."

In the hall, a nurse handed up a printed form and a pen with-

out looking up from her work. In front of her, on the desk, was a
large open jar half-full of thick white wafers—probably the salt-
tablets they had been talking about.

"Right here, baby." Bim pointed his finger at the place to
sign.

Don took the pen. His mind went back to the mornings at
Juan-les-Pins, the agonizing mornings at the bank when often
he spent more than an hour trying to control the shaking of his
hand before he could bring himself to attempt the signature on
the letter-of-credit under the eyes of the watching teller. He
would drop out of line again and again, just as he had reached
the window, and go sit outdoors to stare at the incredible blue of
the sea and take deep breaths and try to calm himself by forgetting the money he needed, the pen, the necessary signature, and
the impassive teller; and when he had recovered enough to join
the line again, the whole unnerving helpless performance would
be repeated. But now, to his surprise—probably to Bim's too—
the hand wrote his name plainly and well. Paraldehyde—he must
hang onto it, never never forget it.

"I'll take you to the elevator, baby."

The walk through the hall and the waiting were a more trying ordeal than he could have anticipated. They went along the
corridor in silence till the nurse stopped and pushed a button in
the wall. Then he leaned against the wall and looked at Don.

Never had he felt so much on trial in his life—on trial for
what, he didn't know. He went hot with exasperation and embarrassment as he felt the nurse's eyes looking him over. He didn't
know where to turn, where to fix his own gaze. He waited in
a foolish suspense—unreasonable, outlandish, bizarre. In all his
life there was no precedent of behavior for such a moment. If that
guy so much as spoke to him, uttered a word of advice, told him
to take it easy— He felt the odd smile and fought to resist. But it
was no use, he couldn't help himself any longer. Involuntarily, he
raised his eyes and looked back.

"Listen, baby." The voice was so low and soft he could scarcely hear it. "I know you."

The elevator doors slid open; he saw the brightly lighted car and the sudden response on the faces of the passengers (the broken blood-vessels, the violent discoloration?); he stepped in and quickly turned his back; through the small glass window of the door he saw the nurse's eyebrows raised in farewell; and the floor gave way beneath his feet.

As he came out into the bright sunlight and started toward the street, an ambulance turned in at the gate. Dang-dang-dang-dang-dang-*gang-gang-gang-gang*-dang-dang-dang. He walked on to a bus stop at the corner, reached into his vest-pocket for one of the four nickels, and stepped into a bus.

He went to the far end of the bus and sat down, on the rear seat. But he might just as well have stayed up front. The passengers turned—and continually turned—to look at him. The driver bent his head slightly to see him in the mirror. He sat back, erect, and gazed absently out of the window, trying to show by his indifference that he had never worn a hat in his life—though a hat, at this moment, was what he longed for more than almost anything else in the world, almost as much as the half-full quart that awaited him on the living room table.

He raced up the three flights of stairs, realizing as he reached the top that exhaustion, and its cure, were at hand again. But the whisky was gone. On the living room table there was no other thing but his hat. There was not even an empty bottle, nor any bottle-wrappings or corks or caps. The litter of the table had been swept away and the entire room cleaned up.

Had Wick come back unexpectedly? Had Helen got in? But Mac would have been here, in the basket; and Helen would have left a note. It was fiendish to have taken the bottle, whoever did it. Mrs. Foley? He went into the kitchen to see if it was on the floor under the sink, where whisky had been kept in the past. He came back through and went to the bathroom. In the mirror over the washbowl he saw how he looked for the first time.

His right eyeball was streaked with red. Around it, for a space as big as his palm, spreading across the temple to the ear, was the discoloration the doctor had so casually spoken of as violent. It was a patch of purple and red and black and shining copper all run together: it looked raw and soft, as if you could poke your finger through it, like a pulsing fontanelle; and it pained now as if he had done just that. He hurried into the living room, snatched up his hat from the table, went into the bedroom and got his wristwatch, wound it and set it by the Dutchman's clock, opened the door to the hall again and ran quietly down the stairs.

Sam's place was locked—it was still a good half-hour before opening time—but he put his face to the glass of the door and peered in. Sam sat at a table in the back, reading a paper, and Gloria stood beside him combing her hair. He tapped on the glass with the edge of the watch.

Sam looked up, came forward a few steps, then pointed for him to go around to a side-door. He didn't know of any side-door, but he looked and found one. He went into the hallway that led to the stairs and the apartments above, and sure enough, Sam opened a door into the hall.

"Now listen, Sam, don't get mad." Sam bent forward and peered at him. "I've got to have a bottle. I've got to have it. Please take this watch."

"Now Mr. Birnam, that's not the thing to do," Sam said. "I've got a drawer full of watches."

"You've got to give it to me, Sam. You've got to. Take this until I can get to the bank tomorrow."

Sam fingered the watch, as if too embarrassed to look at his eye. "I don't know, Mr. Birnam."

"Please, Sam. I've been in an accident. I'm in bad shape."

Something in the desperate strange sound of his own voice

made him know that Sam wouldn't hold out on him. He didn't. He went back into the bar to get the whisky.

Gloria was watching all this from the table. "Nice guy," she said, when he looked at her. "Lovely guy. Do you go around doing that all the time? Standing people up?"

"What are you talking about?"

"You know what I'm talking about. You don't need to pretend. I waited here and waited and waited till half— My God, where'd you get the black-eye!"

It was intolerable, waiting; but he would wait till nightfall, if need be. He heard Sam inside at the bar, rattling a paper-bag.

"Boy, that's a peach! Did Teddy give it to you?"

He glanced at her, immediately suspicious. "Who's Teddy?"

"Your wife, dope."

What was she saying, what the hell was she talking about? Was she making fun of him? Sam appeared at the door with the bottle wrapped in a bag. He snatched it from him, said "Thanks," and ran out. Fool! Where in Christ's name had she got the fantastic idea that he had a wife?...

Coming up the last flight of stairs, he heard the telephone ringing inside. He stood there in the hall, panting, waiting for it to stop before he went in. He turned and kept his eye on the door to the front apartment where the two ladies lived with their dog Sophie. If the knob should turn, if the door should open— The telephone stopped ringing, he unlocked his door and went in.

With the first drink in his hand, he sat down to puzzle out the story of the hat and half-full quart.

Sure. Of course. The two ladies in the front apartment. He remembered it, now. Remembered the polite little tiff on the stairs—after you; no, after you—and the falling, and then falling again. That was the last he remembered of anything. He must have hit his head and passed out then and there.

And what did they do? Call the police? Send him off in an ambulance? He didn't know. But he knew a few things they did do. They had found his hat at the foot of the stairs. They got Dave the janitor to let them into the flat. They put his hat on the living room table. They looked around at the disorder. They cleaned up the place. Cleaned it up and cleaned him out—took away the nasty bottle that was the whole source of the trouble. How nice and neighborly of them to straighten up for him. The dear sweet kind considerate bitches.

Maybe you could laugh about it tomorrow. Maybe you could begin to smile after another drink. Maybe you could even get up in another half-hour and go in and thank them for taking such good care of your hat and your flat, and give little Sophie a kick in the teeth—Sophie who had probably been running around here like mad, smelling for Mac, while the busy ladies were busy cleaning up. He knew what the rest of it would be. A few days later, after Wick got back, there would come a genteel tap at the door; Wick would answer it; one of the ladies would be standing there holding the neck of the half-empty bottle between thumb and forefinger; she would peep over Wick's shoulder to see if Don was about, and then whisper the whole story, her voice rising again to normal on the words "—And so we just thought, under the circumstances—well, *you* understand. . . ."

Wick would understand, all right. So did he. Which is why you made the most of moments like these, why you took it while you had it and took all you could get when you got it, why you made hay while the sun shone.

Now he was in for good. No going out for the rest of the day. There was no possibility of raising any more money (not on a Sunday) or getting any more liquor till tomorrow. So this had to last. Well, a full quart would last quite a good while if you took it easy and read a book. After you had it all in you, in slow easy well-spaced wonderful drinks, maybe you would feel like sleeping and sleep till the necessary joints opened in the morning.

He was in no rush, he could take it easy, already he was feeling much better; but after what he had been through, he didn't feel like feeling too much better too soon. It sneaked up on you, that way, and before you knew it you felt like starting out somewhere. That wasn't the idea today, that wasn't what he wanted at all. For once, maybe, he knew where he was safe.

Now he had himself a good drink, a decent one, and sat back and recalled that moment of departure in the hall, the moment before the elevator came, a moment indeed. *Listen, baby.* The purring Dietrich voice. *I know you.*

Okay, Pal. You win. You know all about everything, wise guy, you weren't born yesterday. He was aware, as Bim was, of the downward path he was on; he knew himself well enough to know and admit that Bim had every reason to say what he said— but only insofar as Bim saw, in him, the potential confederate that was every alcoholic: the fellow bogged down in adolescence; the guy off his track, off his trolley; the man still unable to take, at thirty-three or -six or -nine, the forward step he had missed in his 'teens; the poor devil demoralized and thrown off balance by the very stuff intended to restore his frightened or baffled ego; the gent jarred loose into unsavory bypaths that gave him the shudders to think of but which were his natural habitat and inevitable home so long as drink remained the *modus operandi* of his life; the lush whose native characteristics, whatever they were at the outset, could blur and merge with the whims of every and any companion who offered companionship or worse; the barred one whose own bars were down—the unpredictable renegade to whom *any*thing might happen.

Bim saw all this with the bright eye of his kind. Okay; so far, so good. But Bim's was also the overbright eye which saw signs and meanings where there were none. Don acknowledged his right to say what he said and to see what he thought he saw. But wise guys who weren't born yesterday might very well know all about everything and still be far from the truth.

What Bim did not see was that the alcoholic was not himself, able to choose his own path, and therefore the kinship he seemed

to reveal was incidental, accidental, transitory at best. If the drunk
had been himself he would not be a drunk and potential brother
in the first place. And not to be oneself was a thing incomprehensible to the nonchalant Bim, whose one belief in life was to
be just that, regardless of who or what, to hell with any or all. It
could be such a marvelous world if everyone would only let down
their hair—marvelous for Bim. He could do it; why couldn't
everybody else? But millions had nothing to let down their hair
about, even among drunks, and millions could be themselves by
being no different from what they had always been. For Don,
the avenue where Bim beckoned was a blind alley, not shameful
but useless, futile, vain, offering no attractions whatever, no hope,
nowhere a chance to build. Bim knew better, of course: knew that
one could not moralize or rationalize oneself out of it: the alley
either existed for you, or it did not. Very well, let him know better! Wasn't it possible that one could skirt the alley by very reason of knowing it was there? And not skirt it out of fear, either,
but out of anguished regard for all that one would have to leave
behind if one entered, all the richer realizations of self that would
never be fulfilled. But this was protesting too much, why argue,
why be anguished or angered, why waste time on all that, when
the whole thing boiled down to one simple fact: Drunks were
alike, sure, but no more like Bim (necessarily) than Bim was like
other male nurses or they like him. But could you tell him that?
Not in a thousand years. And why bother, why give him a chance
to raise his eyebrows any higher than he already had? Why bother
with anything but the glass and the whisky at hand. . . .

Oh all the troubling people in the world that could be drowned
in drink without their even knowing it; harmlessly, with no real
damage to them and what satisfaction to oneself; people that you
could drown, thus, here and now and always. Not the least of
them you yourself, of course, but others too, and over and over
again. How they receded and paled and became anonymous as
the livening warmth of the drink quieted your heart; and then,

as the stimulus spread to and awoke your brain, restoring your
critical faculties sharper and clearer than ever, how they emerged
again and stood off from you, apart, seen objectively, coldly, without passion or even concern.

I know you. Oh yeah? His anger rose. That was the trouble
with homos and he didn't mean sapiens either. They were always
so damned anxious to suspect every guy they couldn't make of
merely playing hard-to-get; so damned anxious to believe that
their own taint was shared by everybody else. He never knew
one yet who didn't think that every other man extant, extinct, or
to come, had a dash of it too. Well, who didn't have a dash, or
ten dashes even; but did that moot possibility give them the right
to go through life with the smug smirking knowledge blazing
on their pretty faces as if it were an established fact? As if they
just couldn't wait to tell the world that they knew more about
you than you did yourself? And why, if their glance was one of
recognition, was it also a look of contempt? If they hailed you
as brother, they scorned you for the same reason. Nobody was
quicker with the word "queen," used derisively at that, than the
queen himself—like the Jew who cringes under the term "kike"
but uses it twice as much as anybody else; like the Negro so quick
on the trigger with the word "nigger"; like the TB patient who
smiles from his pillow in secret satisfaction because the telltale
flush on the cheek of his commiserating visitor shows all too
plainly that he will be next. In the same breath that they ridicule their kind, they claim kinship with the great ones of the
world: the Jews with Heine and Disraeli (not kikes now); the
tuberculars with Stevenson and Chopin and Keats; the others
with Wilde, Proust, Tschaikovsky, Michelangelo, Caesar. But
why get worked up about it now? If he wanted to get sore, he
should have got sore at the time—landed one right on that smiling mouth, if it would have made him feel any better. But anger
was just what the nurse Bim would have liked. It would have
given him a chance to say "You see?" and rightly too. And it

wouldn't have made him feel any better either. The only thing that did was this. He drank.

Anger was what the psychiatrist would have been interested in, too. Not the foolish psychiatrist, this time, but the good one, the real one, the one he had never met but knew existed, the doctor whose knowledge and sympathy would have matched his own—and what a relationship that might have been. What might not have come of such a year. It had been his luck (good or bad, what difference did it make now?) to meet up with a fake; but no real damage had been done, since he was as superior to the foolish psychiatrist as the real one, perhaps, would have been to him—the one to whom anger would not have meant anything so glib as "suppressed desires," the doctor whose respect for himself and his calling no less than for his patient could not have permitted him to palm off fraudulent alloys and counterfeits for the pure metal, spurious coin forged by another and scarcely read properly by himself, hoards of phoney wealth whose total value didn't even add up to a nickel, much less to the considerable sum paid out every week for the profitless hour a day—profitless, not worth a nickel. . . .

How was it possible he had only four nickels in his pocket this morning? He knew damned well now—he remembered now—that he had had more than six dollars when he started to leave the flat yesterday to buy that second quart, six out of the ten he'd borrowed from Mr. Wallace at the A & P. What the hell had become of it, and of the good wad of cash he had the day before? Where in God's name was it *going* to? Of course he could go out of his mind thinking about it and trying to track it down but it was funny all the same, damned funny. You just didn't let money slip through your fingers like that, not when money was as important to you as it was at times like these. And you wouldn't have given it up without a struggle to anybody else either. For that matter there hadn't been anybody around to give it up to. Drama. Mystery. Comedy even. Tragical-comical-historical-pastoral, scene individual, or poem unlimited. At least you could think of it as comic while this bottle sat here at your elbow a good deal more than half-full, oh safely and blessedly a good deal more. . . .

The whisky warmed him all inside, as usual; and took away the pain and fatigue and jumping nerves, as usual; and caused his spirits as usual to wake and rise so pleasantly, so reassuringly— the spirits that only this morning, only yesterday, only tomorrow and next week, he thought and would think would never rise again. He wasn't beaten down after all. Who or where was the wee, sleekit, cow'rin', tim'rous beastie now? O what a panic may be in thy breastie a*nother* day but not while you had this in your hand and that on the table. But easy, there; easy this time. Go get another drink if you like but get a book too.

He poured the drink and walked over to inspect the book-shelves. Sleekit, hell! not with a two-day beard and a black-eye like a Rouault portrait. Looking over the brightly-jacketed nov-els, he thought of the volumes at home in his father's library, the books that had never been taken away when his father left and still remained in the shelves in his mother's house: the salesman-sets his father had always fallen for—the green Kiplings, the blue de Maupassants, the maroon Bjornsons (who the hell was he anyway and why a whole set of him?), the small red *Masterpieces of Wit & Humor,* the tan *World's Greatest Orations,* the sickeningly limp limp-leather Roycroft books that almost gave you the creeps to hold, the dark red Mark Twains and the two handsome Trollopes in purple calf or morocco or levant or whatever it was. But all he could think of (suddenly) when he thought of his father's books was that letter to his mother he had found and the sentence that read "I will always fondly remember you and the boys." He had run upstairs then and flung himself down on the bed and cried his eyes out, weeping for the father who would no longer be giving him the cardboards from his laundered shirts to draw beautiful pictures on, pictures his father always admired and showed to all his friends and sent off to the Children's Page of a New York newspaper. How could your admiring father do that to you, go away and leave you forever, did he really not care for you any more, was it possible? And though he sobbed and sobbed on the bed in shame and anguish, he realized too the awful importance of that letter, and he glanced up into the mirror of the bureau to see what a moment of crisis looked like. . . .

He took a drink and searched for a book to read or think about. He had an author, too, in calf or morocco or levant, an author whose works he had had bound himself, both as a kind of personal tribute to the writer he so dearly loved and because he would be reading those nine books (and all the others to come) for the rest of his life. He took down *The Great Gatsby* and ran his finger over the fine green binding. "There's no such thing," he said aloud, "as a flawless novel. But if there is, this is it." He nodded. The class looked and listened in complete attention, and one or two made notes. "Don't be fooled by what the Sunday reviewers say of the jazz-age, Saturday-Evening-Post-popularity, et cetera. People will be going back to Fitzgerald one day as they now go back to Henry James." He walked back and forth, tapping the book in his hand. "Pay no attention, either, to those who care for his writing merely; who speak of 'the texture of his prose' and other silly and borrowed and utterly meaningless phrases. True, the writing is the finest and purest, the most entertaining and most readable, that we have in America today; the nearest anyone has come to it is James Cozzens in *Ask Me Tomorrow*.— Scott Fitzgerald has enormous natural gifts as a writer; but it's the content that counts in literature. I'd rather have someone say of my writing that it had energy than beauty any day. You can write badly and still be a great novelist: look at Dreiser; look at the James Farrell of *Studs Lonigan*." He paused to note the surprised, gratified, or puzzled reactions. "Apart from his other gifts, Scott Fitzgerald has the one thing that a novelist needs: a truly seeing eye. He sees so clearly, in fact, that his latest book has embarrassed those critics who have come to look to him for entertainment, not for such deeply searching stuff as this. What does it matter that *Tender Is The Night* fails as a novel?—which it does. While it lasts, it is the most brilliant and heart-breaking performance you will find in recent fiction. Get the book and read it yourself; it came out last year; and of the four novels so far, it is my favorite. Speaking for myself, it's fatal to open the book at any page, any paragraph; for I must sit down then and there and read the rest of it right through, from that point on, to the finish." (He would not bother to tell the students— too personal, unbecoming—that when he had finished *Tender Is The Night* at nine-thirty in the morning he had telephoned all over the Atlantic seaboard till he finally located Fitzgerald at Tuxedo; and the man had said: "Why don't you write me a letter about it? I think you're a little tight now.") "The fellow is still under forty. The great novels will yet come from his pen. And when they do, we shall have as true a picture of the temper and spirit of our time as any age of literature can boast in the past. One word more. Fitzgerald never swerves by a hair from the one rule that any writer worth his salt will follow: *Don't write about anything you don't know anything about.* Class dismissed."

He put the book back on the shelf, feeling suddenly very foolish and let down. He wasn't that drunk. Was he? It wasn't possible, no not yet, or ever. He could never be so drunk that he would mock his beloved Scott Fitzgerald. Mock? He meant every word of it and more. He felt so deeply about the man and his work— But that was the point. Keep it to yourself. Who cared?

But there was more to it than that. He knew only too well—he had heard, who hadn't?—what was going on with that gifted unhappy man. Would ten years go by again before another novel came out, like the long ten years between *Gatsby* and *Tender Is The Night?* And in the meantime, couldn't something be done to save those gifts and restore the man himself? Would the talent reassert itself and lift the man up, or would it go under still more to drink? Though he didn't know him and never would know him, he felt a personal concern and worry for his welfare, an anxiety as for a well-loved friend in distress of his own making. The very thought of him filled him with such a sadness that he could have wept. Nothing hurts more than to see a soaring spirit brought low.

A crying jag, that's what he'd be going into any minute if he didn't watch out. He poured a drink to bring him out of this state, drank it, and the telephone began to ring from the bedroom.

What is amiss?—You are, and do not know't. Well there was one way to fix that. No-no, nothing so foolish as to lift the receiver off the hook; that would be a giveaway to the guy at the other end. But the door was still shutable and he was still able to shut it and shut out the offending clamor partially. He got up and walked jauntily to the foyer and closed the bedroom door.

Partially was enough. From the big chair in the living room with a drink in your hand and the bottle within easy reach, it sounded like a summer insect back home, the metallic drone of a locust high up in a foliaged tree, fading farther and farther away as the hours passed. . . .

She's a most triumphant lady, if report be square to her.
When she first met Mark Antony, she pursed up his heart, upon the river Cydnus.
There she appear'd indeed; or my reporter devised well for her.

He was into the second Act of *Antony and Cleopatra* and his excitement as he approached the great description was intense. He began to get nervous and fidget in his chair. He sat forward and uttered the opening words as he knew they had never been uttered before: simple, yet cynical; unemotional, yet admiring in spite of himself; faintly derisive, but, in all honesty, forced to concede the triumph—Enobarbus to the life, with something of Iago's intellect, the daring of Lear's Fool, the loyal devotion of Horatio:

"I will tell you.
The barge she sat in, like a burnisht throne,
Burnt on the water: the poop was beaten gold;
Purple the sails, and so perfumed that
The winds were love-sick with them; the oars were silver,
Which to the tune of flutes kept stroke, and made
The water which they beat to follow faster,
As amorous of their strokes. For her own person,
It beggared all description. . . ."

He smiled to himself at the open-dropped mouth of Maecenas, the popping eyes of Agrippa, that pair of visiting firemen hanging breathless on his every grudging syllable, only too ready to believe the last fabulous word. He would dazzle them even more by under-playing to the limit, speaking almost as if he were bored:

" . . . From the barge
A strange invisible perfume hits the sense
Of the adjacent wharfs. The city cast
Her people out upon her; and Antony,
Enthroned i' the market-place, did sit alone,
Whistling to the air; which, but for vacancy,
Had gone to gaze on Cleopatra too,
And made a gap in nature. . . ."

Maecenas gave a low whistle under his breath and shook his head in the disbelief he didn't feel for an instant. But wait. He held up his hand—they hadn't heard the half of it. Hear how our great leader, demi-Atlas of this earth, world-sharer and universal landlord, fell like a ton of bricks:

"Upon her landing, Antony sent to her,
Invited her to supper: she replied,

It should be better he became her guest;
Which she entreated: our courteous Antony,
Whom ne'er the word of 'No' woman heard speak,
Being barber'd ten times o'er, goes to the feast,
And for his ordinary pays his heart
For what his eyes eat only. . . ."

"Royal wench!" exclaims Agrippa of the one-track mind; "She made great Caesar lay his sword to bed: He plough'd her, and she cropt." And the un-understanding Maecenas, the righteous and shocked family-man, inanely adds: "Now Antony must leave her utterly."

He sprang up from his chair.

"Never; he will not."

He walked slowly up and down, deliberating, and out of the corner of his eye, beyond the glare of the footlights, he saw the expectant hushed audience waiting for the familiar words, challenging him to bring them forth as new. Forget the audience; forget you ever heard the words; concentrate on the thing at hand: how to explain to these provincial Romans the secret and mystery of the lass unparallel'd. He faces the two, but he doesn't say it to them. He says it as if thinking aloud, for himself—cold, matter-of-fact, no more than the truth—giving the devil her due:

"Age cannot wither her, nor custom stale
Her infinite variety: other women cloy
The appetites they feed; but she makes hungry
Where most she satisfies: for vilest things
Become themselves in her; that the holy priests
Bless her when she is riggish. . . ."

The only sound is the audible sigh of released breath from the other side of the footlights: and he is, indeed, the absolute

Enobarbus at last, as no actor has ever been able to play him
yet. . . .

He was tired out. He poured a fresh drink. Oh to feel the
power of giving such a performance, or the power of swaying others in any medium, the power of accomplishment. Would it ever
be his? What did he mean would it. Wasn't it now? Did any actor,
any artist in any field, ever strike so to the root and heart of things
as he did now? What matter that no one was around to appreciate
the performance? *You* knew—and that was best of all.

The old pain was back, the head heavy. But the senses were
dull too and you didn't mind a bit, you knew it was there but you
scarcely felt it, you paid as little notice to the ache and the throb
and the sleepiness and the lovely lazy falling into a sleep that was
yet to come but coming blessedly any minute now as you did to
the zinging and faraway metal-like droning of the midsummer
locust in the foliaged tree in the bedroom behind the closed door.
Put the glass down it is heavy it will spill, no drink it, drink it
to save it, then over to the couch keeping your eyes closed not to
spoil the spell or waken, to the couch for a little while for a little
rest. . . .

He stretched out and fell deeply into a dream:

He was in a vast low one-story auditorium like a gymnasium.
Overhead, trapezes had been pulled up out of the way and wound
around the steel rafters that supported the wide squat roof.
Basketball-boards hung at either end of the hall. Horizontal bars,
hurdles, Swedish booms, rowing-machines, leather horses for
vaulting—all the paraphernalia of gymnastics had been stacked
along the side walls to make room for thousands of lightwood
folding-chairs packed in tight rows as dense as thatch. Sunshine
streamed down through the half-dozen skylights, making great
transparent blocks of slanting yellow in the dust- and mote-filled
air.

In the very center of the vast room, Don sat on a rickety
folding-chair—or on the edge of one, for the other half was occu-

pied by a young student in a grey-white sweatshirt. There was no chance that either of them would fall off: to each side, other students sat as closely packed. They sat two to a seat throughout the entire hall; pressed together, shoulders hunched, arms pulled forward between their knees, to make room. They were wedged so solidly in a collective mass that no single one of them could have risen to his feet without dragging up his immediate neighbors as well. Don turned, as far as he was able to, and looked about. Row upon row of close-cropped heads and brush-cuts, blond for the most part, spread in a wide sea all around him—heads of hair clipped almost to the scalp because of their natural shameful curls. Other students stood tight in overlapping file along the side walls, standing on the piled-up gear, craning their necks toward the front platform. The air was heavy with the strong dry sickish-sweet smell of young men.

In all that vast auditorium there was room for not one more student; yet new ones kept arriving. The rear doors opened with a groaning effort and late arrivals squeezed in. Somehow a place was found for each, who immediately became as agitated as all the others before him—stricken by the speaker they were assembled to hear.

A man in a grey suit, grey shirt, with grey hair and grey hands, wearing grey shoes, grey tie, grey glasses— A grey man stood on the platform at the far end of the hall. He had already begun to speak over the restless considerable murmuring of the crowd. He had been speaking, it seemed, before anyone arrived; and there was the feeling, even the certainty, that he would go on speaking long after the last of them had fled to carry out the fearful business which was the burden of his speech. He stood alone in the center of the bunting-draped platform and spoke to the world in deadly monotone deadly clear, like an oracle, the import of whose message is so momentous that he does not stoop to color it by the slightest inflexion or emphasis or shade of emotion: the dreadful intelligence will strike home without his lending it anything but the minimum of lip-service. His talk was punctuated now and again by the muffled crash of a collapsing chair or the shifting of feet or coughing or clearing of throats or the slamming of a door behind one last impossible tardy breathless student, but it did not matter. What he said was heard and felt by all, felt like an electric charge, though none understood.

A silence like infinity dropped finally over the hall, broken only by the fateful monotone. Don strained to hear what held his fellows hypnotized; and as he began to understand, the meaning of all he heard vanished away in the very moment of understanding. It was like a foreign language whose vocabulary he had learned in childhood along with his own native tongue, and forgotten. How rapt he could have listened if, like the others, he had not understood at all! He knew why his attention wandered, why he was unable to follow what he once knew so well, why the gist eluded him precisely because it reached his grasp. For the voice came over the crowd chanting a psycho-analytical lingo that was so familiar to him he could no longer register the sense of the words—the way you can say "Put," "Put," "Put," "Put," "Put," "Put," "Put," or "Take," "Take," "Take," "Take," "Take" over and over till you lose all track of their meaning. So it was now. He heard the complicated once-fascinating polysyllables pour forth from the emotionless speaker (emotionless because no emotion was needed, words took the place of everything) and tried to get back to that state of innocence where these same words had once opened up to him a new world (hardly brave, but such people in it!). He wanted to get back only so that he might belong with the listening throng in more than this crushingly physical way. It was no use. The German derivations, the Latin borrowings, the Freudian locutions, the images torn by the roots from Greek drama and mythology—all the fashionable skimble-skamble from Vienna made no sense to him any more; so that he sat alien and bewildered in the close-packed crowd, who alone of them all would have comprehended and acknowledged the last obscure

point of the harangue but for the melancholy fact that he had trod
that ground too well, too eagerly and hopefully—far too many
times—like the squirrel in the cage.

It was the foolish psychiatrist. Foolish? Now it was plain as
all that daylight, plainer than the dream was real. The man was
neither wise nor foolish, rational or irrational, alive or dead—and
was he indeed man? It was useless to name him, say of him this
or that, call him anything. He *was*, simply. Nothing more. Oh
but nothing less! Oh there was no denying that he was! As Don
sought him through the dust-filled air, he knew that he would
last, remain, be, stand static there for ever and for ever, long
after words like foolish or any signs or sounds of communication
whatever had passed into the language of antiquity. Incredible
that such suspended and everlasting *being* had been achieved; still
less could one credit this triumph, this absolute, in anonymity: for
Don knew him as only the interrogator is known to the interro-
gated, the confessor to the catechized, the questioner whose questions reveal far more than they seek. And knowing him, knowing
he himself was likewise known, Don yet knew—suddenly—that
he could edge himself up from between the pressing elbows and
shoulders of his neighbors, push to the end of the row, pick his
way down the aisle over the thrust-out pant-legs, mount the platform and confront him face to face; and be not known. The man
would never have seen him before in his life.

This was the more shattering because Don now seemed to
sense that the burden of the talk was himself, the speaker spoke
of him, the name named was Birnam. He listened then so pas-
sionately, with such anxiety and intent, that he began to fear he
would give himself away: that his very act of listening would soon
call the attention of the entire hall to the fact that he was here,
sitting in their very midst, giving ear. Without moving his head
by so much as a hair, he allowed his eyes to glance about from
side to side, and was reassured. They were all listening, like himself; never would his presence become known to them while they

continued to listen in such thrall; he could relax, if he wanted to, but for the fact that his shoulders were held up in the vise of his adjacent fellows; he could faint, and not slip down. But he did not feel like relaxing, he was far from faint. Curiosity burned in him, though not for what the speaker was saying (even if he had forgotten the sense, he anticipated every line and could have prompted the speaker himself): he was on fire to know what the others were getting from that unending foreign harangue, they who could not have forgotten the vocabulary because they had never known it. Whatever it was, it was enough. They did not need to understand; they felt. How they felt it! How they took that incomprehensible tirade and translated it into outrage, as yet still dumb. What kept it dumb so long? Why did they not even murmur their revolt? Were they going to be shocked into an eternity of silence, stricken to inaction, unstrung by the enormity of what the speaker was saying, hypnotized and mute *forever*?

No, they were not.

Heads turned. He saw them throughout the hall, beginning to turn this way and that. Students faced one another (many of them having to lean back to do so), who ordinarily would have averted their gaze, dropped their glances, refused to acknowledge one another eye to eye, cowed by the dark meanings they felt sure were lurking somewhere behind those alien dark words. There was no cowing here; these were not sidelong glances. They dared to look each other in the eye— indeed, did so to confirm suspicions. The fellows on either side of Don turned to him, staring; he stared back, first at one, then the other, and tried to match with his own worked-up stare the look of anger that blazed from under their frowning brows. The boy on his right nodded, a short sharp nod. Don did not know what was meant, but he nodded too. Then he noticed that others were nodding in front of him, and up and down his own row. At the same time, a murmur began somewhere (was it outdoors?), a murmur like humming, like a wordless song crooned at a distance. The murmuring grew, till finally he heard that it came from the two on each side of him, and those beside them, and their neighbors, and theirs, and so throughout the hall. The man on the platform talked on, and the murmurings formed a kind of piquant accompaniment to the solo of unending words. It was the first sign of revolt, as yet unrealized; for the murmuring continued to remain nothing but a medley of murmurs, sustained in a prolonged *legato,* as a new note asserted itself: an odd soft clack-clack-clacking that caused him to glance up into the dust-filled air whence it came.

A plane moved over the crowd, not twenty feet up: a frail silly ramshackle airplane, something less than a crate; a contraption of canvas and lath held together by paste and tacks, with a large shiny clacking propeller lazily revolving like the two-bladed fans on the ceilings of old restaurants—an aëroplane; just such a flimsy fake as he himself had ridden in at Coney Island and Riverview, Playland and Revere, Tivoli, Brighton, and the Prater; a counterfeit flying-machine suspended by long cables from a turning swing, and swung gradually out wider and wider into the air over the heads of the gawping holiday-makers as the swing swung faster and faster, giving you the illusion of flying, though flying in a boat. The craft overhead was not suspended by cables, it moved under its own illusory power, on its own rickety all-but-transparent wings (he could see the clots of glue at the seams, the ribs could be heard to creak and give) as it rode the air serene, slow, unpredictable, like a drifting canoe. It floated low over the crowd as if in search; and now and again, capriciously, it would veer off to one side, the way a water-insect, streaking along the surface of a pond, will suddenly turn and dart off in the opposite direction. But the plane did not streak or dart, it meandered, it took its time, it seemed to know whom it was seeking and whom it would find, and it found him.

No other head turned upward beside and besides his own. No one else seemed to have noticed the gently-riding flying-machine or to have heard the propeller's clacking blade. How they would have looked, had they known! In the body of the ship sat three women, resting comfortably with their forearms on the edge of the cockpit or their bare arms dangling over. They were of no age, neither young nor old; they had long hair of an indeterminate color, flowing down about their ample shoulders; they sat together in pleasant, most amiable, most harmonious concourse; and they were naked. Now and again they turned to glance at one another in silent understanding; and often they smiled.

They smiled at Don. Nothing in this or any world could have been more charming, more gratifying or rewarding, than their collective smile. It was not the smile of mirth, though certainly it was good-humored; it was a smile which said that everything they saw, or heard, or knew, everything that *was,* they approved. They approved of Don sitting there, looking up at them; the murmurs, the turning heads, the anger, the sunlight, the foreign voice—all was right and good and exact; all was in order. And under the indescribable sympathy of that approving smile, he could not but approve likewise.

Again he tried to understand the speaker, tried to disassociate the sense from the incredible terminology he once knew so well. Oh, he understood! But how much better did the others understand who did not comprehend at all; who would have reviled the sense even more than they reviled the words; who had only contempt and blind hatred for knowledge such as this; who despised the speaker as they despised the spoken of, because, in their home-bred hearts, they knew and knew rightly that the cold alien passion of the intellect, the passion of detachment which surveys everything and is moved by nothing, lies with the instincts of death.

Belongs with death. Very well, then!—The murmurs increased. They were not murmurs now, they were threat and protest. They grew in volume, gradual and imperceptible, swelling in a vast long-mounting *crescendo*—still low; not loud—all but lulling to the senses. Hardly fearful, almost weary, he sat waiting for the riot to break. His eyes sought the plane. He located it in a far corner of the hall, turning, coming back, dipping now and again to avoid the trapeze-wound rafters. It shone bright gold as it passed through the vertical blocks of sunlight that stood in the dusty air. Now it was overhead, a little to one side, hovering; and again the women smiled.

He looked up at the women—his heart looked up. He had need of that smile now, and took avidly of it. The women glanced at each other as they saw his distress; their exchange was warm, most friendly; concerned, yet unworried; and when they turned to look down at him again, one of them bent further, bowing in assent, in almost affectionate salute. She leaned against the edge, and her blue-white breast drooped over the side, lolling like a water-filled toy-balloon. Did she then, for a moment only, seem to waver between a rueful shake of the head, and a smile? If so, it was a great deal less than a moment, for now she was smiling as before; and strange little chills of apprehension went down his spine. He knew it was almost time; and he tried to smile back to show that he knew, and accepted.

The murmurs had long since passed into muttering, the muttering was now a great roar. A wind seemed to blow through the hall; the building reverberated, the windows shook, he felt the floor beneath his feet vibrate with the noise. One partly-dangling trapeze jounced on its rope; a basketball-board at the end of the hall flapped back and forth like a punkah; the plane itself rippled and dipped overhead, its flimsy wings squeaking above the din; and the women—smiling, unalarmed—steadied themselves with their hands on each other's shoulders. Out of the bedlam a single word established itself, a word cried out by one, then many, and he glanced quickly at the women to see if that was right, too. It was; he knew without looking, knew without their reassuring almost-maternal smile. It was right that the name "Birnam!" should now be chanted by all that angry youth. Short sharp crashing noises, like baskets bursting, punctuated the general tumult as the flimsy chairs broke up. And all the while, on the platform, it was terrible to see the grey man, whom no one could hear now, going on and on with his interminable dark monotonous lecture, as before a somnolent classroom.

One student rose up, and they all perforce rose up also. Don himself was pulled to his feet by the rising shoulders and hips of his locked neighbors. More chairs gave way; the crash of their collapse rattled like volleys of ancient musket-fire. There were groans of release and relief, even from Don himself (yes, that he could share in), and the thousand throats took up the cry in their single atavistic purpose: "Get Birnam! Get Birnam get Birnam! Get birnam get-birnam getbirnam!" Once more he glanced at the women bobbing above, their white arms holding the sides of the weaving plane. They were moving away now, but the smile reached him still—cool, detached, yet affectionate, accepting and denying him at once.

The building caved in. There seemed to have been a deafening explosion. Had their pent-up massed emotion burst the walls apart, blown them down? Where was the alien speaker, where were the women now? There was a heap of flat ruin, and the crowd was on the campus, in the open air. They stood hesitant, dazed. But only for a second. Once outdoors, in the full sunlight, the obscurantism of the dream vanished, and all was suddenly clear as if they followed a planned design.

The fraternity house was located at the far north-east corner of the campus—they all knew that. That's where Birnam was! That's where they would get him! No words were exchanged, no one took leadership. With a herd understanding, they all moved off at a trot. Without a cry now, without so much as a mutter, they started across the campus; and he ran with them.

The ground shook as from continuous nearby blasting. He

knew that while he ran with the crowd, stayed with them, was
one of them, his presence would go undiscovered. But what of
that moment when they should reach the fraternity house and fail
to find him? Would they not then turn about and discover him
there in their very midst? What could save him from their anger
then?—their double anger for having cheated them of finding
him where they had sought him first. He did not think that far
ahead, he merely ran on.

Was this the end at last?—the pattern completed? Or was
some unfathomable providence saving him for a still juster
destruction? It was like all the unreal times he had come so near
it—seeking it, as he had always been seeking it, unrealizingly—
and been always unrealizingly spared. . . . Like the time when he
came-to on the hard iron catwalk high over the railroad tracks
at Basle (awoke in the blue steaming night and saw the murky
yards beneath flecked with tiny piercing lights of ruby and emer-
ald and topaz shining through the steam, and the trains sliding
in from all over Europe or panting there below as they bided
the hour that marked the time-change between Switzerland and
France); that time he had climbed to the wet slippery vibrating
rail of the *Conte di Savoia* plunging westward in the middle of
the night and dared his Norwegian Anna to prevent his leap to
the boiling wake of the ship (she had walked away, amused, and
he had been left standing there, doing what he would have been
unable to do sober and by daylight, till the gale—which might
have done otherwise—filled his camel's-hair coat and threw him
ignominiously to the rolling deck again); or the nightmare-time
at five in the morning, with a tireless barfly Irish friend—the two
of them all that remained after a gala night at the Suvretta, they
and a drowsy fixed-smiling barmaid who awaited their further
pleasure—the way, then, he had exploded a gas-filled balloon
with his cigarette and ignited the twisted crêpe-paper streamers
strung from floor to ceiling: touched off the whole room with
a sudden hellish roar till the place was all one instant flame—

which immediately, miraculously, went out (sparing not only him, that time, but the several hundred sleepers as well who slept in the rooms above). . . .

Was this, then, the end, this lynching now (for so the dream pointed from the start)? No, it was only the beginning, the first of all those freakish nightmare-times, the foundation of the pattern, laid in dream as in fact, to be repeated endlessly till the one ultimate just end or new beginning. . . .

He was not scared for himself (he had never been, ever). He was only frightened because a dreadful thing was about to happen to them all, of which he, the victim, would be the least to suffer. It was horrible that it had to happen but there was no help for it, no other way out for any of them. He ran on blindly, his heart thumping with an intolerable pity. His one fear was that he might stumble and fall and be trampled underfoot, finding his death in a way that he knew was not right, in a way that was against the will of the crowd, a death accidental and anonymous, contrary to the whole intention of the dream as it had shown itself from the beginning. But if the other were intended and inevitable, why fear falling? He would not fall, and he didn't. He ran on, propelled along at a deadly jog-trot by the single purpose of the mob.

The great buildings of the campus were lost in the clouds of dust that went up from the thousands of running feet. The Liberal Arts and Fine Arts colleges, the Hall of Languages, the Library—dimly he was aware that the crowd flowed past them somewhere in the dust-yellow gloom. They became more and more obscured and were left behind. Above the dull thunder of trampling, he heard the bell in the chapel ringing, the alarum-bell.

Then, a little ahead—still a hundred feet off, perhaps—he began to notice there was some small island that the crowd flowed around. The stream separated at that point and closed again beyond it, and ran again on. A tree, a post? But it was an object moving. Something or someone fought there, going against the crowd, cutting through it—toward him? Over the bent backs and bobbing heads, through the spiraling dust, passing maddeningly in and out of view as the crowd wove around it, he saw the young agonized face, the battling arms, the threshing shoulders, the grinding clenched white-shining teeth of his younger brother.

He might have known. Oh he might have known from the start that Wick would turn up, Wick would appear somehow in just this way, Wick of all people in the world would not let it happen.

He thought he would never reach that point where Wick fought, for the further he ran on, the further Wick seemed to be carried off by the onrushing tide. He might even go down, and be lost to him forever, as he himself was about to be lost to Wick. But the distance between them diminished and soon they were in shouting distance, able to exchange excited violent glances, signals that they had seen each other.

They did not shout. Don took silence from Wick who fought silently on, unwilling to draw the attention of the mob to the fact that his search was ended—and theirs too, did they but know it. The throng swept along oblivious of the one as they were of the other, unaware of the straw that was Wick, struggling in the flood.

They touched hands. In another instant they were together, face to face. The din and fury roared around them but they were met, and suddenly Wick showed none of the buffeting he had taken against the mob. He stood before Don, his clear youthful face heart-breaking to see. His hair was combed smooth and cleanly parted, he had on a white clean freshly-ironed shirt open at the throat, he wore grey flannels as well and a sleeveless sweater of soft pale-yellow cashmere, he smiled—and in that moment the dream was over.

It took Don minutes, minutes, to dream all that took place in that last second before the end—all that took place in him, and in Wick, and between them together. It was truly the longest part of the dream, spinning itself out in timeless suffering while the action sped to its crashing climax so fast he had no time to realize it was ended. But in that second, that tick, he lived whole lives. Till then, he had scarcely been touched by the events of the dream at all, he had never even protested its meaning. Now he suffered what could not be borne.

Wick pressed something into his palm. His fingers closed on a tiny tin box and somehow he knew instantly what it was. His way out—Wick had got it to him in time. In time. But they had no time to speak of it, no time for anything but the handclasp which passed the box from one to the other. There was only time for the radiant smile—and Don read in that smile all Wick's joy, all his passionate relief, to have found and reached him in time.

Nor was there time for Wick to sense the full meaning or consequence of what he was doing, there was time only for his first reflex of joy. Later would come the realization—but he would be from thence. Don's heart burst with pity, then, as he knew that a moment from now Wick's suffering would begin—while he, his own suffering ended, would not be there to comfort him. Far from comforting him (O hell-kite!), he was the cause. Unable to bear the sight of Wick's relief, so soon to break into grief as passionate as his joy, he wrenched free the hand that held the box, snatched with his nails at the tin lid, slammed the pills into his mouth, and awoke in a pool of wet on the floor beside the couch.

How he must have wept. The rug was dark with it. He was weeping still, and could not stop. Worse, there was no release from pain even now, in the stunning realization that it had, indeed, been only a dream and the dream was ended. He knew the dream was a good dream, it told him where help lay and would always lie, but that too was no comfort. He staggered to his feet and fell across the couch, the couch he had fallen from at some point in the dream. He wanted now to die, he would never be able to shake the stifling depression the dream had left with him, it would hang darkly over him as long as he remained alive. He got up and went to the bookshelf for the bottle and drank the hot stuff as fast as it would go down, drank it all. Choking and gagging, with tears streaming from his eyes, he groped his way to the bedroom. He opened the door and fell upon the bed. At once he went off again into a dead sleep, a sleep that lasted, then, till the terrible day began, the day of terror. . . .

PART FIVE

The Mouse

Just before dawn he was awakened by the sound of the street-door slamming three flights below. True, it was no more than a muffled and distant thump, but he wondered how he could have heard it at all, much less been awakened by it.

He lay listening. Footsteps came up the stairs. He heard them on each stairway and landing, and along the hall on each floor. He could not be sure, but there seemed to be two people coming. Yes, he was sure of it now. He heard them ascend the last flight and stop just outside the apartment door.

He lay motionless on his back, his eyes closed, to hear the better. There was nothing more for some minutes. Then the conversation began.

"What are we going to do about Don?"

"Such a pity."

"Something's got to be done."

"We can't go on like this much longer."

"He can't either."

"What are we going to do?"

"What's going to be done?"

"What do you think?"

"What do you?"

"What are we going to do about Don?"

The terrifying thing was that the conversation was carried on in whispers, loud stage-whispers, breathful and sibilant, but whispers all the same. The words carried through the closed door, across the little foyer, and into his bedroom as clearly as if they were being whispered at his very pillow.

He knew it was an hallucination. The beginning of break-down? Delirium is a disease of the night, he remembered. He was hearing things. His ears were made the fools of the other senses. When he opened his eyes and looked at the ceiling, the whisper-ing stopped at once. The moment he closed them again, there was the whispering: *What are we going to do about Don?*

The thing to do was keep your eyes wide open and look at something, concentrate on some object, look hard at it. He raised himself on his pillow and leaned toward the desk and stared fixedly at the small plaster bust of Shakespeare that he had car-ried about with him for many years in all the places he'd been and always been able to hang onto and never lose or forget and leave behind or have to pawn or sell, and the whispering stopped. Maybe he could regain control by trying to recall the other desks and dressers, the bureaus and bookcases and cabinets, the man-tels and armoires and nightstands and tables and shelves the little bust had dominated in its time. It was a complacent smug little face and probably looked no more like Shakespeare than he did or indeed not as much, but he was fond of it. He closed his eyes and lay back on the pillow to test how it was now. The whisper-ers said: *What are we going to do about Don, he can't go on like this forever, something's got to be done. . . .*

He got off the bed and stood up; and as he did so, suddenly he realized that he was loudly clearing his throat, as if to warn the whisperers that he was moving about in his room. Nothing could have made him feel more foolish, he could almost smile about it, for he knew, there wasn't even the faintest question, no, not even in his overwrought state, that no one was there. Standing up, he learned for the first time how weak he was. He was barely able to reach the bedroom door and shut it and get back to the bed again.

Had that done it? But not any number of doors, of course, not a thousand sound-proof vaults, would shut the whispering out. He might as well give up, he might as well listen. His imagination was beginning to generate to the point of delirium, and he might as well give himself up to it. He was beginning to hear and see what normally he would merely think. He lay back and clasped his hands under his head and gave himself up to the whisperers, whose sibilant rustling words were almost soothing, now, to his nerves. He was tired. Perhaps if he resisted no longer and heard them out, they would tire, too, and go away. . . .

What are we going to do about Don?
We can't go on like this any longer.
He can't.
None of us can.
He'll kill himself.
He's killing us, if he only knew it.
He knows it.
Something's got to be done.
He's got to be stopped.
For his own good.
For everybody's.
He can't keep this up much more.
Something terrible will happen.
It's already happening.
What are we going to do about Don? . . .

The full daylight finally drove them away. He did not hear them go. The whispering merely became faint and fainter and died out. "Delirium is a disease of the night." As the light filled the room, the whispering vanished. He would not need to listen any more. He could close his eyes in quiet, now, and sleep.

But sleep was out of the question. His nerves and muscles, the tendons in his legs and arms, were taut as if he had been stretched, and were now so stretched, on a rack. He could not release them. He turned over again and again and assumed positions of lassitude, hoping the sleep would come, or at least rest. But in a moment he was aware that his toes were pointed upward toward his knees, straining, or pointed down, as if stretching to reach the very bottom of the bed. The calves of his legs ached with the strain. He could not relax his feet and toes, allow them to lie natural and quiet in whatever position they fell into. In the next second they were active by themselves, pushing, straining, reaching, as if possessed with some uncontrollable reflex, the way the leg of a killed animal will persist with its own movement after death.

He lay on his back and arched his spine for as long a time as possible and then slumped back on the bed again. The effort would start the flow of the stagnant circulation, and the relaxing would quiet him and perhaps induce sleep. But it did not. Every bone in his body throbbed as if he had been subjected the day before to the most violent and unusual exercise, every muscle ached with its own pain. He was in fear of cramps; and to stave them off, he tried again and again, in vain, to lie loosely flung out, or curled up, or limply flat on his back, in all the positions he could think of for sleep.

He recalled the time he had suffered that cramp, that seizure, that constriction of the leg muscles, in the small hotel at Antibes. He had been lying in the wide bed on just such a bright sunshiny morning as this, wondering how soon one of his beach friends would stop by and thus be able to get him a drink. The calves of his legs throbbed and beat with a life of their own, the tendons constantly pulled the toes up as if he were standing on his heels or drew them down in the *points* of the ballet-dancer. He lay on his back and listened desperately for the tiny rickety cage of the *ascenseur* to rattle up and stop on his floor. The ceiling above the bed quivered with little leaf-like patches of sunlight, reflected from the bright sea outside. Time and again throughout the morning (as through all that dreadful night) the stillness was shattered by a raw deafening two-noted screech that could be nothing less than the rusty gates of Hell grinding open on Judgment Day. The grating blast came from somewhere outdoors. It was earsplitting. It sounded as if some violent giant were pumping at an old-fashioned monster pump. Every time it happened he almost sprang from the bed, but his legs went on working feverishly at their own contractions and refused to obey. Suddenly one of them drew up by itself and he felt a stabbing pain in the side of the calf. He flung off the light quilt and leaned forward, grabbing at the bare leg with his hands. A welt, a lump had arisen. Even as he looked, the lump tightened and twisted, the muscles wound themselves into a turning knot under his very eyes, half as big as his fist. In panic he pinched at it with his fingers and thumb, pounded it, thumped on it, and shot his leg into the air. The knot of flesh untwisted, the hot pain died away, and he fell back, exhausted.

Remembering this, dreading now a recurrence of that painful and frightening constriction, he got out of bed. Walking is what he needed; standing. But he was too weak to stand. Sitting, then. He made his way into the living room and collapsed into the big chair by the window. As he did so, he thought of that nightmare noise at Antibes, and recalled how foolish he had felt when he learned it was a donkey braying in the next garden, the first he had ever heard.

It was full daylight now. It looked like midmorning, but the small traveling clock on the bookshelf at his elbow said only 8:10. What was he going to do about liquor, what was he going to do now? He had to have it, if never before in his life. His senses would certainly leave him if he did not have a drink now. He had to have something to carry him through the weakness of that day and the terror. Three drinks would do it, only three. Two, he'd even take two, yes two, truly no more, he'd swear to stop at two, if only it were given to him to get it. Just this once, and one only. . . .

There was, of course, not a drink in the house. He almost doubted he'd be able to walk as far as the kitchen, even if there were a bottle there. Oh, but not seriously. He'd get it! He'd get there! His mind went back to the money again. Whatever had become of it? Had some demon in him caused him to lose it, some demon of the perverse who saw to it that he threw it away? Had he really spent it all? But even if it should turn up, now, he had

not the strength to make use of it. He could never have made the
stairs, much less get cleaned up first to go out. He had reached the
day he had dreaded from the beginning, the day of despair and
utter debilitation when he was physically unable, finally, to get
himself out of the jam. There was only this one thing to face, this
one thing, and the problem would be solved: *Today was the day
you could simply not drink.*

But how could you become reconciled to watching yourself
lose your mind, how could you stand by and let it happen, how
could you face that? How could you sit there and wait for the
breakdown when you knew that a drink, one drink, would avert
it? Would you not instead find someway to destroy yourself first,
yes even in this helpless condition, rather than suffer what could
not be borne?

Like a released spring he was suddenly up in the chair,
crouched against the back, as a line of fire ran across the rug
toward his feet. He stared in fright, and it was gone. Was this an
hallucination too? No, not in this daylight. Delirium is a disease
of the night. It was an illusion, a prank of the eye, the result of
his over-strung nerves. You often saw flashes out of the corner of
your eye, dancing lights that vanished when you turned in their
direction. Such a thing was this, nothing more, he was sure of it.
He glanced toward the fireplace, and again the streak of fire raced
across the rug. It was as if a path of gasoline had been poured
along the carpet and then touched with a match. It was so bright,
so like flame, that it seemed to be the only color in the room,
like the orange-red fire in the Aetna advertisements. Tentatively
he lowered his feet and sat watching, then; watching the whole
length and expanse of the rug. So long as he kept his eye on it—

Physically he knew he was in dangerous shape. His pounding
heart seemed continually about to stop. It thumped and missed,
but did not go all the way to oblivion. It pounded with such frantic insistence that he was unable to get in any position, sitting,
lying, leaning, where he could not hear it. He felt it strike against

the wall of his chest in irregular alarming tattoo, but what was more intolerable still is that he heard it, heard it as plainly as if his own ear were pressed against his breast: a disorderly thumping, sometimes loud, sometimes soft, sometimes even missing whole beats—and quiet for so long that he would sit up in sudden panic and listen wildly for it to go on.

"He died a thousand deaths"—aaah! Worse by far than a thousand, it was *one* death drawn out in endless torture, a death that didn't die. You kept on dying, and dying; you died all day and all night; and still there was dying yet to do, and more dying ahead—it simply did not end and would never end. It was more than the human heart could bear, or the brain: it was conscious insanity—any moment now his brain would burst with terror and he would go mad. But it didn't burst, he didn't go blessedly mad, he crouched there raw and alive, his eyes staring to see if the familiar room would go blank in breakdown, his ears straining to hear the first crack or rattle of total collapse. The telephone rang.

The noise stabbed his bladder and bathed his thighs with hot urine, but he was unable to move or care. The telephone rang from the bedroom, and rang out, and rang out. It sounded red; orange-yellow; like the nerve-shattering bell that rings in the subway when a train is about to pull out; like the screaming alarm of the prison-break. It was not bad. It could be borne. He knew what it was and that it would be no worse. Present fears were less than horrible imaginings. This was something he could take, perhaps even pin his mind on.

He did not think who it might be. He merely listened. The still rooms rang with the metallic summons but he had no intention of answering. Certainly he had not the strength. Finally it ceased. At once the silence became as clamorous as the lately-jangling 'phone. He undid his belt and his fly, unbuttoned his shorts, and slid both pants down his legs to his feet. For the time being, this was as much of an effort as he could make. He sat back in a trance of exhaustion.

The 'phone rang again. It was like a sting. It stung him to alertness as before. He listened, raw with suspense, to the long ringing beat and the long pause, the long beat and the long pause, over and over in the nerve-wracking monotony of the automatic dialing system. To regain control, he tried to concentrate on listening to the silent spaces between. Were they longer than the rings? He tried to measure them by counting. During each pause (and each time he was more hopeful), there was a moment of breathless anxiety when he began to hope the pause might extend itself another second, and another, and still another, or one more, till the stillness erased the ringing altogether and took over the house once more. The ring came again.

Telephones didn't ring like that at home, not in his mother's house when he was a boy. They were short, or long, or anyway irregular, depending on the operator; and sometimes you even knew which operator was on duty by the way the 'phone rang. Madge always gave three short rings, Doris a couple of long ones. . . .

It was good thinking of home. He thought of it deliberately now—thought of home with passion. . . . He saw himself sitting in the front-pew of the chancel, on the men's and boys' side, wearing his clean-smelling choir-vestments: the long black cassock and the white linen stiffly-starched cotta—he felt the pinch and chafe of the Buster Brown collar as he turned to watch the minister preparing the communion. From across the red-carpeted aisle, on the women's side, he heard his mother's voice among all the others, the warm alto voice that reached the farthest corner of the nave as surely as the most piercing soprano. He looked at her where she sat among the other women and girls. She smiled back at him, her perfect teeth gleaming, and gave him the smallest wink. He had heard it said that Mr. Harrison often declared, yes even to his wife, that he only came to church on Sundays to look at Mrs. Birnam in the choir; and he wondered if it were true. . . . The church was filled with sunlight, it was a wonderful summer

Sunday morning. The sun streamed in through the yellowish-green stained-glass windows and bathed the congregation in a soft sub-marine light, as if the whole place were under water. Beyond the communion rail, his little brother Wick knelt at the altar, his hands at his side, not leaning against anything, and Don could see that the hem of his white cotta trembled ever so slightly. Wick was waiting to help Mr. Brittain with the service, and Don was waiting to tell Wick after church (and so too, probably, was their mother) that his sloppy plaid socks showed beneath the skirt of his cassock. Behind the wall in back of the men's side he could hear the muffled thump and pound of the wooden pump that sustained the breath of the organ. . . . The minister was ready to serve the choir. His mother rose with the other women and went to the altar rail, where they knelt in a row on the red-carpeted step. All the heads were bowed, now, except hers. She looked straight before her, her elbows on the rail, her hands clasped under her chin. She seemed lost in thought, and so was he, as he gazed at his beautiful mother, lovely with the clear profile, the straight nose, the soft cheeks—the soft, pink, rose-like cheeks. . . .

The telephone was ringing again. He had no way of knowing how long his little excursion into the past, his deliberate revery, had lasted. It had not been refreshing or helpful; or if it had, the ringing of the 'phone wiped it at once all away, woke his aching nerves, his rioting heart, his fears of what was going to happen to him now. The telephone rang on. Was there possibly one small infinitesimal sip in the bottom of the sticky bottle standing there on the table? If there were, he was unable to reach it; and he knew only too well that the sip or drop, had there been one, would in his present need prove a greater aggravation than none at all.

Now it came to him suddenly that he had not eaten. He had eaten not a single bite of food since before Wick left—how many days ago? He was never able to eat when he was drinking; it was the last thing he ever thought of and the last thing he wanted; and the thought of food now—even knowing that food, if he had it, might help him out of his weakness and so enable him to go out and get drink somewhere—made him retch. Was it possible to go without food so long and still be upright? He knew it was, it had happened many times. He thought of the sandwich he had started to buy a day or so ago (when was it?) and wondered what had prevented him. No food in all that time. But he couldn't think of it or wonder about it, because now a new thought possessed him: Interminable and agonizing though the long day would be, it was bound to end, sometime, somehow, and darkness would finally fall. What did that not mean? Delirium was a disease of the night, yes; but also—oh, worse!—delirium never came while you were drinking. Only after you had stopped. That was the terrible thought. He had stopped. And there was no way of starting again. Unable to go out and get liquor, trapped here the whole day without it, what would tonight be like? It was a prospect so terrifying that at once he tried to busy himself, occupy his mind, with something to do.

He leaned down and disentangled his trousers and shorts from where they lay in a heap over his shoes. He lifted them up and dropped them a little to one side, off the rug. Some men there are, when the bagpipe sings i' the nose, cannot contain their urine. . . . That's the way it had been when the 'phone rang that first time, the 'phone that had been ringing ever since; that's the way it nearly always was in the subway when the suddenly screaming bell, like a spurt of white metallic fire, struck at your brain and your loins. He looked at the pants and shorts lying in a heap beside the bookcase, and wondered: was it the first time he had had them off—since when? He dimly remembered changing his clothes once, when was that?—and then wasn't it only his shirt? In the bathroom sometime? It was useless to try to remember. He recalled nothing, not one thing, of all the events of all the days since he had started drinking, the day Wick left. Each day's drinking had wiped out the day before, it always did, always—and who could understand the blessing of that? The blessing and sometimes the terror—terror because you lived always in a state of mortal apprehension of some dreadful deed committed for which, though you were called to account, you could never bear witness. And who would ever believe that? I'm responsible, yes, but I'm not responsible; I did it, I; but it *was* not I; it wasn't *I*. . . .

Only one understood this, only one out of all the people he knew, the few friends he had left. Helen. She and she alone knew that he was literally not himself when drinking, knew that he was not to be held accountable for what he said and did. It was somebody else who did and said these things, not Don. When he turned up at her house drunk and asked her to marry him, she wouldn't listen; wouldn't listen to him at all, though that was what she wanted of him more than anything else in the world. She knew better than to listen to him at such a time. (What matter that he never asked her otherwise? She wouldn't have him that way.) She knew a great deal better than a romantic friend of theirs who had the oh ideal solution, why don't you live with him, that's all he needs, take a place together and live with him, he's lost and lonely, he needs love, he needs you, why don't you just live with him? Helen wouldn't listen to that, either. He needed love all right (who didn't?), but he had to get back to himself first in order to know what love was and to know that he wanted it. She knew better, too, far better and wiser and more honest (with herself as well as with him) than those who advised her: "Marry him and reform him." Many a woman would jump at the chance, they'd love the idea, they'd marry the guy and reform him. Not Helen. She spotted it at once for what it was: taking advantage of a man when he was down; and certainly she wouldn't have him under those conditions. If any "reform" was to be done, she knew it would have to be done on his own entirely—not for her, but for himself first. If that should ever come about, *then* she might listen; but until then—

In drink, he was not Don. Helen knew this even to the extent of knowing that he himself would be just as shocked or upset as she was by some reckless act committed while he was in his cups, when he learned about it later (for certainly he didn't know about it at the time). Which is why she never reproached him for drinking when he was drinking, why she never uttered a word of complaint or protest, at least not to him. She would string along with him patiently and pretend to believe his lies and his fancies; sit listening to him when, out of whim, he wanted to read to her, even though she understood scarcely a syllable of his confused babble; go with him when he suddenly wanted to take in a movie or play which he was in no condition to comprehend and which, in the middle, he would up and leave; follow him as best she could in all his impulsive caprices and inspirations, patiently waiting the while for him to come back to himself, and to her. She would take him in when he came to her house very drunk, take him in and take care of him (though it was like having as house-guest an elusive and cunning hysteric), feed him and nurse him without blame through several days of hangdog hangover, and then, when he was restored and his ego began to function once more, kick him out. The times he had been kicked out of Helen's house and told never never to come back again, she was belly-sick of it—her word; a word all the stronger, all the more telling, because it was so unlike her. He often complained that she was so much nicer to him when he was drunk than when he was sober and behaving himself, what was the idea anyway, what was the use of trying to make an effort, what did it get you but a kick in the teeth? And she would reply, with that simplicity of hers that spoke volumes: "When you're all beaten down with drink, you need me. You're humble then, and want me. But soon's you come out of it, you don't need me any more."

The telephone was ringing but he was thinking of something else now and almost didn't hear it. He was thinking of the plays they had suddenly gone to on the spur of the moment and as suddenly got up and left, how he had talked all the way uptown from the Village about what a gifted actress the star was, hadn't Helen

seen her in *Sandalwood* and *Spellbound,* or *Mariners* hadn't she
seen *Mariners,* or God *They Knew What They Wanted,* lord what
an artist, the greatest woman in the theater of our time; and then
at the play, his wandering attention, his increasing restlessness,
his feeling that he would suffocate if he didn't get another drink
at once, his suddenly having to get up and leave before the second
act and Helen leaving too without a word, oh she'd leave all right,
of *course* she would leave, wasn't she afraid of his going out and
getting started again, didn't that come before all the artists in the
world? And even as his anger rose (the two of them going up
the dark aisle), his pity rose too, it was such a rotten shame that
Helen couldn't once, just once, enjoy a play with him. . . . He was
thinking of those times when he felt the necessity of reading to
her, when he read to her for her own good, read something she
ought to know, something he himself was crazy about and damn
it *she* had to know it and love it too! He would read on and on
(the favorite short-story or the passage out of the great novel) and
the words wouldn't come right or at least not come out of his
mouth right, he himself heard the unnatural elisions and the con-
sonants slurred and blurred but went right on just the same, just
as if he were articulating perfectly; and Helen, though she was
a poor dissembler, ignored the stumbling thick speech the same
as he and pretended to understand. And when he had finished
and exclaimed "Isn't it *wunderbar*" and accepted her nod, how he
could curse himself then for having mutilated the beautiful passage, for not having been sober enough to take advantage of this
opportunity to reveal the passage to Helen, for having ignored his
own dreadful speech, for having pretended to accept Helen's pretense, and for having used the word *wunderbar.* . . . He was thinking most and bitterly of those times when he had asked Helen to
marry him, call up your father, let's call him up right now, this
very second, tell him we're going to get married this weekend,
or tonight! He felt like a hound, then, when he saw the tears in
her eyes as she smiled and shook her head and refused to talk,

and he wanted to marry her all the more, wanted to marry her at once, now more than ever (and the thing that hurt him as he said it was that he knew she wouldn't take him and he didn't blame her a bit, no not one single bit, though he loved her more than he ever did before, truly loved her now, right now at this moment, and ached for the day when they would somehow, someway, get together). And while she turned away to busy herself with something so that he couldn't see her eyes, he would go on and on picturing the wedding (to cover her embarrassment as well as his own, yet knowing that he was wounding her more than ever and for Christ's sake why couldn't he stop!), the wedding that was to take place as soon as it could be arranged, they'd get his brother as bestman, Wick would be so happy, Wick would be so pleased (God was he marrying Wick!), they'd go to The Little Church Around the Corner, he'd always wanted to be married at the—oh Jesus didn't he ever know when to stop!

No wonder she would kick him out as soon as he was able to be on his feet again, no wonder she wouldn't have him around to mock with his silence the theme he couldn't harp enough on the other night, the imperial theme that was always happy prologue, nothing more. . . .

But that was all long ago. Years. Two anyway. He never went near her house any more; not when he was drinking. He knew better; thank God he knew enough to avoid people when he was drinking now, especially Helen. He was never going to let her see him like that again, give her a chance to take care of him only to throw him out. The times she had thrown him out! He wished he had a dollar for every time he had been kicked out of Helen's house! He wished he had a bottle for every one of those times! or a glass! or a jigger!

The telephone began again. It had been silent for a while, but now it rang as if for the only time that morning, as if this were the most important call of all. He shut his eyes and gritted his teeth. He thought of how Central at home (was that another world, another lifetime?) had sometimes given him a ring on Sunday afternoon and said he'd better hurry if he wanted to get Dorothy for a date, Harry Fox was trying to call her now and her line was busy. . . .

Reveries of home. . . . Sentimental tears slid out from under his closed lids as he saw himself standing, now, in the new Scout uniform, his first, with a crowd of other children of all ages on the wide front lawn of the vast old red-brick high-school. The Scoutmaster and principal and some of the teachers were handing out stiff cotton flags to each one and arranging the children into groups according to grade, in double-file. It was Decoration Day, a bright hot May morning, full summer already. How proud he was, then, when the Scouts were all taken out of their respective grade-groups and moved up front to head the procession. He did not even envy Harold Jenkins who carried the big flag of the Troop with the gold eagle on top and a white bathrobe-cord swaying around the fluttering folds. It was enough to be in uniform and up front with the rest—let somebody else lead or carry the flag; time enough for that when he was older. Down-street the band began to play. His heart nearly burst. They were to join the old soldiers and the band in front of the park and march from there to the cemetery. The Scoutmaster blew his whistle and they started out. . . . The stores were all closed, the long shades drawn, sunlight glared hot and white on the store-fronts. People lined the sidewalks, waving flags. Ahead of them, several open cars moved slowly off, carrying the mayor and the ministers and the superintendent of schools in their Sunday clothes. They each held a small flag and waved it to the crowd; they wore big badges on their lapels with forked satin ribbons; the cars were festooned with red-white-and-blue streamers and the wheels were wound with them. Behind marched the old soldiers, some thirty or forty wonderful white-haired old men, straight and proud. Their uniforms were dark blue, almost black; some of them had on funny little tilted caps that looked crushed-in at the front, one or two

wore those long pointed hats like fancy-dress admirals, the curv-
ing top edged with a kind of white brush. All carried swords.
Harold Jenkins' grandfather was there, and Melvin Ostler's,
and a lot of the kids'. . . . At the cemetery, under the elm trees
and willows sifting sunlight down on the flower-decked graves
that were each like individual gardens, they grouped themselves
about the uneven ground and the mayor said a speech from the
bunting-draped platform and someone read a prayer and taps
were sounded: old Mr. Bickerton came forward and raised his
dented brightly-polished bugle and blew taps. Everybody took
off their hats. He stood there listening, while chills ran down his
spine. He looked at Mr. Peech the Scoutmaster standing a little
apart with bowed head, and a wave of affection, of love, swept
over him. What a wonderful and good man he was, what a fine
father he would make! To have a father like that— The sound
of the taps died away, and a group of eight old soldiers came forward and fired a salute. The bright morning was shattered by the
crash; and a second later, in the stunning silence that followed, the
sharp *craack* came again as the volley was given back by the railroad embankment beyond the graveyard. The faint blue-white
smoke curled out of the rifles and rose in the sunshine, drifting
among the trees and turning light and dark as it floated through
sunbeam and shade. His nostrils tingled pleasantly with the wonderful pungent smell of the gun-power. . . .

His longing to be home, home at last, home for good, was so
great it became despair, then desperation. The telephone rang.
Christ he was going *nuts* with sentimentality! Self-pity like this
would drive him to suicide! Or was it someone else he wished to
destroy in destroying himself? His interest in this, his knowledge
that it might be so, his consciousness of it at all, made him believe
it would never come to pass—just as his belief that a drunk is
capable of violence short of murder might prevent that violence
and certainly that murder. But did this include murder of oneself?

If his mother knew that he sat here now thinking wanting needing death; if Wick knew, or Helen; if Mrs. Wertheim, Sam and Gloria, the Kappa U brothers, the ladies in the front apartment just beyond that wall, M. Mc., the teller at Juan-les-Pins, the foolish psychiatrist, any Mr. Rabinowitz—who would believe it? Every one! Not one had reason to doubt he would ever reach such a pass; not one but knew (if they were wise or knowing at all) that this was his logical end and what was he waiting for? Every one of them had seen or could have seen that he had had the seed of self-destruction in him; and given time— All who had known him surely knew; expected nothing less; waited merely for the word. All were ready with the "Too bad but he's much better off" or "Only wonder is he didn't do it sooner."

All? Dorothy too? Anna? Miss Dawson? No, never Dorothy. Not Anna, really. Certainly not Miss Dawson. Dorothy he had deliberately not been in touch with since he was in his 'teens, Dorothy he had let believe what she would believe always. Anna had pushed him away from her before he got to be the mess he was now, while he still had a chance. Miss Dawson could go on building a rosy life for him (and probably had) beginning and ending with the charming childish promise he showed (oh lord it made you sick to think of it) at eight. Eight for Christ's sake!

"I honestly think you're going to amount to something rather wonderful," Dorothy had said when he left home; and then added, but as if to herself: "even though I'm not sure of my own place in the picture." And he? What had he answered. To his shame he spoke as if in bashful protest (hearing only the first half of what she had said, not hearing at all the rest of it, the little rueful thought of self): "*Dor*othy!"—as much as to say "Oh go way with you" or "Flatterer." To his shame. But everything about Dorothy was to his shame; not because he had allowed her to love him as he had not loved her, so long that she had never been able to love anybody else again, but because he had allowed her to believe in him. Would she believe in him now? Believe that he was finally about to put into effect the one real accomplishment that had been delayed too long? . . .

Or Anna—would she? Anna who had said "I am not good for you, go back and find that Helen you talk about so much till I am bored," meaning it of course and thinking thereby to do him the final good she hadn't been able to do him in any other way. But how much more good had she done him (without knowing it) when she uttered that pronouncement on the boat, the question and indictment she couldn't have begun to appreciate the full meaning of herself, though the answer and sentence if honest would affect her as much as it did him. . . . The week before they sailed they had played around for five days in Paris, played with Kees all over town, here and there all night and most of the day; and one evening, dancing with Anna at Armenonville, she had said, suddenly serious, "There is a question I will ask you when we are on the boat." His heart sank, but he smiled and said "Tell me now." She shook her head. "No, I want to wait till we are away from here, by ourselves. On the boat I will ask you." He wanted to hear it then, he asked her again when they got back to their table, because it was bound to be serious and he wanted her to bring it out with Kees there, Kees to whom he could turn and laugh and kid with about the whole thing, kidding Anna out of it whatever it was. But no, she would wait till after they had sailed; and then, the first night out, in her cabin, while his heart thumped because of what it might turn out to be, she said it: "Why do you only come to bed with me when you are drunk?" He roared with delight. He knew damned well she had reason to ask; but in his relief that it had been no worse he was able to laugh as if it were terribly funny and he almost shouted "Because I'm *always* drunk!" She wasn't convinced, he knew that, not the way she looked at him; but at the end, because of the way he neglected her in New York, Anna had seen that he was finally in Helen's hands again and probably safe, his European education over at last. Certainly he was headed for no such fulfillment as this. . . .

No such thing had ever entered the dreamy head of Miss Dawson either, who took such a fancy to him in the 2nd Grade that he hadn't been able to live it down for the rest of his life but would today for good and all. "My dear Mrs. Birnam," she wrote in her lovely Palmer-method hand, "I would just like to say something which no doubt you already know and that is that you have a boy whom you can well be proud of on his eighth birthday. He is the most perfect child in the schoolroom I have ever known and the most winning and sweet besides being so bright. I sincerely hope that Dame Fortune will smile on him and Good Luck attend him through a long and happy life. Most sincerely, Ruth Dawson."

Eight! Fool that she was, idiot, maudlin old maid to write such a letter! the letter that hung over his head ever since, preserved and shown to him every time he went home. Let her see him sitting here panting sweating shaking now, let Anna see him! *Good creatures, do you love your lives? Here is a knife like other knives. . . .* You people who build fond hopes for the promising, who look on the well-favored young and know—know—that here is one that will go far (oh far indeed)—let it be a lesson to you all! What right had they to take such advantage of him at eight? What right at eighteen? Sickening words that actually had pleased him. Miss Dawson and Dorothy (and how many more?)—*I need but stick it in my heart. . . . And all you folk will die. . . .*

Eight. It was scarcely the age of reason, much less the beginning of wisdom. That had come at ten, when his father left. Wisdom of a sort. And not when he left, either; but months after, when he began to realize he was never coming back. Okay for him to realize it, he could take it; but nobody else must know—nobody. People did, though. They stopped him on the street to ask, neighbors called him in their back doors to give him a cookie and ask, "Is your papa coming home for Thanksgiving?" "Oh yes, Papa's coming home, he always comes home on holidays." "He wasn't home for Labor Day." "*That* isn't a holiday! Not like Thanks*giv*ing." "The 4th of July is." "Yes, but Papa couldn't get a—I think they call it a reservation. But he's coming home Thanksgiving, all right." He kept it up, right up to the very day, knowing all the while— And then, Thanksgiving over, people began again. "Is your papa coming home for Christmas?" After a while, they stopped asking; and then his shame began in earnest, because then they knew.

At noon the doorbell began to ring. The sound froze him in his chair. What was the foul-fiend up to now? The buzzer that released the lock on the street-door was in the kitchen, but he could not have made it if his life depended literally upon it. And what of it? He would not have pressed the buzzer even if it had been at his elbow. He listened to the long insistent drone of the bell. What had he done yesterday, what recklessness or tampering or damage had he been up to, what outright crime? Was it someone come to question him, accuse him, take him away perhaps? Finally the bell ceased, but it left a void of silence that was heavy with threat. Now what, now what. . . . He was soon to find out.

There were footsteps in the hall, ascending the last flight. Someone rapped on the apartment door.

He looked wildly about him. It was broad daylight, the room was filled with sun, there was no question this was real. He knew it was true, was happening, even as he thought—almost longingly, now—of the whisperers of the early morning. He crouched back in his chair and stared across the room and through the foyer at the doorknob of the outer locked door—fixed it with his eye, in panic. The rapping came again; to his horror he saw the doorknob turn back and forth; and Helen's voice called softly: "Don. Don. Are you in there, Don?"

If he coughed now, if his heart thumped any louder, if he so much as let go his breath—

"Don. Won't you let me in?"

Oh, it was her voice all right!

"You are there, aren't you Don?"

The doorknob rattled.

"It's Helen, Don. Please open the door."

The voice was low and pleading; not loud, not demanding, not even reproachful.

"I've only got a little while, Don, I wish you'd please let me in. Please."

There was an uncertain note in the voice now, he was winning, he was fooling her, she had begun to believe he wasn't there. If he could hang on another moment—

"Don, are you there, won't you answer? I want to help you." A pause. "I only want—"

She didn't finish that one. He waited in agonized suspense; and after a moment, only a moment more, the doorknob stopped turning, the footsteps moved off.

He was almost faint with relief. But as he heard her going down the stairs and away—taking with her the help he needed so badly—he wanted to cry out "Come back! come back!" The Helen he knew so well and for so long, who loved him and whom he loved and would always love, she who had been through so much with him that they could never grow apart, no, no matter how much he shut her out and shut himself out too— He wanted her now, wanted to call out "Come back, don't leave me! Come back!" Wanted to but never would, never in this world, never never, not if he were sitting here bleeding to death from twenty wounds. He would gladly have died at this moment rather than face Helen, or anyone. But Helen above all.

He understood it, now; saw what had been going on. It was Helen who had been ringing him all morning. From the office; from work. Perhaps she had been in touch with Wick, by 'phone from the farm; Wick had asked her to find out about him; she would have done it in any case, on her own, knowing he was on the loose. She must have been convinced he was there in the apartment and would eventually answer, or was out and would soon return, the way she had called so often. During her lunch-hour she came over to see for herself. When he didn't answer the doorbell, she had gained admittance by ringing some other apartment, perhaps, or seeing Dave the janitor. Then she had come upstairs and rapped on the door and tried the knob and called to him, thinking her words—thinking the sound of her voice—might—

How little people knew! How little they ever knew or understood! (His fists closed in anger.) How could they know what he was suffering! How could they know he would never be able to answer the door or the telephone! How could he explain it to them even! Would telling them tell them why! (He poured the words out in anguished angry whispers.) How could they ever understand! How could people—anyone!—those walking by on the street outside—the two ladies cooking their lunch in the front apartment—the ignorant innocent riders on the L train half a block away—how could they know the hell that was going on in this room! His friends here, his brother at the farm, his mother at home, how could they sense or know of the gathering panic that was any moment about to burst the walls out! How could Helen if she came into this room and saw him with her very eyes, how could she see the breaking-point that had been reached here or the taut brain that was ready to snap! The telephone rang.

She was back. Back at the office, back at work, back at it, back at him. Or she had stopped in a drugstore—what difference does it make? She would 'phone and 'phone and 'phone, the bell would ring him into the next world, *that* was the way she was helping him—could she possibly know that? Or know it even if told? His mind recoiled and plunged again into the past, as into a cooling stream. . . .

Holidays, Sundays, days of no school. . . . He was coming down over Wylie's Hill, coming home, after a hike into the country to his favorite haunt. He had lingered there half the morning, reluctant as always to leave the lovely spot, his own discovery and place. It was a little glen. There was a willow grew aslant the brook, that showed its hoar leaves in the glassy stream. He could daydream here forever, imagining that beautiful and muddy death—realer to him by far than anything that took place in life. The fantastic garlands had floated off and were now wedged at the rim of the tiny dam, the coronet of weeds still hung from the drooping bough, and here was the reed-like broken limb that had dropped her to the brook. He saw the thin clothes spread wide, ballooning with air; he heard the tunes, so innocent, so ribald; and then the garments, growing heavy with water, lowered the frail figure to the gentle mud beneath. But still the pretty dress billowed around her, the hands moved restless and fitful, the lovely zany face still showed in the stream, quivering and blurred, but smiling still. . . . He had lingered there too long, as usual; past noon. It was Thanksgiving, a freakishly perfect day, balmy and dry as early fall. From Wylie's Hill he could see the town spread out below, the familiar loved town where everybody in the world knew him and had always known him, where he had so many uncles and aunts who were no relation to him whatever that the neighborhood, indeed the village, was one great family. As he came down the hill and crossed the railroad tracks, he began to smell the dinners cooking, the dinners that today would all be alike, yet none so good as the dinner cooked by his mother. She would be working at it now, as she had been since early morning. When he got home he would go to the kitchen and help himself to celery and radishes and take them up to his room while he read and waited for dinner. . . .

The defaulters, the renegers, the backward-lookers, the adolescents, the ungrownups. . . . He was a life-term member of that motley and ludicrous crew: uncles cousins fathers husbands brothers sons dear friends promising friends—always promising. Not so damned motley either, since they were all crossed the same, following so consistently the same pattern and history from oh way back. They were the loved ones (usually); oddly, too, the well-favored. As children they were loved of their parents, their mothers especially; and if they were one of several, they were the ones most loved. ("I've wept over you more than any of the others"—but all they felt was a guilty pride and pleasure at their power to damage.) They were the brightest in school (usually), the intelligent, the quick to learn, never the studious. They tried their hands at many talents; and though they didn't get anywhere, their friends cover this up for them now by speaking of them as "clever," they say they have "personality," they say "So-&-so would go far if only he'd apply himself," or "So-&-so is a queer duck, what he needs is a good wife," and often "*Sure* he's got brains but what good does it do him?" Brains indeed and indeed what good does it do them? Dreamy tosspots, they stand all afternoon in a 2nd Avenue bar looking at the sun-patterns under the L or their own faces in the mirror; they do good but not good enough work on the paper and dream of the novel they're certainly going to get around to someday; they stand behind a desk on the lecture-platform lecturing with loving and fruitless persuasion to students watching the clock; throughout whole evenings with sinking heart they sit watching their wives over the edge of a book and wondering how, how, how had it ever come about; they live in and search the past not to discover where and at what point they missed the boat but only to revel in the fancied and fanciful pleasures of a better happier and easier day; they see not wisely but too well and what they see isn't worth it; they eat of and are eaten by ennui, with no relief from boredom even in their periodic plunges from euphoria to despair or their rapid rise back to the top again. They wake up on mornings such as this, all but out of their minds with remorse, enduring what others call and can call a hangover—that funny word Americans will joke about forever, even when the morning-after is their own.

The humor of the hangover: the hilarious vocabulary: the things other drinkers call what they suffer then—the things *they* can call it who endure the normal reaction, merely, of a few hours of headache, butterfly-stomach, and (crowning irony!) nausea at the thought of another drink. The jitters, the ginters, the booze-blues, the hooch-humps, the katzenjammers; the beezy-weezies, screaming meemies, snozzle-wobbles, bottle-ache, ork-orks, woefits, the moaning after. It was ghastly funny, oh hilarious!—He looked about the room as if he had not seen it before, as if he had just come awake. On the floor by the fireplace where he had flung it was the James Joyce that had started the whole thing, if start he had needed: the spell that was ending in anything but riot. Riot, God, it was lethargy, torpor, stupor! Atrophy; except for the violent heart, gradual petrification; slow death. And there on the table were the souvenirs of the spree (spree!), the trophies of the toot (bat, bout, binge, bender, bust, tear, souse, lark, pub-crawl, wing-ding, randan), the empty sticky bottles, the dead soldiers. Dead soldiers—Christ how could they joke or make light of such a taunting crazing thing as an empty bottle, the bottle so lately filled with that which was his hell to have but his life all the same, empty now before his eyes, mocking him with its shouting emptiness, degrading him, reducing him to a shattered broken wreck which could only be restored by the very stuff that destroyed him again. But to be thus destroyed! What would he not give for such destruction now! A jigger of it, two fingers, no more!

And yet was there one soul, among all the people he knew, who would give him that drink, if they could? Would Wick, would Helen? Even knowing, as they did know, how he needed it, what it would do for him? There was not one.

In a kind of self-abuse that was almost ease to his torment, he allowed himself to dwell, for as long as he could stand it, on the dream of drink.

Suppose a bottle should materialize before him full and unopened. Once assured of its reality, how calmly then, all excitement gone, he would open it and pour, almost not needing it in the security the sight of it gave him. But he would drink it, of course. He wouldn't care how bad it tasted—un-iced, without water or soda, lukewarm, stinking, throttling. He would drink a good half-glass at once—and at once the pricking nerves would die down, the thumping heart quiet, the fatigue and ease come warmly over him at last. That's what liquor and only liquor could do for him on the mornings after, that's why he had to go on and on, it was necessity. Half a glass and he would be at peace, as calm as if he had not been drinking for weeks. With a drink under his belt again, he would see differently, hear right, feel normal and relaxed. His mind would begin to work and notice and take stock. He would be aware of hunger, and wish to do something about it. He would get up and bathe and dress. He would certainly answer that ringing telephone, walk right up to it and pick up the receiver and answer it, saying (his voice composed and friendly, showing no trace of tension or guile): "Have you really been calling all this time, I'm so sorry, I've only just come in, fact is I was about to ring you up myself, how are you, Helen, what is it?" He knew how it would be. He knew he could get away with it, fool her, fool anybody, it didn't make any difference what he said, it cost so little and made her feel better, might as well reassure her now, he was safe with all that distance between them, safe while they were at two ends of a telephone wire, she wasn't going to be around to check up on him or reproach him; for he knew he was bound to miss or avoid the appointment they would make to meet later, the appointment he himself would propose, to reassure her—just as he had missed being here when Wick came back to take him to the farm. He knew all that; and he knew, too, that that one drink would not be his last, nor that bottle, now that he was on his feet again.

So much for the beginning. Then he would have another, because he knew that the effects would shortly wear off and he'd be right back where he started, raw and shaking in this chair. He would pour a larger drink, this time, and maybe take more time with it, while his mind began to pick up alertly, alarmingly (he knew that), and suggest a hundred different things to do. He would feel great, then, and ready for anything. He'd have another drink before he started out, his hunger would vanish and all thought of food would vanish too, he'd grab his hat and give a last

look in the mirror and run lightheartedly down the stairs, bound
for who knows what pleasure or danger? That, he did *not* know.
From then on, only one thing was certain. Tomorrow morning
(provided he got home safe) would find him in this chair again,
more desperate, if possible, than now; on the borderline itself.

No one knew this in all the world better than he did. But no
one else in all the world knew, either, why he would do this, or
what he would get out of it. What if he did end up in this chair
again, in this same crazed state? The hours of respite were worth it
even if they flung him back worse than he was now—and besides,
he lost all track of that fact during the respite hours. The curse of
the thing, and the blessing too, was that he promised himself to
take one drink, or at the most a couple, only to relieve the fright
of his tension and stave off collapse; he took it as a medicine; and
then, the medicine in him, he was whole again, ready once more
to start out. An endless chain, of course; a vicious circle if ever
there was one; a helpless series of processes in which the original
disorder creates a second which aggravates the first and leads to
a third, a third which makes inevitable and necessary a fourth,
and so on till the nadir of such a day as today is reached—and *this*
is not the bottom, this unhuman torture of now, this wanting to
start all over again, even though he well knew that a fifth depth
and a sixth were yet to be sounded. He knew all that, he was no
fool like other people (they who believed his promises when he
knew better than to believe them himself); and knowing it, he
yet craved the drink that would bring the whole ruin down upon
him again.

And what of the passing and lost, the uncounted and unre-
coverable days used up in those depths, the time that went down
the drain and never came back? What thing was there in all the
world that could ever repay you for those days? Who knew besides
yourself the panic-feeling of stopping suddenly in the middle of a
morning's fright to ask: What day is it? Often what month, what
season? To ask, but to ask no one but yourself; because you could

not have admitted you didn't know. Had you lost track of ten
days, or one? Not only lost track, but not had them at all. Was it
March or September? And wasn't that using up life frightfully
fast, or—worse than fast—unaware? Time was all you had, all
anyone had, and you weren't counting, you let it slip by as if the
unused day or week might offer itself over again tomorrow. But
it didn't and couldn't—it had been used even though you hadn't
used it. Had you no better use for precious time than that? What
are you if the chief good and market of your time be but to drink
and sleep? Hadn't you in youth often cried out what a day to
be alive? And how many days had there been, since, when you
weren't even able to long for death? Why ask how many? You
could never say, you had lost count too long ago. The lost lost
days, so many that you were something a good deal less than your
thirty-three years, many months less, whole gaps and periods of
your life taken out in blank—most shameful and wanton waste of
all, because nothing could ever give them back again. Compensa-
tion for your loss, recovery of time itself, lay only in re-entering
that blank once more where time was uncounted and time didn't
count, drinking yourself out of the middle of the week and into
your timeless time-out.

   The telephone had been ringing for minutes again. Was
somebody calling him from Budapest? Was it Betty in Cleveland
or Gösta in Borås? He thought of the calls he had made in one
hour of one afternoon (and immediately forgotten) to Santa Fé,
Chicago, Berlin, New Orleans, Murray Bay and Villefranche,
how the letters came in, some a few days, some weeks later, asking what had become of him, hadn't he been just about to leave or
sail, had something delayed him, they had had no further word
and were waiting. The first of these letters had puzzled him, he
didn't know what they were talking about; then Wick had presented him with the 'phone bill (before the other letters came in
from abroad) and pleaded how could he, how could he. . . . How
could he? It had been an inspiration of the earlier drinks; it gave

him a sense of power, he supposed, to pick up the telephone—just like that—and ring up Kees or Poupée and surprise them by saying he was coming to see them. He was lonely or something, he did it with the best will in the world, the friendliest motives—but how could he explain that to Wick? How could he, really, because he didn't really know, or remember.

The 'phone had stopped ringing, but he knew that in the next room it was merely gathering itself to stab again. What of it? He would not be there, he wasn't here. . . . He sat in the tub, both taps running full, getting ready for a long idle Sunday morning bath before Sunday-school. The din of the water was pleasant, the steam rose and obscured the tiny Dutch scenes repeated endlessly in the bathroom wallpaper. Someone was calling him. He turned off the faucets and shouted "Yes?" There was no one. The noise of the water running full had created new imaginary sounds in his ear, as it always did, sounds in which someone was forever calling his name, or pounding on the wall, or rapping on the bathroom door itself. He sat back and turned on the taps again. He busied himself with the soap and washcloth; and again, over the din of running water, he heard his name called. Did someone want to get in, was he wanted on the telephone? He shut off the taps and yelled "What *is* it!" . . . It was the telephone ringing.

Hadn't she had enough? What was she trying to do, anyway? What did she mean, what did she think she was doing! He tried to think it out, calmly. He went over it all again, trying to think if he had it right. She and Wick had been in touch with each other and Helen was trying to keep tabs on him. Wick had stayed on at the farm, the whole long weekend, as planned. He didn't want to come back in the middle of it because he knew what he would come back to. Helen was trying to get hold of him and perhaps help him get back in shape before Wick came home. She would keep on 'phoning until he answered. If he was out, he wouldn't stay out forever. Not if he was still alive, or out of jail. He'd be bound to be in at least once when she called. But what if she tried some other means besides 'phoning, what if she came over here? No, she had done that this noon and it hadn't got her anywhere, she wouldn't do it again, she couldn't, God, would she? And if she did, what then? If she found some means of getting in—! Nothing in this or any world could make him face Helen today. Not even her opening the door could make him do it. He wouldn't be responsible if she tried. All he wanted to do was die here alone, without anyone, because he could never explain, he could never even say goodbye. If she tried to get at him again, tried to help him or reach him—well, let her try, he wouldn't be here, alive, if she should succeed.

The excursions into the past (willful and deliberate before, because they were all he had) had become spontaneous, the automatic reflex of his anxiety and over-taut nerves. . . . He lay in his bed at home, sleepless, alert, for in another hour or so it would be Christmas morning and he had to know, somehow, if what he wanted most in all the world was under the tree. Wick was sound asleep beside him and would not wake until wakened. The sky outside the window was so brilliant and clear that he was sure it was daylight, or would be daylight soon. The stars glittered hard and fast as if on a blue ceiling, a ceiling that was surely bluer now than it had been half an hour before or even ten minutes ago. Tense and rigid in his bed (for it was very cold) he gazed at the sky and wondered how long before it would really be dawn. . . . Now and again he heard noises from outside, the crackling sharp noises of the bitter cold. The wheels of a wagon ground and groaned in the icy street, and then came the hard ringing rattle of milk-bottles clinking together in their steel basket and the sound of the milkman going up the walk—*grutch, gruntch, grutch, gruntch* along the solid snow. He listened. The wagon started and went on again, and the frozen wheels gave out hard, slow, but musical sounds as they moved on, like the sound of pendant panes of glass being knocked together—like the little Chinese wind-bells that used to hang on the side porch, but exaggerated, now, and harsh.

The sounds continued as the wagon went up the street, but always they seemed to be just below the window, so sharp and clear did they ring upon the frosty air. Everything was intensified a hundred times: the stillness of the house, his awareness, the noises outside, the cold, the glittering fast stars, his anxiety and need to know. . . . He got out of bed, being careful to put the covers back over Wick, and stole downstairs. The house was dark, the shades in the living-room were drawn, he stumbled over something on the floor. He listened, breathless. His mother slept in the downstairs bedroom just off the living room. Through the closed door he heard her bed creak. Then she said, "Who's there?" He did not answer. "Is that you, Don? Shame on you!" There was a pause. "Now listen. It's under the tree. You can take one look, and then I want you to go back to bed and stay there till you're called, do you hear?" All this low, not loud, she didn't want to wake the others any more than he did. "Don't turn the lights on. Just pull up the shades. You can see enough." He picked his way carefully across the room and raised the shades. Then he came back and looked at the tree. On the floor, right in front, was the fat oblong package wrapped in thin tissue-paper. He picked it up and took it over to the light. By its size and weight he knew at once this was it. He pressed the tissue-paper close to the book with his fingers and read the title through the white blur: *Idylls of the King.* It was the same as the large illustrated copy he had coveted so long from the Fine Books shelf at the public library. "Hurry up," his mother said, "now march!" He put the book back and went upstairs. He crawled into bed beside Wick and took his hand, as they always did when they were ready for sleep. Now let Christmas come whenever it was ready, let it take its time, let all the other presents wait, the book could wait too, now that he knew he had it. . . .

Curious that he could have taken to drink, who after his first communion refused to take part in the service again because he hated the taste of the wine. Odd that he of all people should ever have turned into a drinker, he who had been not only bored but actually impatient with the chapter on the evils of alcohol and what it did to the brain-cells, in the 6th-grade Hygiene book—impatient because all this stuff would certainly never apply to him in a thousand years and it was a waste of time for them all and not very nice besides. Nice people didn't talk about such things or have such things happen to them, not in their town or among their kind of people. Nice people didn't go into saloons, nobody he knew ever did, except he himself once, yes at the age of fourteen, as a sacrifice and gesture of patriotism. He and Eddie Richmond were distributing posters through the downtown stores during the Boy Scout drive for the Liberty Loan, he was covering one side of the street, Eddie the other, when he noticed that Eddie had skipped McGill's saloon. He crossed over to Eddie's side and they talked about it. No sir, Eddie wouldn't go in there, not in a saloon. But not even on account of the Liberty Loan? Not even for the Allies? No sir! Well, *he* would, then; and he did, knowing Eddie would marvel at his courage and tell all the others. He walked straight into the dark foul-smelling place and said "Mr. McGill, can I hang one of these up in your window?" He felt wonderful doing it, all the more so because the two or three men standing at the bar with their tiny glasses of whisky looked at him sheepishly; and when he pushed the two half-doors aside and came out, he knew proudly that he would never again in all his life be inside a saloon but *this* was all *right*. He didn't even care if anyone saw him coming out, in fact he hoped they would, hadn't he done it for the Liberty Loan?

Was that funny, could you laugh at it now? Let others, if they could, but it was heartbreaking only. He thought almost with tears of that priggish self-righteous lad walking through the swinging doors, so innocent, so unaware that someday— Heartbreaking hell! The thought angered him instead. Little prick, that's what he was! Smug little bastard who— He sat up suddenly, his senses straining, his nerves on edge. The telephone had stopped ring-ing. But not only that, he now realized it hadn't been ringing for some time. Was she on her way over here again? He looked at the clock.

It was ten minutes past five. Had the day really gone, had it really managed to pass, he was still sane, still alive? The room was cool, the sunlight had long since left the carpet, though he hadn't realized it till now. He turned to look out the window. The sun had withdrawn also from the apartment building across the way, it was getting dark. Now what? What about the night, how was he going to survive it?—for he knew that sleep, in this keyed-up state, was beyond possibility. Or was Helen going to arrive and attempt again to rescue him from that night? He knew, knowing her, remembering all those times (O times!), that's just what would happen, she was on her way even now. Never! He would face a nightmare night of devils and creeping horror and shrieking empty bottles twenty times more dreadful than the dreadful day, rather than face Helen, rather than open the door to her. Let her ring the bell, let her ring her head off, he was beyond reach now. He clutched the arms of the chair, fixed his eye on the door, and waited for the bell to ring.

Was there a limit to what he could endure? It seemed not. He was more vulnerable to suffering—and at the same time, paradoxically, he had a greater capacity for it—than anyone he knew; and this was no idle or egotistic boast, something he merely fancied to be true and was proud of because it set him apart, spoke of a superior sensitivity or sensibility. An occasion or period of suffering in his past which, reckoned now in perspective, was a mere incident, one out of many in a long chain, would have stood out in the average life as a major crisis, perhaps indeed the only one, a moment where the victim had reached a peak or depth from which recovery was a lifelong process. But such moments, such peaks and depths, were his very pattern—natural, it seemed, perhaps even necessary, to his development. Why had he not been destroyed by all that happened to him? How is it he could take it over and over again and yet again? What capacity, vitality, or resilience did he have that others did not? Was it that his imagination laid hold of that suffering and transmuted it to experience, an experience he did not profit from, true, but experience all the same: a realization of who and what he was, a fulfillment of self? Was he trying to find out, in this roundabout descent to destruction, what it was all about; and would he, at the final and ultimate moment, know?

So his whole history had tended. He had been led on through good and bad, fair and foul, by nothing more than his own insatiable appetite for experience, an appetite part curiosity and part desire (but never three-parts coward). Not for nothing had he glanced up again and again from the bed to look in the mirror and see what a weeping boy looked like, a stricken boy weeping his heart away, that time he first learned his father had gone off and left them all and would never come home again (it was an important and awful moment, his childish but native prescience told him it was maybe the most important moment in his life, and he had to see what it looked like, even while his heart was breaking). Not for nothing had he stood by, when he might so easily have escaped by deceit or treachery or merely walking out, and let the fraternity disaster come down upon him, come down with all the nightmare forces of evil that nearly wrecked his life at the very start. Not for nothing had he ignored his secret morning hemorrhages until it was too late, then embraced both the prospect and the actuality of the long years in the tuberculosis sanatorium as if they offered a rich and rewarding experience. (Childish of course; anything but adult; self-dramatization, sure!—but who was more important or interesting to one than oneself?—and perhaps because of that very thing, that dual nature of participant and spectator, he had never gone down truly to the bottom, never gone under entirely, not yet.) He had come out of that dark confinement as he had gone in, wholehearted, and knowing more about himself than it was given to many others to know.

Had it done him any good? Had he got anything out of it?

He needn't credit himself with self-knowledge as though it were a rare and special virtue; or, if he must, for Christ's sake let him keep it to himself. For what was the good of knowing he was a fool and an adolescent if he went on being an adolescent and fool even more than when he didn't know it? That kind of wisdom wasn't virtue nor that kind of virtue wisdom. Neither had prevented the floundering as before, nor deterred him from the other things, realer and less real than illness, he had faced or gone into: the dangers, the dubious pleasures, the serious undertakings, the disappointments, the trying-anything-once; the mistaken loves and the terrible mistakes in love; the thousand times he had seemed to go deliberately out of his way to get in a jam, while others skirted these same troubles almost without knowing it, almost by instinct, their natural protective sense the very opposite of that instinct of his which led him inevitably and willy-nilly to the trap. Was it really self-destruction; or was it a kind of misguided self-search, self-quest in a blind alley, an untimely extension of the interminable slow pain of growing up, retarded, even cherished, too long? "You are like a plant of slow growth," Anna had written him once (in words he couldn't have used in a thousand years), "but the flower will be beautiful." Slower than many, later than most. . . .

Too late?

Too late, too late, by default; he knew it and accepted it in his helplessness, even though he might protest it with passion: too late because there was at last a limit to what you could endure, and that limit at last would be reached tonight. Physically alone he was finished. The day of terror would break him down into madness at last, when the day was over; his brain would snap and the one rash and final thing would be done.

But oh, this is not the end he had imagined for himself as a kid! or even at thirty. To the adolescent boy, dreaming romantically of the gifted tormented men who had thrown their lives away, suicide had been a glamorous thing, a gallant flinging down of the glove, a refusal to submit, to conform, to endure, a demonstration that the spirit with honor is unwilling to go on except in its own way: almost a gesture debonair.

Romantic rubbish!—had he ever believed it, even as a kid? An end like this was abject, nothing more; cringing, groveling, ignoble, contemptible, vile; a way out shameful and ashamed (could you open the door to Helen?); unbecoming, immoral, worse than unmanly. But you could reach a point, too, where the body rebelled though the spirit still stirred, where physical endurance was nearing its limit, where you no longer actually had the *strength to care* how abject you were, how base or despicable; and that point had been reached hours ago. The painful day had unmanned him, and all that was left was the small weak will (but will all the same—all he had left) to end the despair as well as the pain, somehow, someway. A bottle would do it; but the bottle was empty. A window, then; or a knife.

It had been a knife before that had almost done it and then not done it. It wasn't the first time he had reached this point. Not the first by any means. But always something had lifted him through the moment and beyond it and on safely to the other side. What was it that had carried him over and past it? Most often nothing more than mere curiosity, an interest in his own plight, narcissism itself, a curiosity and interest to know what was going to happen next—even the time he had reached bottom that black week in Provincetown, the very depth of spirit, when the will was so weak he could scarcely write the two or three notes he felt were necessary to leave behind. In a state of depletion, cut off through his own carelessness without a single nickel left and unable somehow to get in touch with anyone who would help, he had stayed on after the season was finished, stayed on out of exhaustion and sheer inability to get away, like a derelict abandoned, stayed long after the last summer visitor had gone and the street lights had been turned off at night for the rest of the year and no one lived in that part of the town but himself. The shack he had rented at the tip end of Whoopee Wharf and no longer had the money to pay for (but who cared? who even knew?) was as isolated from the world as the lonely melancholy bell-buoy that rang dolefully all night long somewhere out in the bay. With no food, no money, no drink, no possibility of getting himself out of there, he had gone into a fit of depression, a weariness of life, that was illness, that was each day worse, that had lasted longer and struck deeper than any depression he had ever suffered before. Three or four days usually saw the end of such a spell, but this had lasted a week now, this must be meant, this was supposed to be the one. His only visitors were a group of violent Portuguese fishermen who, drunk and predatory, began now systematically to terrorize him. Out of an absolutely silent night (save for the sad clanging harborbell and the querulous wail of the seagulls) they would come thundering along the wharf at two in the morning shouting his name, demanding money, demanding to be let in, yelling for booty, clothing, drink, his very person. They would pound on the flimsy walls and curse him with laughter, calling him names he didn't dare listen to or think of the meaning of. He would lie breathless in the dark, knowing only too well what they would do to him if they got him (he covered his ears as they shouted insanely: "Donnie boy! Come out and get your breakfast!") He was the more terrified because he knew he had brought this on himself, it was a kind of grotesque retribution, he and he alone was solely responsible for their wrath. He had carried on wastefully, wantonly, with all kinds of people, for weeks, throwing money away, drinking up more money in a weekend than the Portuguese made in seven days of hard work. They knew all this; they had seen it happen all summer; they had watched meekly, even sheepishly, envying him his continual holiday, his Mrs. Scott and his Doris, his gay shirts, his long idle afternoons, and his nights; and now that he was left behind alone and the others had abandoned him, all their hatred and contempt came out in these night maraudings, these ineffectual but terrifying raids. When they had got tired, convinced perhaps that he himself had finally managed to get away maybe the evening before, they clumbered off down the wharf to the town again. He listened to the footsteps and laughter and violent talk dying away, and then the tolling bellbuoy and the seagulls took over once more, their plaintive thin cries sounding like chalk scraping fitfully, intermittently, on some vast blackboard raised high in the black night. When daylight came at last, his despair had reached its peak. He wrote his three notes, exactly alike; he got out the Bavarian huntingknife that had come with his *lederhosen* and which he used to wear stuck in the little leather slit provided for it just below the right hip; he drew the still-sharp blade tentatively across his wrist a few times, till the thin skin was streaked with three or four tiny hair-like lines of red. He gazed at the wrist lost in thought, almost without interest, almost with indifference, and the silly notion came to him: "Maybe tomorrow I'll regret this, maybe tomorrow I'll wish I hadn't. . . ." He put the knife away and promised himself that if he felt like this tomorrow he'd do it then, he'd give himself one more chance, he'd wait one more day; *then* if his despair demanded such a way out, it was right that he should go through with it. He went out on the pier and lay in the sun, too weak to walk farther. During the morning he saw the fishermen. They came along Whoopee Wharf to look over their idle boats and nets. They nodded politely to him, saying quietly, "Good morning, Mr. Birnam." He looked at them and answered hello. He knew that these same men, now so mild and respectful, would be back again in the night, derisive, ribald, dangerous, shouting the obscenities that were as much a part of their nature as these shy and gentle daytime manners. He knew they would be back in full and maybe greater force, next time; and he knew, too, that tomorrow morning he would go through the same performance with the knife, like a ritual, trying to see how it was or how it would be, and telling himself that if the *next* day he felt this low again. . . .

Thinking of this now, he suffered almost a nausea of shame

for the infantile curiosity that always had, in the past, carried him
safely by and beyond such a moment. He had never had the guts
to see it through, not even when he wanted it, deserved it, and
had to have it. Or that is, he had the guts; but his self-interest and
self-absorption had refused to allow him to take himself from the
scene, to erase himself for good and all, and thus not be on hand
to see what happened afterwards. What was the good of carrying
off such a thing if its full effect was to be lost on the one person
most interested?—himself. If he weren't there, he of all people, to
appreciate the result of what he had done, it was all wasted and
gone for nothing, lost to him, lost on everyone else. The thing
that saved him was as inane and trivial and contemptible as that:
he couldn't stand not being around to know all that would happen, all that would be said and done, because of his death. It was
shameful to think of; but, if that's what he owed his life to now—if
that's what had given him back his life to throw away again, or
preserved it till just such a day as this when the effect would *not*
be lost, when the full shock of his death or his dying would strike
Helen between the eyes as she opened the door—

When the doorbell rang, he was utterly unstrung. He couldn't
believe it had happened, this very thing he had been waiting for.
He seemed to go to pieces because the last enormity, inevitable
though it had been all day, was finally at hand. He slumped in the
chair half in faint and waited for the doorbell to ring itself out, as
it would very soon with no one here to answer it. The bell buzzed
and buzzed and finally, abruptly, stopped.

He lay in the arms of the chair, almost patient, now, for the
rest of it. He knew what was going on. Helen was on her way
down the filthy stairs into the cellar to get the keys from Dave.
He saw her standing on the lower step explaining, and he saw the
West Indian face of Dave eyeing her stupidly, trying to puzzle
out whether he should or shouldn't. But he always did, no matter
how well you tipped him, no matter how many times you told
him that under no circumstances, no matter who it is—

There were steps in the hall, on one of the landings. Not the two ladies going out and down. Somebody was coming up. He lay helpless now, soaked with sweat, unable to do more than stare at the doorknob to the outer door still plainly seen in the dusk through the little foyer. He held it with his eye as if his life depended on it, as it did indeed. If he saw it turn—what could he do? When he saw it twist and turn, as it was bound to do any minute now, would he be able to spring to the violent action, come sharply alive out of the demand and desperation of the moment and put to instant use all the strength that could not now lift his hand from the arm of the chair? His breath came in painful gasps; he was almost smothered in panic.

He heard the footsteps on the last flight. There were two, not one; two of them. They were not talking. They merely came on, slowly enough, but on till they reached the landing outside his door. He saw (as one too sick or weak to protest the surgeon's knife that will kill or cure) the doorknob turn.

Helpless rage swept up in him because he was suddenly sobbing now and could not stop. He was going to pieces in spite of himself and not in the way he had meant to; he was breaking up as if before his own eyes, entirely apart from and beyond his own control or power to stop it.

Somebody was rapping on the door. Then there was a silence in which he listened too. The doorknob turned again, and then again. Then a key was put in the lock.

The door opened and there was Helen and Dave. But only for a moment. Helen turned. "That's all, Dave. Thank you very much. You can go now." Dave tried to peer around her into the room but Helen quietly closed the door and came in.

"Hello," she said.

He was dog-sick. His stomach began to rise, his throat retched; but nothing came. Only noises like a dog somewhere out of his chest. Helen didn't seem to hear. She merely said Hello and went into the kitchen and set down some package on the kitchen table. She came back and turned on the light near the bookcase, then the floor-lamp at the end of the couch. As the glow spread in the room, making a light in which he could be plainly seen now—in which he was exposed raw and helpless for anyone to see—a quaking shook him like a chill, his arms flopped up and down off the arms of the chair as if danced or dandled on wires. She could see him now if she looked—and his legs waggled and knocked at the thought. If she looked at him now his head would begin bobbing like the Japanese toy.

"I've brought you something to eat, Don," she said as she went back to the kitchen. She emerged again and came toward him with a glass of milk and half of a sandwich on a plate.

He couldn't look at the food, or her eyes, he could only shake his head.

"How long since you've eaten, Don? Yesterday? Two days?"

He shook his head and the tears streamed helplessly down his cheeks. He could die of shame for crying, but he couldn't help it. He sank back weak in the chair.

"Your poor eye," Helen was saying. "Is it sore, does it hurt?"

He tried again to shake his head no, and he felt his chin bobbing up and down, the whole head shaking till he was dizzy.

Helen looked away from him—(she knew, she knew thank God, and damn her too, damn her! she knew how he was hating her looking at him)—and found something to busy herself with, to leave him alone. She picked up the wet shorts and damp trousers lying in a heap at the foot of the bookcase and took them into the bathroom. He heard her at the washbowl, probably washing out the shorts. She went into the bedroom and opened his closet door. In a few moments she was back with a pair of clean shorts and some trousers to another suit.

"Here, Don, put these on. I want to take you down to my house."

He shook his head.

"Can you put these on yourself? I'll help you, if you want."

He sat shaking his head and looking at the floor and wishing he might die—anything to end this misery of shame and pain and exhaustion, this rattling in the chair as if he was suffering a fatal chill, this agony of knowing now, now, now he was caught and finished, the spell of riot or escape was over, the terror hadn't even begun. The night ahead without drink was a threat that scared him out of his wits. What could one do, what could be done to avert or avoid the oncoming night? . . .

"Please, Don. Try. You must get dressed. I want you to go with me."

Finally he was able to speak. "I can't."

Helen sat down. "Listen, Don. You're sick. You're not well. You can't stay here alone." She spoke so quietly and calmly, without even any pleading, that he was sick with shame. Why, he couldn't have said—for her words and her tone of voice and her whole gentle manner were as far from reproaching him as it was possible to be. "You need help, Don. I want to take you down to my house and take care of you."

"I couldn't" was all he could say.

"Why can't you, Don?"

"I haven't the strength. I couldn't get up."

"I'll help you. Here, let me help you put on your shorts and your pants."

"I couldn't stand. I couldn't make the stairs. I can't get up."

"Yes you can, Don. Please take a little milk first and I'll help you."

"Go away. Won't you please go away and leave me?"

"Not like this, Don. I can't leave you. Not here alone. Come down to my house, Don. You can take a bath and I'll put you to bed. I'll be able to take care of you there."

"Helen, I can't. I'm not strong enough. Please go away."

"Wick will be back tomorrow, Don. You really must try to get back on your feet before then."

"Tomorrow? Is today Monday?"

"Yes, Don."

She got up and went into the kitchen. In a moment she was back again.

"Don, if there were any food in, I'd take care of you here. But there isn't. And I don't want to leave you while I go out and find something. Listen, Don, I'm going into the bedroom now and get your pajamas, and then your razor and toothbrush and a clean shirt. If I bother you looking at you, try to pull yourself together while I'm getting your things. I'm sorry, Don, but you've got to come down to my house. We'll get Dave to help you on the stairs, if you like," she added, as she moved off to the bedroom.

His breathing came harder and faster as he made the effort to pull on his shorts. But that was all he was able to do. He couldn't even raise himself to slide them under him. They clung merely around his knees and his thighs. What had become of all his resistance, his anger, his defiance, his threat and promise of death now? Nothing could be more abject than the despicable shameful helpless creature he knew himself to be. He couldn't even protest; and he knew—curse or weep or shake his head how he liked—that in another hour he would be in Helen's bed and glad of it. How that impossible move could be brought about, was beyond him; and perhaps that was the very reason it could be done. Everything was up to Helen now.

She was back. She put down the little bag she had packed, and bent over to help him pull on his shorts and trousers. He pulled on her shoulder for support and managed to stand.

"I've got to have a drink of water," he said, "that's all I want."

"I'll get it for you."

"No, let me try to get to the bathroom."

Leaning against her, his arm across her shoulder, her arms around his waist, he crossed the room. In the bathroom, he braced himself against the washbowl and poured a glass of water. But he had barely got it down when suddenly it shot out of his mouth like spray from a hose. He collapsed on the toilet-seat, retching and gasping.

"I'll get Dave," Helen said.

"No, leave me alone. Oh, go away, go away. . . ."

Helen left. He folded his arms on the edge of the washbowl and lay his head down against them. In the bedroom, he heard Helen telephoning for a taxi.

A cab-driver. Seeing them leave the front door and step into his cab. Or passers-by on the sidewalk, seeing Helen helping him. Or Dave. Or Mrs. Wertheim. Or the boy from the tailor's. How could he be seen? In this condition. How could Helen want to be seen with him? But she didn't seem to care, she was ready to go through with it apparently without a qualm. If she didn't care, why couldn't he not care? But it was so different. She wasn't the one who was helpless, the cab-driver wasn't the one, Dave wasn't—they weren't the ones who suffered spasms of sudden fright at every sound, or at every glance directed their way. Only he was the bundle of exploding nerves and panic.

Not quite an hour later, he was in the tub. His clean pajamas hung on a hook by the door. Helen had filled the tub for him and he had managed to pull off his clothes in her bedroom and stumble along the hall in his shorts. Now he lay back in the hot water and felt so soothed and calm that he could almost sleep.

He would never know how they had got here. He remembered having to sit down again and again, a dozen times, before he could get up enough strength or courage to try the stairs. On each landing, sometimes in the middle of the flight of stairs, he had had to sit down again and rest. In the cab, terrified by the noise of the traffic, he had passed into a kind of oblivion, so that he remembered nothing of the trip down to the Village. Had they driven through Charles Street, he wondered? If they had, he didn't know it. Could they actually have driven by Jack's and he not know it? Not feel, even without knowing where he was, that the upstairs bar and the French-speaking waiter were somewhere near?—as if the place gave out some kind of vibration that he alone, of all the millions in the city, was sensitive to. Was he going to be bothered by that for the rest of his life? Could he lay that ghost—ever?

Helen tapped on the door. "Don? Are you all right?"

"Yes. Why?"

"Nothing. I just wondered." He heard her go back down the hall.

That was only one; that was one he happened to remember. How many other ghosts were there that he didn't even suspect? Who was going to turn up and thunder at him "Look here, you did this and that, how about it, what have you got to say for yourself?" Whoever it was or would be, wouldn't turn up here. He was safe here. Or if they did, Helen would never let them in; not now; not for days. He had escaped at last, escaped beyond the reach of all; all but one.

In the hall, now, he heard Helen on the telephone. Apparently she was having trouble getting her number, but eventually the call came through and she began to talk. He could not hear what she was saying, but instantly he knew she had called Wick. Don was okay, she had him here at the house, he was in the tub now, soon she was going to give him some light food and put him to bed, don't worry, everything's all right. That's what she would be telling him; and Wick mustn't worry, he didn't need to worry any more. That's what she would think and that's what Wick would think too. The bat had flown his cloister'd flight and come to rest at last. Well, he was willing, why not? He was too weak to do anything about it but accept, he couldn't have fought or protested or run out on them if he tried. It was infuriating to be so helplessly at their will and command, now; but that's what he wanted, too, in a way. He was too exhausted and depleted to want anything else.

Helen came to the door again. "Are you all right, Don?"

"What's the matter?"

"You were so quiet, I wondered."

"I'm just lying here."

"Don't stay in too long. It will weaken you too much. Please get out soon. I've got some milk-toast for you and then you can get into a clean bed and rest and sleep as long as you need to."

"I don't want anything."

"You must eat, Don. And I have a couple of sedatives, too, if that will help."

The thought of food made him retch again, but perhaps with the help of the sedatives— Or perhaps, if they made him finally sleep, he could eat tomorrow, in the morning. He let the water run out of the tub. But that was a mistake. He should have got out first. With the water gone from around him, he felt weaker and heavier and more helpless than ever before. He lay in the empty tub like a dead weight of bones; and then, as he began to be chilled, he hauled himself up.

Wrapped in an enormous towel, leaning against the wash-bowl, he saw his face in the mirror, and his eye. It was a sickening sight. He regarded it with awe, objectively, not feeling it at all—amazed by it all over again because he had forgotten it for so long. No wonder Helen had said "Your poor eye"—and he had thought she was speaking merely about his bloodshot eyeballs, always streaked with red at the end of these bouts. What had happened to him to give him such a blow? Who? And where? Whatever it was, it was a wonder it didn't fracture his skull, or finish him off for good.

In his pajamas, in bed at last, in Helen's bed, he lay back against the propped-up pillows and felt clean at least. Helen came in and turned off the ceiling light and snapped on the little shaded lamp that stood on the night-table near his head.

"Why don't you lie flat," she said, "and be comfortable."

"I can't. My heart— Maybe later."

She brought him a glass of water and two little pills. "Perhaps you should take these before you eat. They'll work better."

"What are they?"

"I don't know. Something the doctor gave me this afternoon."

So she'd been preparing for this all along, certain of the outcome, certain that before the day was over he'd be safe in her bed at home. He pretended not to notice. He put the pills in his mouth; but under her gaze, he could not hold the glass in his hand, he would shake the water all over the bed. He looked up helplessly. She held the glass for him and tilted it so he could drink. Then she went to the kitchen and returned in a few moments with a soup-dish of milk-toast.

"No, I can't. Really. Please."

"I'll just leave it here, then," she said. "Maybe you'll feel like it a little later." She meant After I leave the room, after I'm not here to watch you. She left him then and went to eat her own supper in the kitchen.

Just as he was about to reach for the plate, a streak of fire ran out of the hall and across the rug to the bed. He stared at the floor and it went out suddenly, like a flame extinguished. The old illusion, the nervous twitch in the eye, the dancing flashes and lights that were seen just beyond the edge of your vision. But you could face them down, and they vanished. Perhaps they would vanish utterly when the sedatives got working.

He recalled the time the foolish psychiatrist had given him a little envelope containing fourteen sodium amytal tablets, yes, he did that, and told him to take two each night when he went to bed—and two in the morning, if he must—during his hangover period; and he had taken them all at once, on purpose to put himself out for as long a time as possible or for good, even. He remembered Wick's fright as he came to, two days later, and Wick's anger at the doctor, and his own disappointment and chagrin at waking up, mixed somehow, and curiously, with relief because of Wick's concern. He reached again for the milk-toast, but the shaking plate spilled milk in the bed, and he was forced to put it back again, on the night-table. He leaned on his elbow and bent his head down to the plate and spooned up a few mouth-fuls. It stayed down, and even warmed him inside. He spooned up some more, and after many minutes, had eaten it all.

He had come out of that as he had come out of everything else. The fourteen tablets didn't finish him off—nothing ever did or had or apparently would. He reached the limit of his endurance, the absolute physical limit, and then picked up and went on for another twenty-four hours or a week. He took a dreadful fall or suffered a blow somewhere and all he got was a black eye. He went out to pawn a typewriter on Yom Kippur and came back with ten dollars he got for nothing from the man at the A & P. His heart didn't stop in the chair or his brain explode; instead Helen came along and saw that he was bathed and fed and saved from a night of terror alone. His very nightmare was synthetic: a dream by Thomas Mann. He got caught in the act of stealing a purse, caught red-handed before a whole mob of people, and what happened: he merely apologized, and they all but apologized themselves, and sent him on his way scot-free. He threatened he promised himself death, and when the doorknob turned that was to be the cue, when the door opened and in walked the victim, the victim of his suicide, all he did was sit helpless as before, more spineless if possible, and wait to be scooped up and taken care of. All that ever happened to him was that he mislaid some money somewhere and mislaid it all over again the next day and the next or lost it or threw it away or something; and even that didn't mat-ter. He always came up with cash. The same evil genius who took it away from him in his cups was waiting the next morning to hand him some more.

What was the intention or sum of any of this? It wasn't even decently dramatic or sad or tragic or a shame or comic or ironic or anything else—it was nothing. He was being made a fool of by some perverse fate or that evil genius who didn't consider him important enough to finish off one way or the other. He was always left dangling and safe in a way that was merely ludicrous—

ludicrous but not worth laughing at, something merely to put up with and bear with because there was nothing else to do about it. It was worse than insulting, it was inane, vacant, empty, lacking sense or meaning whatever. "Helen!"

She came quickly into the bedroom from the kitchen.

"Do you suppose I could have— Are there any— Have you got another one of those pills, by any chance?"

"Oh Don, do you think you need it?"

"I—I do, terribly. They aren't working at all."

"Well," she said, "I'll see if I've got another."

"Let me have two. I need them, Helen. I've got to have them. I can't stand this."

She didn't argue. She knew it would be no use. She could hold out on him, of course, but what would be the use of that, either? If the pills would do him any good, put him to sleep—

She got them and set them down on the bed-table, with a fresh glass of water, and left him again.

He took the pills and the water, and was gratified to see that his shaking had stopped considerably. He looked at his hands. His fingers were covered with burns. He noticed them now for the first time. There were three or four small burns between the index- and middle-fingers of each hand where he had held cigarettes too long—always the surest sign that he had been drinking himself unconscious and for days. There were probably burns in the trousers he had left at home, too, and perhaps even in the shorts. The wonder is that he hadn't yet burned himself to death. But he'd never do that, either—he was always going to be spared that too, like everything else. Whenever he got close to it, the smell of the burning wool or cotton or his own sometimes serious burns always awakened him, like the time he had burned up his bed in both the Grand Hotel Dolder and the Hotel Quisisana; like the time he had awakened in the stench of burning feathers in his cabin on the *Lafayette* and found the *édredon* aflame on top of him. The cover was one great hole, the feathers were burning all down inside, he sprang up and flung the thing off his berth, dragged it into the bath and turned on the shower. What to do with it then? The porthole, of course; and in the morning, the aged steward not even asking, shaking his head over the ways of the tourist and wondering silently, perhaps, in whose cabin the *édredon* would later turn up. . . .

What was Helen doing? She had gone into the living room now, what was she doing there? It didn't matter, he knew what it was. Helen wouldn't sit here and sew or sit here and read or sit here and anything, though this was the room she ordinarily sat in, in her comfortable chair by her work-table there in the corner. Helen wouldn't come into this room any more than was necessary. She was keeping out of his way because that was what he wanted; she wouldn't talk to him because he couldn't stand being looked at, not like this; she would make up a bed on the sofa in the living room and sleep there tonight, and chances are he wouldn't even see her when she left for work in the morning. He would sleep, and sometime around noon she would 'phone and ask pleasantly (not too pleasantly, just matter-of-fact, as if nothing were wrong at all) how he was. He was grateful for this, more grateful than he had ever been in his life, but he couldn't have uttered a word about it. He was feeling calmer, now, not sleepy or drowsy yet, but more relaxed, peaceful, almost good. He felt keenly what Helen was doing for him by staying out of the room—but forget it, as she was forgetting it; pretend it wasn't so, and thus spare both their feelings and thus prevent the tears—on both sides.

Helen hadn't uttered a word of reproach from the moment she turned the doorknob and came through the door. She had never said You've been drinking. She hadn't said Have you got any more liquor anywhere? She hadn't asked How long have you been at it? Have you got any money left? Are you finished now, or are you going to start again tomorrow? She hadn't said Where'd you get the black eye, or What in heaven's name happened to you? She hadn't mentioned the matinée he had missed or said Sure, you weren't feeling up to it, you had *other* plans for that afternoon. She didn't remind him of the several dozen 'phone-calls she had been making for days. She hadn't said At least you could have answered the 'phone and saved me that much worry. She hadn't said Look at you, look what a sight you are. She hadn't called you a fool or a drunk or a liar or anything. She didn't say Why can't you think of your brother Wick, if you don't care anything about yourself? And of course she would never have said What about me? She had merely said "Let me help you, I'll take you down to my house, I'll put you to bed in a clean bed and you can sleep as long as you need to."

What was she thinking as she sat in the other room. Was she thinking any of these things? Yes, all of them, and probably more and worse, as she had every right to think; but she could never have brought herself to utter a syllable of these reproaches while she saw that physically, if not inwardly too, he was already so beaten down. And what was he going to do about it? Take it in silence and say nothing, promise nothing—how could he, how could he in all honesty promise anything, it would be so easy when he was feeling so low. Too easy. Keep the promises to himself, hold them until he knew what he was talking about—and then, of course, never say a thing.

He was reminded, sickeningly, of something that had passed through his mind hours before, sometime that afternoon. Some such thing as his capacity for suffering and always suffering more than anybody else. Well, he did, maybe; maybe his vulnerability was more exposed and raw than what was normal in others; but if thought could make one ashamed, he was ashamed now. Some minor incident of suffering in his past would have stood out in the average life as a major crisis—he had actually thought and said to himself some such thing as that. How true could it be? It was true, all right, but only true to the extent that his imagination heightened these things and made them greater in retrospect than they ever were at the time. Christ knows other people suffered too; but did their self-centeredness, their self-absorption and pre-occupation with self, magnify their troubles or experiences out of all proportion to the actuality and blind them to the fact that trouble was the lot of all? They knew what he never knew: one's troubles mattered only to oneself. What happened to him was no greater or no worse than what happened to everybody else; if it were odder or more bizarre or more out of the usual, that's because he went after it; and if he suffered more, he also had the capacity to understand and place and take that suffering without weeping and wailing about it forever and ever. "I haven't got time to be neurotic," he had heard Helen say once; and the words had made him go weak with anger. He had thought it was the most stupid and reactionary remark he ever heard in his life; but was it any more stupid than the sneering thrust he had made in reply: "Time! You haven't got the imagination!"

Even as he submitted himself to this castigation, this chastise-ment and searching of self, he knew it was all merely part of his present low and depleted state, symptomatic of his physical condi-tion only, and that tomorrow or next week he would bounce right back, all ego again. He knew it and he was tired of it, tired of that interminable process and recurring cycle; tired now, though, of thinking about it. He sank back among the pillows and tried deliberately shutting all thought from his mind, in the hope that sleep would come.

But it was no use. He was still wakeful, still jumpy and alert, still sensitive to the slightest far-away noise from the street, for all the false calm that had been induced by the sedatives. And the mind refused to die down: it worked at the top of its bent, piling reminder after disturbing reminder upon him. He became poi-gnantly aware of Helen sitting in silence in the next room.

What was she waiting for? Oh, not now, not this minute, but tomorrow and yesterday and last month and last year and the long while they had been tied up inextricably together. What did she expect to get out of it, what did she want, what did she think it would lead to—in short, what was she waiting for?

She loved him. It was as simple and final as that. What difference did it make what she was going to get out of it, she loved him and she couldn't help herself. Nor could he. He had learned that, one night—and learned, at the same time, that she knew its finality too, and accepted it as inevitable, as he must. Whether he must or not, he did. After that.

One evening, as he was leaving her, he had planned a question, premeditated a little test. Through that week, one of his soberer weeks, she had been on his mind continually. He was painfully conscious of the kind of life he was leading her, the pain he was putting her through, the impossibility of her ever finding happiness through him. He loved Helen, wanted her, needed her far more than she ever needed him; but what did he have to offer, when tomorrow or next week he was bound to yield again to the downward pull and destroy a little more of himself and of her? Something had to be done. A clean break and an honest one, a break that would be clear and open, wounding her as gently as possible—for she was certain to be wounded when she grasped the import of his question. He thought it out carefully. He would ask her, at the tail end of the evening, just as he was leaving, "Are you taking me seriously?" and then wait for the answer. And when her answer came, he would say, "Well, you shouldn't." No matter what her words were, they would provide the necessary cue. If she replied "Yes," or if she answered "No," or even if she said "I don't know," all he needed to say, then, was: "Well, you shouldn't"—and they would both be answered, both understand, from then on.

At the door, he moved up to her in the darkness and took her in his arms. His heart pounded. But it was a necessary thing, it had to be done. Perhaps she would see, one day, that it had been kindness. He released her from his arms. He lighted a cigarette to still his nervousness. He put his hand on the doorknob.

"Don't go," she said.

He let go of the doorknob and took her chin in his hand. "Helen. Are you taking me seriously?"

Her arms went around his neck, the answer came without hesitation—tired, whispered, but one he had never counted on, one that did not fit into the little scheme at all: "I love you, darling—what difference does it make?"

What was she waiting for? What was he! But of course there were too many answers to that one. Wick expressed it in a word. "It's all right for you to ruin your life; that's up to you," he said; "but you have no right to ruin someone else's."

Why did there always have to be some woman hopelessly involved with a hopeless drunk, so that the Helens of this world numbered into the hundreds of thousands?—But from there you went on to: Why were drunks, almost always, persons of talent, personality, lovable qualities, gifts, brains, assets of all kinds (else why would anyone care?); why were so many brilliant men alcoholic?—And from there, the next one was: Why did you drink?

Like the others, the question was rhetorical, abstract, anything but pragmatic; as vain to ask as his own clever question had been vain. It was far too late to pose such a problem with any reasonable hope for an answer—or, an answer forthcoming, any reasonable hope that it would be worth listening to or prove anything at all. It had long since ceased to matter Why. You were a drunk; that's all there was to it. You drank; period. And once you took a drink, once you got under way, what difference did it make Why? There were so many dozen reasons that didn't count at all; none that did. Maybe you drank because you were unhappy, or too happy; or too hot, or too cold; or you didn't like the *Partisan Review,* or you loved the *Partisan Review.* It was as groundless as that. To hell with the causes—absent father, fraternity shock, too much mother, too much money, or the dozen other reasons you fell back on to justify yourself. They counted for nothing in the face of the one fact: you drank and it was killing you. Why? Because alcohol was something you couldn't handle, it had you licked. Why? Because you had reached the point where one drink was too many and a hundred not enough.

There was no cure. It was something that would ail you always, as long as you lasted (and how long would that be, the way you were going?). But—you did have this: you could recover and stay well. You could recover and become an "arrested case," like the TB patient whose doctor will not commit himself to a cure more certain or permanent than that. "Your case is arrested, provided you take care of yourself," or "provided you don't break down again." When the patient is discharged from Davos, he is bidden God-speed with the cheery farewell: "So-long till your next relapse"—and the nurse Bim, saying goodbye to the lovely advertising man for the sixth time that year, looks forward to his early return. But the patient does manage to keep away from Davos for good (and the advertising man need see no more of the alcoholic ward and Bim): provided he takes care of himself, provided he doesn't break down again.

Who knew better than himself how true these reflections were, he who had had cause—on a hundred such evenings of zero as this—to puzzle them out and think them through and promise himself to remember, remember. Oh, he could promise himself; but when the state of well-being was restored in him again, the nightmare of the latest long weekend paled and dimmed and became unreal—unreal as that streak of flame racing now, this minute, along the carpet to the bed, the path of blazing gasoline that went out when you looked at it, because it wasn't there to begin with. . . .

The light in the room had seemed to become a wash of grey-yellow, a lifeless glare almost without light in itself, like the livid dead color that stands in the air before a late summer afternoon thunder-shower, the light seen along the clapboards of country houses when the atmosphere becomes oppressive and thick and heavy with storm. It was a distillation—a dilution, rather, a weakening and watering—of the yellow-red flare of the gasoline on the carpet, thinned and spread out through the still air of the room, like a fog. The little bed-lamp itself had become a feeble yellowish glimmer, anemic and unnatural, like the white glow of a cigarette in the murky red gloom of a café. . . .

The thumping erratic heart had died down to a lethargy like stone. He was calm outside; but suddenly so restless within, unquiet, all but unruly, that he longed for something on which to fix his attention and so take his mind off himself—longed, almost, for the tremors and panic of the afternoon and morning and all that long day, tremors and fright which had given him action, of a sort, and distraction. . . .

His eye seemed to be attracted by a stir or rustle near the foot of the bed. He turned, and saw nothing but a small hole in the wall about a foot above his eye-level. It was an opening with cracked plaster around it, as if a big nail had once been hammered there and later yanked out—a spike or bigger. After a moment he saw, with a start, the little stir of movement that had drawn his attention.

Was that a mouse which appeared at the mouth of the hole? He saw only its snout first, pointed and twitching, assaying the light. He lay flat on his back, uneasy, and did not move; it grew bolder; and soon he could see the mouse entire, hesitant in the opening as if timid about the difficult descent to the floor. It trembled there, half-in half-out of the hole, the little beast that might have been his poor earthborn companion and fellow-mortal if he had not had an irrational feminine abhorrence of mice. He tried now to control this, knowing the mouse was safe in the wall and could not get down. He kept his eye fixed on it, and gradually relaxed. Though he did not like it, he found he could watch the mouse with equanimity, even interest, so long as it was not running around on the floor, under the bed. There was even a certain pathos in the way it peered from side to side—something pathetic in the tiny nose twitching in nervous apprehension, the sensitive whiskers strained for danger, the infinitesimal shining bead-like eyes that held so much alarm. In fascination and pity he watched, and forgot for the moment his own terrors.

Curious the way he began, then, to like the little creature. From time to time it looked at him, as all the while he looked at it, never taking his eyes away. He wondered if the mouse really saw him, and began to hope that it did or would. He believed that if he turned his head ever so slightly, or made some small movement, the mouse would really see him, see that it was he; yet he was afraid, too, that some stir on his part would frighten it away, and he did not want to cause the mouse any more anxiety than he could see it was already suffering. Besides, he was beginning almost to feel its company. Finally he wished he could get up and help the little grey thing to the floor, if that was what it wanted: still more, that the mouse might know he intended it no harm—or, foolishly, that they might nod to each other in friendly trust and fellowship. A foolish fancy; but it grew, he felt, out of the mouse's loneliness no less than his own. . . . And now the mouse did really see him. For some time, then, the two of them lay looking at one another, as if in quiet recognition, and unaccountably he felt contented and relieved.

He jumped. There was an almost soundless noise at his ear as something brushed by his temple—a sound like the soft *flik* made by a light-bulb when it burns suddenly out—and a bat flew by. The tip of its hooked wing nicked his forehead as it sped in swift but fluttering flight straight at the mouse. Like a sprung snare he was off the pillow, upright, staring from a sitting position at the two locked in titanic pygmy struggle.

His throat seemed to burst apart as he cried out. He could not stay and be helpless witness to the horror and injustice of that spectacle. (Oh that at this moment the world might end and they and he with it!) His breast was on fire with passion and grief but he could not protest or help. Tears blurred his sight, but he had to look.

The obscene wings hid how the contest went. They were folded around the opening of the hole, hooked into the plaster, deathly still; then they stirred with a scratching sound as the bat shifted for position. There was a smell. His breath stopped in his agony to see. The wings spread as the bat began to squeeze the small bat-body of the mouse—he could see the gripping claws like miniature nail-parings. The horrible wings lifted, the round ears of the bat disappeared, as its teeth sank into the struggling mouse. The more it squeezed, the wider and higher rose the wings, like tiny filthy umbrellas, grey-wet with slime. Under the single spread of wings the two furry forms lay exposed to his stare, cuddled together as under a cosy canopy, indistinguishable one from the other, except that now the mouse began to bleed. Tiny drops of bright blood spurted down the wall; and from his bed he heard the faint miles-distant shrieks of dying.

Helen came running.

"Don—what is it!"

He was pointing, stammering in terror. "The mouse—bat—!"

She took the rigid arm in both her hands and pressed it down, slowly, to his side. She held it firmly there. "Lie back, Don," she said softly. "Please try to relax, won't you please? Don't sit up."

He struggled. "There, in the hole—that hole—!"

Involuntarily she turned her head in the direction of his stare, apprehensive herself; then sat down on the edge of the bed, still holding his arm. She took the handkerchief from his pajama-pocket and mopped the sweat from his face. Her voice was low and comforting. "Don, there's no mouse, no hole"—and she was right.

He lay back, gasping; and tears of exhaustion streamed from his eyes, tears of pity for Helen's quiet sad bewildered concern, tears of helpless fright for what might happen to him yet.

In a few moments he had closed his eyes. She put out the light and tiptoed out of the room and shut the door behind her. He lay finally in a wakeful drowse, just this side of sleep. The telephone rang beyond the closed door. He was aware of Helen hurrying down the hall to answer it before the repeated ringing would wake him. He heard her talking, and knew that Wick had called back to see how things were. He did not hear the words but he could tell that she was reassuring Wick; and he knew by the tone of her voice that she thought he was safe. . . .

PART SIX

The End

I hope you had a good night. I saw you were still sleeping so I didn't disturb you. The coffee is made. Just warm it up. And there are eggs in the ice-box. Holy Love comes in at 10.30 so if you wake up after that, she can get your breakfast. I'll telephone around noon. I hope you have a quiet day and more rest if you want it. Don't let Holy Love get in your hair. Just chase her away if it bothers you having her around. The house can go till tomorrow. Love.—H.

Eggs. He couldn't imagine anything more sickening at the moment than eggs. He looked around for Helen's clock. But she must have taken it to the living room where she slept. He heard someone moving about in the kitchen and after a moment realized it was Holy Love. That meant it was past ten-thirty, maybe around eleven, or even noon. That meant Wick would be coming back very shortly. That meant the long weekend was over. Wick had said they'd come back Tuesday morning (they!) and it always took a good three hours to drive from the farm.

He had slept soundly since—when? He had no idea when it was he went to sleep, but certainly he had been sleeping twelve hours and maybe more. He should feel very rested. But he didn't and he wasn't. The moment he stirred in bed, tried to get up, made a move with his legs, he felt how weak he was. His heart didn't thump like yesterday but it was irregular and it hurt. He was dizzy in the head. His responses and co-ordination weren't what they should be. When he made a move he moved too far or not quite far enough. His breathing still came in panting gasps, even after the long sleep.

He settled back among the pillows and lay still for a moment, and the swaying room came to rest with him. Flecks of sunlight rippled on the ceiling or maybe it wasn't sunlight at all maybe it was something in his own head or vision or something that lingered on from sleep. If he opened his eyes wide or sat up again—

He sat up and the whole room seemed just slightly ajar. That wasn't what he meant. Slightly off center. That wasn't it either. Whatever you called it in a two- or three-color job when the frames hadn't quite jibed and the color stood just above or a little to one side of what it was supposed to color. He couldn't think straight this morning or apparently see right. The outlines of things inside and out were a touch blurred. So was his vision unless he looked straight at something and held it for a moment. When he moved, the object moved too, for a second, and then settled back. The effect of the paraldative maybe. Sodium amytive. *Sed*ative. Whatever the hell it was. Anyway something like an intoxication, a little whoozy, not at all unpleasant. You could lie back and kind of float just off the bed and enjoy it. Except that he had things to do.

Intoxication. Pifflocation. He remembered going to a movie with his mother so many years ago that he was too young to have been there at that kind of movie at all, but his mother didn't know what the movie was about until they got into it; and then, during an awful scene in which a man reeled and staggered across the floor of an awful Western saloon and fell down and came to rest with his head on a spitoon, his mother laughed self-consciously and said aloud to a neighbor "He's pifflocated," making a light-hearted joke of it so he wouldn't take the awful scene too seriously or think too much about it. Every time he had heard the word intoxication since, he thought of the other. Both words connoted something very unpleasant. Not nice. Something one didn't mention. He had never identified himself with either of them.

Ever thought of himself, in any stage, as being one or the other. He honestly didn't believe he'd ever used or spoken either word. Why say intoxicated anyhow when drunk was what you meant and said it better.

For that matter why think of such a thing now when you were so far from drunk that you could bridle at the term as you bridled at the other. But not far from drinking. How far depended on how fast he worked.

So Helen was going to 'phone at noon. He couldn't not answer the call. She'd know that he heard it no matter how soundly he still slept, or that Holy Love would answer it if he didn't and go in and wake him. The thing to do was not be here. But then he'd had that clear in his mind from the moment he opened his eyes. It was the only thing this morning that was clear.

He waited till he heard Holy Love go down the hall to the living room. Then he swung his feet over the edge of the bed and stood up. It wasn't too good. He felt strong enough but uncertain. His whole body felt cool inside as if his blood didn't run warm any more. He swayed slightly, and when he took a step he wobbled. Perhaps this would pass when he got some coffee in him. He opened the door to Helen's closet, got out a wrap of hers, and put it over his shoulders. He went to the kitchen.

Sitting at the little enamel table drinking the hot coffee, he suddenly had the odd idea that somebody was standing behind him, towering above and in back of his head. He knew better, but involuntarily he looked around. He felt a pressure weighing on his spirit, an almost physical weight pressing down on him. He kept wanting to dodge the heavy hand that was about to be placed on his shoulder, or wheel around suddenly and stop the voice that was about to speak out and thunder his name. He bent down to the coffee again, getting right down to it so that he could sip it from the cup without picking it up.

These were not hallucinations. He wondered if they might not be something worse. He remembered waking up in his room

at the farm one morning and finding on his desk a volume of
the medical dictionary open at the page describing what alcohol
did to a guy. Shy Mrs. Hansen (shy hell!) who never would have
spoken a word to him on the subject or admitted to his face that
she even knew he drank, had looked it up, marked the passage,
and left it there for him to see for himself. Amused, he read it
through.

ALCOHOLISM: Edema of brain with serous meningitis
in both acute and chronic cases. Thickened dura and pia
mater, some tissue degeneration. It acts, at least in part, by
inhibiting the ego-ideals and revealing the anti-social. Con-
sequently a great variety of clinical pictures present themselves, especially in the acute intoxications—i.e., coma,
amnesia, furor, automatism. The persistent drinker devel-
ops delirium tremens, chronic hallucinations and dementia.

ACUTE: Symptoms: Flushing of face, quickening of
pulse, mental exhilaration, followed by incoherent speech,
deep respiration, loss of co-ordination, dilated pupils,
vomiting, delirium, slow pulse, subnormal temperature,
impaired judgment, emotional instability, muscular inco-
ordination and finally stupor and coma.

CHRONIC: Symptoms: Fine or violent tremor, mental
impairment, disturbed sleep, injection of conjuctivae, red-
ness of nose, etc. If long continued, atheroma of arteries,
cirrhosis of liver and chronic interstitial nephritis are apt to
develop.—This brings mental deterioration in its wake and
change in the central nervous system resulting in impaired
memory, failure of judgment, inability to carry on business
and lower moral ideals and habits. Natural affection disap-
pears.

Furor. Delirium. Disturbed sleep. Mental deterioration. As
for that natural affection disappearing, it was so damned true that

he was offended. He was far from amused when he finished the passage. For once in his life he got a scare. The only thing he ever feared was losing his mind or destroying the responses or functions of his brain, and it looked as if he might be doing just that. If anything could ever deter him from drinking, it would be this fear. Is that what was happening now? Or, if it was happening, would he realize it? Or would it sneak up on him without his knowing, make a babbling idiot of him all of a sudden, sometime, somewhere, without a moment's warning? Was this weight, back of him, above him, on top of him, a premature sign? Could it be, thus, a blessing in disguise, a signal that there was still time if he would only yet use those waning wits to pull himself together before it was too late? Okay, Mrs. Hansen, but it's been too late for years—and I'm *still* whole. For instance:

The pressure that weighed upon him, the feeling that someone stood behind him, spurred him also to gather his thoughts and map out his plan. What he did he'd have to do quickly. Speed was what counted today. He got up from the table and went down the hall to see how the land lay.

He stuck his head in the living room and said "Good morning." Holy Love was probably thinking the worst (he and Helen had spent the night together) because she replied Good-morning without calling him by name or without looking up from her dusting. He went to the bathroom and, in passing, tried the door to the closet in the hall. It was locked.

He went into the bathroom and sat down on the edge of the tub. Helen had seen to it, of course, that the hall-closet was safely locked before she went to work. She never had any great supply on hand but one bottle would have been enough. There was a key to that lock somewhere about the place but where? Maybe Holy Love had it or knew where it was. He didn't feel like facing her again but he could call. He stood up, looked at himself in the bathroom mirror, and called out "Holy? Would you open the hall-closet for me, please?" His heart sank at the sight of his eye.

"Sorry, Mist' Birnam," she said from the other room, "I don't have no key."

He pretended not to have heard. "I left something in there last night, and I need it."

"Sorry, I don't have no key."

She was a liar, of course, but what could he do about it? He felt himself begin to sway and he hung onto the washbowl. Well, now he could only go back to the bedroom, try to dress, and wait his chance. If Holy Love should produce a key from her apron-pocket and open that closet door behind his back, God help her. God help him!

He pulled on his socks and his shirt and pants and then lay back on the bed. He had begun to breathe hard again and he felt a rising excitement grow in him, an excitement he couldn't control or understand. Probably physical. He closed his eyes and tried to quiet the heavy breathing. He had to be calm in order to get out of here and on to what he was about. He thought deliberately of his objective and named it to himself: He must get back into that bed of his, his own bed at home, before Wick returned.

When he got back into the house it was going to be for good, this time, there was no getting around that. It meant bed for several days, bed and frightful hangover and shattered nerves. And it was something he wasn't going to go through without liquor to help him, liquor to taper off with gradually, a few bottles cached here and there in secret places about the flat, aid that he could turn to when the mornings got too bad. He'd get half a dozen, somehow, somewhere. Nobody would believe, of course, that it was liquor to be used medicinally only. Nobody would believe that he would drink just enough of it and no more, just enough to keep his sanity. They'd be certain that it meant he was off again and that the long weekend was to stretch to another long week or longer. But he knew better. Knew when he was licked (temporarily). Knew when it was time to stop and recoup and get back on his feet and stay that way for a while. Knew that another such day as yesterday (he couldn't remember what it had been like but it must have been frightful—he knew that from past experience) would, at this stage of the game, knock him out entirely, pull his brain apart piecemeal, and leave him a lunatic staring in his chair not knowing himself or anybody else. Only way to stave that off was to have a supply on hand for the dreadful three or four days to follow, and then, with the aid of the drink as medicine, gradually work back to normal, taking fewer ones and smaller ones daily, till you didn't want it or need it any more. Would anybody believe that? But did they ever believe you, ever, about anything? So pay no attention. They always made such a fuss, anyway, whatever you did.

He sprang up. He had heard Holy Love in the hall. She was just closing a door. He ran to the hall and saw her dragging the vacuum cleaner into the living room.

She certainly hadn't got it out of the bathroom. She couldn't say it had been in the medicine cabinet. He went down the hall.

"How about it, Holy?"

She looked up at him. "How about what, Mist' Birnam?"

"Are you going to open that closet for me?"

"Sorry, I don't have no key."

"Where'd you get that vacuum cleaner!"

"From the kitchen."

He went in and sat down on the sofa. He looked worse than undignified in his stocking feet but what difference did it make, she was treating him like a child anyway. "What's the idea, Holy? Were you told not to let me in that hall-closet?"

She avoided looking at him from now on. "I wasn't told nothing."

"Then give me the key. I've *got* to get into that closet and get something *out!*"

"Sorry, I don't have no key."

"How did you get in, then?"

"Get in where?"

"You've got the key right there in your apron-pocket. Now give it to me! Do you hear?"

"Mist' Birnam, if I had a key I'd give it to you. But I don't have no key."

Could you take it from her by force? He got up and hurried back to the bedroom and lay down on the bed again. If he had stayed there another minute he would have choked her.

He lay listening to the wail and hum of the vacuum cleaner. She wouldn't be cleaning all day. She'd get through sometime and have to put it away again. From what he'd heard of Holy's sloppy work she'd be through in five minutes. She was.

He heard the noise of the vacuum cleaner die out like a run-down record. He sprang up again and stood listening, every sense and nerve on edge.

Then began an idiotic duel over the hall-closet. Every time he heard her step in the hall, he passed through into the kitchen. Stayed there until he heard her again. Then back again to the bedroom. He moved noiselessly in his stocking feet but at no time did he catch her about to unlock the door. Once or twice she seemed to change her mind and went back into the living room as he returned again to the kitchen.

He was hot with rage. Angry with himself mostly for going through such an idiotic performance, for submitting to such an indignity, for ever being in such a position at all. He could have killed her without a thought.

He heard a step in the hall. He looked out of the kitchen. She was gone. The vacuum cleaner was lying on the floor in front of the locked closet door, and he knew it would go on lying there till Kingdom Come so long as he stayed in the house. He hurried into the bedroom and put on his shoes. He put on his tie, his coat and his vest. He found his hat and put it on his head. He was certainly going to go in and have a showdown now, have it out with her for good and all.

She was on her knees in front of the fireplace, her head in

the hearth, when he came into the living room. With a brush she was sweeping up the ashes of the night before. He stood looking down at her and wondered how best to begin this time. There was no sense in antagonizing her any further. She couldn't be browbeaten. But it went against him to plead with her, begging for the key. He had demeaned and humiliated himself enough.

His eye fell on the bronze Romulus and Remus on the mantel.

It was a small statue about eight inches long and four inches high, a replica of the famous symbol of Rome, the mother-wolf suckling the two children crouched beneath her. The base was a solid oblong of bronze, with sharp corners. He had picked it up in Italy and brought it home for Helen.

His hand went out for it. He loved the little statue, had always loved it, had loved it when it was an illustration in his Latin grammar, had hunted for it in Rome on his very first day there, but he had never thought of it like this. All shaking was suddenly gone from his hand and arm and whole body. He was deathly calm and aware. He looked down at Holy Love on her hands and knees in the fireplace and saw her neatly-parted hair. His stomach went cold and he turned and fled back to the bedroom.

Melodrama! In all his life he had never been in any situation so corny, so ham. He felt like an idiot. His taste was offended, his sense of the fitness of things, his deepest intelligence. For once, the foolish psychiatrist had been right. The drunk will go to any lengths to get his desperately-needed drink. Any. But not *that* far.

He looked wildly about the room. He had to get out of here quick. Helen's typewriter was gone from the desk. Had she taken it with her on purpose? God they thought of everything.

Not everything. Fitted over the back of the chair beside the desk was Helen's short leopard jacket which apparently had just come back from summer storage. The furrier's tag still hung on the front button. He snatched up the jacket and hurried into the hall.

Just as he slammed the front door and ran down the stairs, he heard the telephone ring behind him. Ring ring let her ring now forever, or let Holy Love try to explain that one!

He turned to the left and ran up Bleecker Street toward Abingdon Square. He'd find a Mr. Rabinowitz along 8th Avenue somewhere and the place would be open too. They could never fool him again. It wasn't Yom Kippur today.

He had no thought for anyone along the way, scarcely even for himself. He didn't care who looked at him or who wondered at his speed or at the leopard jacket under his arm or at the black eye or who thought what. He was hurrying against time as he had never hurried before. He felt dizzy still but it was probably now only from the headlong rush.

He suddenly had the queer feeling that he had done all this before, traversed this very same route, in just this way and at just this speed, for the same reason. But no, that was another place, certainly another time—and now he remembered.

The night he left the Kappa U house for good, he had hurried downtown without even knowing where he was going or why. His only thought was to go somewhere else and quick. He walked along the dark side-streets of the business section until he was tired and had to stop. He came to a brightly-lighted shop-window. It was a bookstore, and the floor of the window was piled high with some new book just out, in a gay jacket. He leaned against the glass to rest a moment and absently looked in. His eye fell on the title, *Tales of the Jazz Age,* and on the crazy collegiate figures by John Held Jr. that adorned the white wrapper. He was amazed. This was news to him. He hadn't heard that Fitzgerald had brought out a new book. Down in front, close to the glass, was a propped-up copy held open with rubberbands at a story called "May Day." He bent down to the glass and began to read. He read down the entire left page, and then down the other. That was as far as he could go with the story but it was great stuff. He stood up with a sigh and promised himself to come down here, first thing tomorrow morning, the moment the store was opened, and buy himself a copy. He turned then to go on—and stopped dead in his tracks. Suddenly he had never felt so good and so foolish in his life. You God damned fool, he said to himself; if you've got enough curiosity and interest to know what's in that book, then what the hell are you running away from? . . .

But that was all different. This time he was running to, not from. Wasn't he? Just above 15th he found the place and turned in.

Fat Mr. Rabinowitz (or Weintraub or Winthrop or whoever he was) in a shirt grey-wet with sweat turned the leopard jacket over and over and felt of it and looked at the lining and examined the label. He thought he would collapse standing there waiting for the decision. A vivid brunette in the cashier's cage looked at him and drew in her breath audibly. Sure, the eye. Well? What about it? He raised his head and stared back at her coldly.

Mr. Rabinowitz flopped the jacket over again and rubbed it with his finger. "Is it hot?"

He didn't follow. "Hot?"

"Did you steal it?"

He went dumb with surprise. He had never expected anything like this. He was so amazed he didn't even react. His anger only began to grow when he heard his own voice saying meekly: "No, it belongs to my wife. I'll pick it up next week if you'll only give me—"

"Okay, I guess it's worth five dollars."

"Five *dollar*s—why, it's—"

"I'll give you five." He handed him a ticket and five of the filthiest one-dollar bills he had ever had in his hand and the most priceless.

He hurried out of the shop with the bills wadded inside his palm.

In the street, he ruffled through them again to see if there were really five. Everything was in order, everything was wonderful. He rolled them up and stuck them into his outside breast-pocket as if to get them out of sight as quickly as possible.

Thrusting the money inside the pocket, his fingers ran into opposition. Something blocked the opening. He reached in with his hand and pulled out a fistful of bills.

He was thunder-struck. Instantly he jammed the bills back out of sight and glanced around in panic. Something preposterous and fantastic was happening to his brain. Was he going to go to pieces right there on the sidewalk? His eye fell on the blue light of a subway-entrance at the corner. He ran for the entrance and dashed down the stairs.

He had to get where he could look at that windfall of bills in private, count them without anyone seeing. He changed one of his dirty dollar bills at the window, put a nickel in the slot, and bumped through the stile. There was a Men's Room down the platform to the left. He slammed against the door and rushed in.

Two men who had been standing inside stepped back suddenly from the urinals. He looked up at them in alarm. Both averted their faces in casual fashion and assumed the most unconcerned expressions in exactly the same way. He ducked at once for one of the toilets and let the doors fall to behind him. Then he sat down to wait, crouching and holding his breath, listening intently to hear if the two men should leave.

There was not a sound. He peered through the crack between the doors and saw the two standing against the wall, several feet apart, ostentatiously disclaiming any connection with each other. What the hell was this. They were spying on him. They were detectives or something. They knew what he was up to in there. Knew he had all that cash he had no right to have. Why didn't they go. How was he ever going to get out of here now if they didn't go. Or were they going to open the doors in a moment and drag him out and lead him away. Were they waiting for him to take the money out of his pocket before they suddenly sprang forward, pulled back the doors, and surprised him with the cash in his hand. One of the men cleared his throat slightly and he heard the other give a little answering cough.

He peered through the crack again. Both men wore overcoats. Both had their hands thrust down deep into their coat pockets and held slightly to the front. Did they have guns. They were waiting for somebody. Was it him. Nobody stood around in a Men's Room. You didn't wait for trains there. They weren't looking at a paper or anything. They didn't talk or even look at each other. They were pretending they had never seen each other before, knew nothing about each other, were unaware of each other at all—for his benefit. That was obvious. How long would they wait before they acted—or left. How long could *he* wait. Involuntarily he reached to his breast-pocket and fingered through the roll of bills. He had no idea where or how he could have got so much cash. Was he imagining it? One of the men began to hum. The other shifted his feet and leaned back more comfortably against the wall. Both tilted their heads now and again and looked at the ceiling.

How long was this to go on. Every few minutes a train rumbled into the station and the whole place jarred and shook. He heard the old nerve-shattering bell that announced the train was pulling out but they still stayed. So did he. Nothing in this world could have dragged him out of there. He wasn't fool enough to walk out and step right into their waiting arms, or have one of them tip his coat-pocket up toward him and say "How about it, Buddy. Fork it over." He'd stay in here all day if necessary while his nerves got worse and worse but he'd stay.

They were getting impatient. He saw one of the men glance upward around the room in a wide arc ending in a little nod and the other nodded too. He bent down and gazed at the floor so they wouldn't see him looking. Another train came in. When it pulled out again, the silence was unbearable. He waited in intolerable suspense for minutes, then raised his head ever so slightly to look through the crack as inconspicuously as possible. They were gone.

Nobody stood there. There was no one at all. Had there been

anybody? He had neither seen them go nor heard them. They may have left during the thunder of the last train, but he was beginning to doubt his senses entirely. If they had stood there all this time waiting for him, why had they suddenly gone? Maybe even the money was an illusion. He pulled it out of his breast-pocket.

It was real, all right. There was twenty-seven dollars in bills. Not counting the money he had just got from the pawnbroker. Deep down in the pocket (he could barely reach it with his finger-tips, he'd have to turn the coat upside down to get at it) was a pile of silver that must have amounted to another few dollars. He waited for the rumble of the next train, then ran out through the doors, across the platform, and stepped onto an E train.

He got off at 3rd and 53rd and hurried to a liquor store, not the one at the corner of his street but another one he seldom went to on 56th. He paid for and grabbed up six pints of rye and tried to walk out of the shop as calmly as possible.

The old Lincoln was not in front of the house; but when he got upstairs and opened the door, Mac barked from his basket. He ducked at once into his bedroom, dropped the package into the laundry hamper in his closet, and stood listening.

There was no sound from the other rooms. He swallowed to steady his voice, and then said: "Wick, are you there?" He heard the tap-tap of the Scottie's claws on the bare floor of the foyer and Mac came in to see him.

In his relief he began to shake. He was faint with exhaustion and soaked through in sweat. He needed a drink at once. He had worked fast but not fast enough apparently. Still, he had had the breaks. Wick was home, yes, but he was out again. He'd have to work fast some more. The drink would have to wait a little. For once something else was more important.

He stripped to his shorts and fired the wet clothes into the cor-ner of the closet. He got the package out of the laundry-hamper and tore it open, thrusting the wrapping back into the hamper

again. He took two of the pints and went to the bathroom. He
lifted the heavy enameled lid of the water-tank and put it on the
toilet-seat. He took one of the bottles by the neck and carefully set
it down inside, in the water, fingering around till he was sure it
was out of the way of the plunger. He slowly lowered the second
bottle in on the other side, and with his hand he pushed the ball
up and down till it rode free. Then he picked up the heavy cover
again and set it back where it belonged. He flushed the toilet to
see how it would work. If it didn't stop, if it kept on running, the
bottles were interfering with the mechanism. Without waiting
for the flushing to stop, he ran into the kitchen.

He got some string out of the table-drawer and cut off two
pieces about a foot-and-a-half in length. While he was putting
away the string, he heard the flushing of the toilet come to a sighing stop. He grabbed up an empty glass and hurried back to the
bedroom.

He laid two of the pints on the bed and tied a piece of string
around the neck of each. He opened the window a few inches
and lowered one of the bottles till it hung just under the outside
sill. He fastened the end of the string to a tiny cleat that was used
for the awning in summer. He did the same with the other bottle,
on the opposite side of the window. Then he closed the window
and adjusted the curtains, allowing them to fall naturally over the
radiator in veiling folds.

He had two pints for himself for now, one to be taken away
if necessary, the other to start on at once. He opened one of them
and poured a full glass of whisky. He tucked the other bottle
into the bookcase where Wick was certain to look for it when he
found him drunk and asleep.

He sat down on the edge of the bed and began to drink. In a
very few minutes he was tired. He filled the glass again, set it on
the floor by the bed, and crawled in.

He thought of the money. It was a laugh, all right. Shoving
it away, all those days, into his outside breast-pocket. For safe-

keeping. So damned safe that he had never found it himself. Who would ever have thought to look in his breast-pocket. Who ever kept anything in his breast-pocket but a handkerchief and a handkerchief that was never used at that. All those bills stuffed in there so tight that the change in the bottom didn't even clink or jingle when he ran frantically about in search of money. An inspiration came to him.

He sprang out of bed, fished through his pockets for all the money he had left, every last cent, and ran with it into the living room. He spread the bills on the table, fan-shaped, each one of them showing. In the very middle he stacked up the pile of change in a neat little tower. He admired his steady hand, his untrembling hand, as he arranged the half-dollars on the bottom, then quarters next, then nickels, then pennies, with the dimes on top. That would satisfy Wick. Satisfy anybody.

He hurried back to his room. He poured another drink, drank it, and crawled in, feeling like a million dollars.

He lay listening now for Wick. Let him come any time now. The thing was over. He himself was back home in bed again and safe. God knows why or how but he had come through one more. No telling what might happen the next time but why worry about that? This one was over and nothing had happened at all. Why did they make such a fuss?

Printed in the United States
by Baker & Taylor Publisher Services